CRISIS AT THE KODIAK STARPORT

CRISIS AT THE KODIAK STARPORT

BY JUSTIN OLDHAM

SHADOW FUSION LLC
ANCHORAGE

Published in the United States of America by Shadow Fusion LLC
http://www.shadowfusionbooks.com

Cover images courtesy of NASA/JPL-Caltech and NASA Visible Earth (visibleearth.nasa.gov)

Translations from English to Mandarin Chinese courtesy of Google Translate

Library of Congress Control Number: 2015908753

ISBN: 978-1-935964-69-8

Dedicated to the men and women who work at the real-world Kodiak Space Launch Facility. Their pioneering spirit will make this fiction into a reality we can all be proud of.

PROLOGUE

Political calculations made by the elected leaders of here and now may harm future citizens, who have to live with the unforeseen consequences of those policies.

The rise of conglomerates at the end of the 20th century posed a problem for elected leaders that endangered the sovereignty of their governments. Twenty-first century private sector interests had more potential to affect human destiny than their national competitors once did. Multinational corporations had greater influence than many of the countries that disagreed with their stated goals.

Country representatives derived their power from ideologically driven voters influenced by popular causes rooted in societal values that were liberal or conservative. The institutions they administered used their legal authority to tax and fine in an effort to regulate the behavior of corporations.

Big business exerted its own form of influence, derived from the products and services that corporations offered to customers. Lobbyists, lawyers, and strategists, tasked with countering the restraints placed on their employers, used after-tax profits to buy goodwill inside the governments that attempted to change their behavior.

Social activists, in favor of increased government regulation, claimed that the greater good was served by communal approaches to natural resource management stressing preservation over development.

Green entrepreneurs advocated a conservationist agenda that could maximize renewable resources while, at the same time, limiting the use of exhaustible metals and minerals that could not be replaced with recyclable synthetic substitutes.

Advancements in agriculture, industry, and other fields began to reveal solutions for these and other problems, appearing to vindicate the corporate argument in favor of managed exploitation. This fact alone gave the companies holding patents for those emerging technologies even more influence over terrestrial governments.

The stage was set for an international conflict. Extremist regulatory policies gave consumers a false impression that their leaders were doing something to prevent catastrophe. Aggressive commercial practices appeared to be safe because they made the most of what was available to be exploited.

There was no single event that defined the start of this decline. It occurred over the span of several decades. Growing populations gradually outstripped regional food production capacity as consumerism became an accepted philosophy in most countries. Changes in global climate coincided with a rise in militant environmentalism. Blights and droughts resulted in shortages of fruits, grains, and vegetables.

Every aspect of the worsening crisis was luridly documented and caustically commented upon by media organizations around the world. A well-known presenter of the day joked, "We are presiding over the demise of our own species. Stay tuned for more. Updates at the top of every hour. I'll be back with more in-depth interviews after this short commercial break."

Long-simmering border disputes between countries devolved into low-intensity skirmishes as massive refugee migrations threatened what little remained of international civility. Conflicts on land quickly spread to the seas as fishing fleets scoured the oceans in search of what little harvest remained. Minor boundary disputes grew to become regional wars as cash-strapped governments with small armies fell prey to larger countries with bigger armies. Fights broke out over water that could be used to irrigate crops. These battles claimed thousands of lives each month as the crisis reached a level of intensity that threatened the Kodiak Starport.

Experts agree that the geography of the Kodiak aerospace facility is ideal for commercial activity. The same location that is ideal for rocket launches and ballistic airliner traffic also happens to be vulnerable to attack by hostile naval forces, if they should be on their way to North America. The Asia-Pacific conflict that took place during this period is thoroughly documented. China and the United States were just two of many combatants in the region asserting their claims to underwater boundaries.

Post-conflict allegations concerning certain activities at the Kodiak Starport are still under investigation. Researchers continue to examining many of the drastic decisions that were made by corporate staff and contractors during pivotal instances of controversy. The right or wrong of what was done there at that time will continue to be debated by historians and lawmakers because national interest collided with corporate imperatives.

What you are about to read is a dramatic reconstruction of those events, as extrapolated from official sources and first-hand accounts taken from published memoirs.

CHAPTER ONE

Storm clouds hung low over the Tanana Valley. September winds whipped the branches of birch and black spruce trees located on and around the University of Alaska campus. James Cook's tilt-rotor aircraft roared in to make a fast three-point landing at the hillside air park. Attendants in bright yellow rain gear rushed out to put wheel chocks in place and open doors.

A man in the dark blue uniform of a United States Air Force officer approached the aircraft as the prop wash subsided. His dress coat flapped in the breeze. He kept one hand on the top of his head to secure his peaked cap. He used the other hand to open the right side passenger door.

Jim looked up from what he was doing. "Aren't you Avril's son?" he asked.

Norman Ahgupuk smiled. His dusky features beamed. "Yes, sir. He's my father. I'm glad to meet you."

Jim handed his laptop computer to an aide. "You're still a major," he noted.

"Promotions are hard to find," Norman grinned.

"That's what I hear," Jim sighed. He unbuckled his seat belt. "Do you have an appointment to see me?"

Norman stepped back to shield the executive from shifting wind. "No, sir. I'm here for career day, handing out brochures, and taking applications. I asked your security for permission to come out and greet you."

The white-haired starport administrator stepped out of the luxurious interior. "How does your dad like retirement?" he asked as he put on his coat.

Norman frowned. "He doesn't."

Jim took a moment to up size up the younger man. "What your business with me?"

"I want to build your squadron."

"What makes you think I need one?" Jim queried.

The aviator backed off. "I watch the news and my dad tells me things when he shouldn't. I was just a kid when the Chinese made their first play in this part of the world."

"Don't believe the hype," Jim growled.

Norman tilted his head. "They didn't do much damage last time. Your predecessor, with a little help from my dad, gave them a bloody nose. It's not the kind of thing they're going to forget."

Jim smiled. "Travis Griffin is a good man."

"You're in charge now."

"How old are you?" Jim asked, stalling.

"Forty-one," Norman replied.

"What's your qualification?" Jim asked politely.

"Anything with rotors or wings," the flyer asserted.

Jim stretched to get the kinks out of his back. "You've got brass, I'll give you that. Did your dad tell you to see me?"

"No," Norman lied.

Jim adopted a stern pose. "What *did* he say?"

The younger man lowered his head. "Nobody likes a smartass. I should be happy that I've got a job. He also said you liked personal initiative."

Jim laughed. "What makes you think I have the parts to make a squadron?"

The pensive man looked around. "I have a friend in the private sector who says you bought a dozen F-15s last year, just before Christmas."

"They're for my wife," Jim quipped.

"She needs people to fly them," Norman insisted.

The executive turned in his tracks. "We don't *officially* have any such aircraft on the books. That would be illegal. Treaty violation. We don't officially do that kind of thing. Not on my watch."

"No, sir," Norman concurred quietly.

"That's my official story. Yours?" Jim inquired.

"My enlistment is up in 30 days."

"As in retirement?"

"I'm out," the pilot admitted.

"Why do I want golden oldies like you?" Jim criticized.

"Who else are you going to get?"

The perturbed executive rapped his knuckles on the cold skin of the VTOL. "Does the 'anything' you fly include this?"

Norman looked over his shoulder. "I'm serious. My papers are already in. I've still got a few years left in the cockpit. There isn't—"

Cook shook his head. "I didn't ask for a dissertation on your motives. I want to know what else you can fly. I need to know what you can do, just in case I'm interested in having another headache on the payroll."

"I can fly VTOLs if it'll get me onboard with your program," Norman responded, nodding.

Jim rubbed his chin. "Your dad was quite proud when you got accepted to the Air Force Academy."

"I'm done with that," Norman reiterated.

"This thing with China is going to get real. They'll call you back when there is a fight," Jim warned.

Ahgupuk fidgeted. "Yes. They'll retrain me for air transports because somebody upstairs thinks I'm too old for fighters, or they'll chain me to a desk because somebody else thinks I'm too old for flight duty."

"You still sound like a bad investment."

Norman sensed that he was being tested. "I don't want to fly a tanker or a desk. Let me help you."

Norman's persistence impressed Jim. The younger man was offering him a piece of the puzzle he'd need to make his defense plan work. Each month that passed brought the West closer to conflict with the East. The starport's last brush with history had resulted in dozens of deaths.

Jim arched an eyebrow. "Suppose you're the man for this job. Talk to me about filling cockpits."

Norman exuded confidence. "I can get pilots, if you don't care who they are or where they come from."

"Sounds like international recruitment." Jim scowled.

"Some of it would be."

"I hear 'mercenary,' even though you don't actually say the word," Jim frowned.

The Alaskan Native shrugged. "It's a tough market. The U.S. defense budget has been down for decades. It's not that much different anywhere else. The best of a very small bunch are kept and the rest are let go."

It was the truth and Jim knew it. "I want instructor-grade. People who can teach on the ground and in the air."

Norman cackled. "Nobody with that kind of resume will work for you. Not when they can get contractor's rates from half the governments on this planet."

"What does that leave me?"

"I think you know."

"Prove that you a good investment," Cook challenged.

Norman looked him in the eye. "You're gonna get washouts. Mavericks and knuckleheads who couldn't stomach the chain of command. Some will teach, after they've been properly incentivized. The rest will just be hard to keep on a short leash."

The administrator looked at his watch. "The rules are simple. This is totally off the books. I don't want to know. I don't need to know. Screw up and I'll throw you to the wolves."

Norman touched the brim of his hat. "I was never here. We never had this conversation. How do I meet with your inner circle?"

"Come with us when we're done," Jim suggested.

"No time like the present," Norman enthused.

"We'll drop you off at an undisclosed location to speak with some people who don't have names."

"Shady," Norman protested.

Cook gave him a mean stare. "Take it or leave it. This isn't what it looks like. There's more at stake than the fate of a corporation or 3,000 jobs. I'll spare you the speech because all of that will become clear soon enough."

Norman raised his hands in a show of surrender. "How does the new guy earn some goodwill?" he asked in an attempt to lighten the mood.

Jim turned back to the aircraft. He stuck his head inside. "Are you driving with a co-pilot today?"

The startled man shook his helmeted head.

Jim pointed over his shoulder. "Mr. Ahgupuk thinks he can fly. Get yourself a cup of coffee for the ride back to Anchorage and let him drive when we go."

"What happens if he spills my brew?" the flippant man asked glibly.

"Gain altitude and throw him out."

"Thanks," Norman beamed.

"Okay then. I understand you. You understand me. We're done." Cook turned to leave.

"No worries," Norman replied.

"Always worry," Jim griped and broke free to meet his approaching hostess.

"Welcome to Fairbanks!" Chancellor Helen Hathaway offered.

The irritated man forced himself into a more temperate posture. "I hope you appreciate what it took to rearrange my schedule."

"I do," Hathaway replied.

"We came in through the rain," Jim complained.

A gust of wind ruffled Hathaway's conservative coat. "Our top ten donors are on campus today."

He checked his tie. "The owner's manual for that bird says these things can take a lightning strike. I'd rather not put that to the test."

The chancellor stepped back. "I'm hoping others will follow your lead."

The starport boss took the briefcase handed to him by an aide and followed Hathaway into the terminal. The rest of his entourage trailed at a polite distance.

"I read the fisheries forecast you sent."

She ushered him into the spacious lounge. "Harvests are down for the tenth year in a row. Every kind of fish you'd care to name is getting harder to find. Deep sea crab beds have been picked clean."

"Times are tough."

The chancellor led the way into a large elevator. "All I know is that the Chinese are spoiling for a fight. They sank *both* of our research vessels last year."

"Survivors?" he asked as the lift began to descend.

"None that we know of," she whispered.

The grim news left him speechless.

Hathaway continued, "I'm sure they'll take another crack at the starport, if they can."

They rode down three levels and got off.

Chinese, Japanese, and Korean fishing fleets had been pillaging Alaskan waters for more than half a century. Extensive overfishing had resulted in depleted harvests that were threatening to destroy entire species.

Fewer jobs in the fishing industry meant fewer enrollees in the university's marine science programs. Half of all Alaskan fishing vessels were sold for scrap or in foreclosure because their former owners couldn't make the loan payments.

Lack of cash had forced the school to look for funding in other areas of private sector interest that didn't rely on resources from the sea. The starport on Kodiak Island was just one of a few big donors that could bridge that growing gap.

"No more government grants?" Jim asked.

"None to be had in the last two years," Helen confessed.

"I'm aware of the legislature's mood," Jim muttered.

Hathaway giggled. "The kids in Juneau don't see things our way. Oil traded at $400 a barrel this morning and state geologists have verified two new natural gas fields. You'd think they could be a little more generous, with that kind of windfall."

The administrator followed her out of the elevator. "You read my quarterly financials and I read yours. We're already your single largest amalgamation of donors. What makes you think I can bully my board into being more generous?"

The chancellor stopped in the hallway. Overhead lighting reflected off her silver hair. "Generosity from you shames the others. They'll follow your lead."

"We can't be any more helpful," Jim protested.

The tenacious woman held out her hand and somebody gave her a small tablet computer. "You've got a cash surplus and you've got a decent credit rating."

"Since when?"

She tapped the screen and held it up to eye level. "Page five of your latest profit disclosure. Paragraph six, government contracts. Half of what you do is paid for by Uncle Sam."

Jim blushed. "Yeah. Well. There was a time when all of what we did was funded by federal and state sources."

"Fifty percent," Hathaway repeated stubbornly.

"Doesn't mean anything," he grunted.

Helen handed off her visual aid. "It matters. You're the gold standard around here. Please, don't back down from last year's commitments. The others are already making excuses. I can't go to the legislature with another hole in my budget. They'll crucify me."

Jim and his staff were directed to the end of the corridor. "We can do that, but I'll want something in return."

"Such as?" Helen asked, bracing herself.

He touched Hathaway on the shoulder. "A favor to be named by me at a later date."

"Why so secretive?" she whispered.

Jim slowed. "You're not the only one who has to make deals. Desperate times do call for desperate measures."

Helen snickered as she walked. "This from the man who's in bed with the military-industrial complex. You really should find a better way to pay for what you do. We'd all be better off if you did."

He kept his voice low. "Every starport on the planet has the same problem. Each new regional war puts our installations at risk."

"Stop making weapons," she suggested sarcastically.

Jim grinned. "Want to, but can't. Look. Between you and me, this thing with China is going hot someday and we're trying to be ready for it. It's in our best interest to help you maintain the science and engineering programs. You educate. We employ."

"The noble defender of spaceflight," Hathaway sneered.

Jim was too cynical to let the barb reach him. "Our T.V. commercial does say 'gateway to the stars.' Who gets to be the gatekeeper? Who *should* be the gatekeeper? How long does that gate stay shut if we let it close?"

Helen stepped aside to let a security guard pass. "You say that like the barbarians are at the gates and you expect to have your precious kingdom burnt to the ground any day now."

The analogy made Jim laugh. He slowed to a stop. "That did sound a bit imperious, didn't it?"

"Only just a little."

Cook pulled the wrinkles out of his coat with both hands. "Really want to know what I think? Worst case is, they occupy our facilities. Winning the war means they keep the starport and all our secrets. Losing means they take everything that isn't nailed down and go home with whatever they can carry."

"Crude."

"Practical," he confessed.

Chapter Two

The starport's delegation waited behind the elevated stage as one guest speaker after another made presentations to the restless audience.

Jim's entourage swarmed around him. A stylist combed his hair and applied light makeup while he read from a series of small devices that were handed to him.

"When did *this* happen?" he asked when a news headline caught his attention.

"Half an hour ago," somebody clarified.

Jim checked his watch again. He wasn't due to speak for another five minutes. Alaskan news groups were reporting the loss of a 130-foot fishing vessel. It had sunk near the southern tip of the Aleutian Islands, close to the international boundary between the United States and Russia. Amateur video, allegedly taken from the bridge of the beleaguered boat, streamed through popular web sites.

He selected a feed and touched "play." The long, dark silhouette was visible through a rain-streaked windscreen. Panicked voices provided narration.

"Why are they so close?"

"Keep turning. Warn 'em off!"

Radio static crackled through intercom speakers in the wheelhouse. A stern voice bellowed in Mandarin Chinese.

"What's he saying?"

"Does it matter? I think they just shot at us!"

"I told you we shouldn't have come out this far."

The camera view swung wildly to reveal a trio of men dressed in bright orange water survival suits. A gloved hand reached for the camera. A bearded face appeared.

"Can't see anything from in here," he complained.

Sounds of pounding feet and the squeak of an opening door accompanied three seconds of blurry footage. The image cleared as the camera came up to reveal the full length of a dull gray naval destroyer less than a hundred yards off the boat's starboard beam.

"There's your proof!" the cameraman screamed.

A sudden flash from the front of the warship dazzled the camera. The sound of a loud crash ended with the shriek of twisting metal as the video froze.

Jim gave the device back to his aide. "Fishermen out of Dutch Harbor have said for a long time that they were being harassed by the Chinese."

"They're not the only ones making that claim," one of his staffers reminded.

Jim adjusted his tie. "One crisis at a time. Let me get past this unruly mob and then we'll deal with the Chinese."

The chancellor was on stage, introducing the starport representative. He walked out to face the applause.

Jim laid one hand on the multimedia controls built into the pedestal. He began his speech with an overview. Holographic projectors over his head presented static photo images as he spoke. The podium's wireless microphone system broadcast his voice through every speaker in the chamber.

"Kodiak Starport is one of the best known locations in Alaska. Our story began in the late 1990s. The corporation started as a quasi-private, state-funded venture. What this means is that the State of Alaska provided seed money." Still photos of the early space launch complex bloomed and faded.

"The Kodiak Starport was involved in that scuffle with Chinese. Leaders on both sides managed to bring that conflict to a halt before it got totally out of control. Shots were fired. Lives were lost on both sides."

Newspaper headlines and web site banners scrolled to form a grim narrative. Jim touched a screen on the podium to refresh his speaking notes.

"That was 16 years ago. We've taken some flak from the media about our use of private security forces. It's been suggested that we should rely on the U.S. Army garrison that now squats on our land."

Video clips from old news programs played silently.

He gauged the mood of his audience. "Every starport in the United Stated has a mandatory 'relationship' with the federal government. It's not one of our choosing. We've tried, and failed, many times to break this dependency. I won't hide my distaste for this kind of behavior. Neither should you."

He waited for the elaborate images over his head to change. "Four years ago, we put up a space station. *Gold Rush* will have the honor of being Alaska's first zero gravity manufacturing site when it's fully operational. A lucky few of you might work there someday."

Many listeners in the diverse crowd nodded their heads. Jim decided to skip the remainder of his potentially militant remarks. "The rest, as they say, is history. The company has been in private hands for quite some time now. I am actually the fifth person to hold the position of Senior Administrator. Some of my predecessors served for a very long time.

"The 'administrator' part of my job title is a holdover from the early days of the American space program, when NASA was the leader in rocket launch technologies. I have full executive authority over the starport's day-to-day operations. The chain of command is presently five on-site department heads, three off-site department heads, nine division chiefs, and an army of lawyers.

"We employ 5,000 people. My boss is the board of directors for our parent company, Shadow Fusion Enterprises. The offices are located in Anchorage. It's a publicly traded company, ticker symbol SHFE.

"Our expense and profit reports are a matter of public record. I'd like to remind the donor representatives who are in the audience today that we—the starport—are still the biggest single for-profit contributor that benefits this university.

"I want to be quite clear. This university, and its extensions, provide us with a lot of skilled professionals. Every donor that supports the U.A. system gets the same benefit that we do in some way. Don't be stingy."

Chancellor Hathaway smiled from her seat in the audience. Members of the faculty nodded their approval.

Jim shuffled his feet in an effort to relax. "You might be interested to know that the Kodiak Starport provides work spaces, assembly points, and manufacturing facilities to more than 70 businesses. Some are big; others are small.

"All of these companies pay some form of tax to the State of Alaska. These range from two percent, upwards to fifteen percent. This includes revenues from all licenses permits and inspection fees.

"I'd also like to point out that many of Alaska's indigenous people are heavily invested in what we do. Alaska Native corporations own 44 percent of SFE stock. We are the largest employer of ethnic Alaskans in the United States.

"No starport has paid an environmental damage fine in three years. Some of our wastewater retention ponds are actually leased to local fish farmers. Their effort to restock the Bering Sea salmon run is noble. We're glad to support it."

He paused to let the last multimedia sounds and images to fade. "Some of you have already texted questions. Let me get to those now."

Jim put on his glasses so he could read the small monitor on the podium.

"The future of space flight. All the starports around the world are now leading the way in this field. Our biggest obstacles can be found here on Earth. The one thing that threatens our success, more than any other, is the fighting that goes on between nations.

"Most governments have thrown in the towel. Space flight is just too expensive for their tax bases to afford. Even so, a handful of countries continue to reach for space to gain a military or political advantage."

He cleared his throat. "All starports are still taxed and regulated by the nations they reside in. We're not charities, though we have become the principal source of revenue for some small countries. Tax us too much, or harm us with your petty wars, and we *will* relocate. It's that simple.

"The local media makes a big deal out of the troubles we with have with Washington, but I can assure that you that our relationship with the federal government is about as good as it will ever be."

A ripple of laughter went through the spectators. Jim gathered his thoughts, then continued. "Out there, in the convention hall, you've already seen the booths for the job fair. I'm just old enough to remember when this part of this campus was built. The starport can't hire all of you, but we're ready to employ a lot of you."

Applause filtered through the crowd. Jim rested both hands on the lectern. "Times are tough. Unemployment is high. Education is no guarantee of success. The oceans in this part of the world are a mess. Fish and crab are in very short supply."

He coughed. "The…the inordinately high price of oil and other commodities that are extracted on dry land give the false impression that all is well in Alaska. That's not true. The whole country is in a condition of what I call 'free fall.' What goes up must come down. Nobody appreciates that fact more than we do.

"Renewed tensions between China and the United States over the issue of sovereign waters and international fishing treaties threaten to make things worse. There's even talk of war. None of us want to be caught in the middle of that because might have to defend ourselves."

The auditorium became solemnly quiet. Jim realized that he'd just ad-libbed something that wasn't in his prepared speech. He let one arm fall to his side. "We have to think long-term. *You* have to look beyond this crisis, into the next decade. Today sucks, but tomorrow can be all peaches and cream if you're willing to work hard enough. Remember it. Believe it. Want it. Don't settle for anything less."

The soon-to-be graduates looked at each other. "Who's he kidding?" somebody joked loudly.

"Thank you and good night," Jim concluded. Half-hearted cheers followed him off the stage.

"Tough crowd," somebody jeered.

Jim didn't stop until he was in the hallway. "My fault. They need some hope. Couldn't help myself."

He took a breath to continue speaking when a warbling sound interrupted his discomfort. Jim turned to see a serious man in the urban camouflage that had been adopted by starport security making his way through the throng of moving people.

"Coming through!" the specialist barked. He stopped in front of the administrator, holding a stainless steel briefcase.

Jim put his thumb on the DNA-sensitive lock to make the case snap open. A bright red satellite phone popped up. Small red lights on the handset flashed on and off. He checked his watch. "Alert the air crew to start refueling."

The device continued to warble. Jim picked up the handset and typed in a five-digit access code. Some of his aides loitered nearby in an effort to find out what was happening. He glared at them. "Don't be so obvious." Staffers scattered in every direction to carry out orders.

The uplink went through with an urgent chirp. A video screen in the briefcase came to life. The face of Billy Richter came into view, wearing a headset.

"Afternoon, Jim. What did I interrupt?" he joked.

"Career day," Cook replied stoically.

The chief of security sobered. "I'm calling to report an ongoing cyber-attack that started 15 minutes ago."

"Damage?" Jim queried.

Billy grimaced. "The internal operations network was breached. Somebody knew our system. The nerds are telling me that data has been copied from the personnel archives."

"Somebody wants to know who they're dealing with," Jim guessed.

The old soldier shrugged. "I hate computers. We've pulled the plug on all terrestrial inputs. E-SEC is going to shut down the satellite relay when I terminate this call. They want to scrub everything to get ahead of any lurking viruses. I just thought you should know why we've gone dark."

Jim thought about the chaotic video he'd been watching before his presentation. "How many times is this now?" he asked.

"Three in the last 30 days," Billy told him.

Jim turned to see Chancellor Hathaway approaching. "Okay. Thanks for the update. Give the nerds whatever they want. Keep this in house. No media. I'll get back to you in six hours."

Hathaway and her staff assistant stopped at a respectful distance. She waited for Jim to hang up. "Is there a problem?" she inquired.

"No," Jim replied.

Helen relaxed. "I was afraid you would run off."

"Never," he fumed with false indignation.

She pointed down the hallway. "We've arranged a press conference just for the in-state media. If you'll be so kind as to follow me."

Jim waited for the man with the satellite phone to fade back into the crowd. He motioned for his people to follow him. The chancellor moved closer.

"Are you sure there isn't a problem?" she asked quietly.

"It's nothing we can't handle," he assured.

CHAPTER THREE

September gave way to October as the state of Alaska became shrouded in winter snow. Diplomatic actions between the United States and China became more heated as United Nations intermediaries tried to head off another clash of arms.

Laura Andrewyuk sipped hot coffee from a gray stoneware mug while keeping an eye on the starport's busy operations center. Sensors in the large gyro-stabilized chair adjusted the seat's angle and fabric density to comply with her preprogrammed comfort settings.

Her view was panoramic. Massive panels of auto-tint polycarbonate surrounded the compartment on three sides, tucked into a high corner of the cavernous control room like a skybox in a sports stadium. Monitors and holographic displays flickered with a thousand terabytes per hour of real time audio and visual data that was being eagerly examined by hundreds of highly trained and experienced specialists and technicians.

Overhead speakers in the dimly lit birdcage ceiling softly broadcast a constant stream of monotone chatter from a dozen voices.

"Weather alert. Storm is confirmed. Gonna get wet."

"Module secured. Package is ready for roll back."

"Booster ignition in three…two…one…"

A display on the big desk lit up as distant rumbling filled the sky. Automated cameras carried out their duty, documenting the launch of another commercial payload.

The executive turned in her chair and raised her mug to toast a line of color photos on the back wall. "Money in the bank." She raised her cup a second time to the picture of Travis Griffin. "At least one of us got to retire."

Desktop alarms sounded when a multimedia update she'd flagged earlier began to stream. A quick pivot and a swipe at a touch screen allowed her to watch the report as it was broadcast live to the service's subscribers.

Several screens around her came to life with the image of a brown-haired woman in a yellow rain coat. "This is Beatrice Brown for Polar News, coming to you live from the docks in Dillingham, Alaska. We are getting sporadic reports from the Small Rock gold mine, about 65 miles from where I stand."

An earpiece with microphone hung from her left ear, swaying in the blustery weather. "State officials are now warning that several layers of the containment wall around that mine's arsenic lake have collapsed. An employee at the mine has told me, off-air via wireless phone, that he thinks the levies will break within the hour."

Text crawled across the bottom of the screen. *Tragedy threatens Small Rock mine in Southcentral Alaska. Governor prepares to meet with disaster planners. Stay tuned for details.*

The correspondent put both hands in her pockets as a gust of wind hit with enough force to make her flinch. "Polar News hasn't been able to reach anyone at the mine. Communities in the affected area, as far south as Port Heiden, are scrambling to get the word out."

"Bloody hell," Laura murmured.

The reporter pointed to a ship behind her. "Evacuations are expected to begin later in the day, using vessels like this to move hundreds, or even thousands, of displaced people to safer locations. Fears have run rampant in this part of the state for decades as local leaders have tried, and failed, to come up with a disaster response plan for an event that this mine's investors said would never be needed."

Laura stroked the screen to mute the sound. She put her mug down on the broad black desktop and frowned while fidgeting with the ruffles on her red blouse. Images of state officials and angry residents flashed across the silent screen. "There's always a fire," she reminded herself.

A phone on the desk chirped. She used a touch screen on the armrest to answer the call. A small holographic image coalesced in midair just three feet away.

The calm countenance of Billy Richter nodded back at her from his office on the far side of the starport. His indigenous features, dark hair, and easy-going smile gave him an air of youthful energy, despite being middle aged.

He coughed into his hand. "You see the news?"

"I do," she confirmed.

"DNR wants our VTOLs and some of the fuel carriers."

The request from the Alaska Department of Natural Resources wasn't unexpected, or unreasonable. Laura's expert eye roamed over the displays in her field of view. "Looks like a normal day at the office for us, but we've got another off-the-books load for *Gold Rush* going up in five hours. How long do they want those assets?"

Billy shook his head. His official title was Chief of Security, disguising the fact he also commanded the starport's unofficial military contingent.

Richter knew what was on Laura's mind. He rocked back in his chair. "Hey, you wanted to be the president of the company. Now, you are. It's like Travis used to say. There is always a fire, somewhere."

Laura bristled at the reminder she'd already given herself. "Don't quote Griffin to me. You were still in high school when I hired him. It's that damned space station. It sits up there, never quite finished, costing more money than we ever thought it would."

"Gateway to the future," he poked.

She sat up. "Your butt is going to be the gateway for my boot if you let anything slow down the special shipments to *Gold Rush*. Tell me straight. Can we lend DNR aviation assets without compromising security?"

"We can do better than that." Billy's face was replaced by an animated projection. His voice continued to flow through speakers around the room. "We, I mean you, have controlling interest in two air taxi services, one air freight company, and the only hovercraft manufacturing plant in the state."

Laura saw the point he was trying to make. "Enough civilian capacity to respond without tapping military assets. How do the hovercraft tie in?"

Several company logos danced across the desktop as Billy spoke. "Five tour operators and six heavy lift outfits use what we build. Call these guys and ask them to pitch in. You should be able to put enough air and water transport in Bristol Bay within 24 hours to make the kids over at FEMA downright jealous."

The jab made Laura laugh. Federal regulations had put a stranglehold on many international businesses trying to conduct commerce on U.S. soil. Decades of continuously intrusive legislation expanded the government's authority. Thousands of restrictive laws had forced the starport's administration to house and accommodate staff from more than a dozen federal agencies, including the armed forces.

The Federal Emergency Management Agency, commonly called FEMA, was tasked with responding to natural and man-made disasters. Recent changes to the agency's mandate gave it authority over state and federal resources when combating environmental mishaps of the type that were now playing out in southwestern Alaska.

Laura clasped her hands together, thinking. FEMA was just one of many organizations that didn't play ball with starport officials, even when federal and state regulations worked in favor of the aerospace corporation.

"Let's get ahead of this thing," she said decisively. "Jim's not here right now, but I have the authority to make these decisions. I'll send you an action order. Get those civilian resources moving towards Dillingham." Laura waved her hand emphatically. "No direct calls. Don't say anything to the Feds until they call. Be absolutely certain that they get billed for every single thing we do. We need the cash and they need the paper trail. Everybody wins, nobody dies, and our troops stay out of the spotlight."

"I hear and obey," Billy quipped, then signed off.

Laura sat back as the call winked out. Displays around the office quietly reset. Images from launch control played in time with softly babbling background sounds as the executive considered her options. Keeping the starport safe seemed easy enough, especially with government-funded military units on site.

Corporations that ran starports employed thousands of people from all walks of life and made billions in profit every year. That fact made them dangerous in the minds of many politicians who coveted and feared their patronage. The net result was an uneasy relationship. No legitimate government could afford to allow starports to operate independently on their sovereign soil. The belief in every country was that these multinational corporations couldn't be trusted.

SFE's starport, located on Kodiak Island, wasn't the biggest of its kind, nor was it the smallest, though its reputation as a hub of innovation was known far and wide. Even so, the federal garrison that took up 50 precious acres near the northern end of the complex was quite typical of similar facilities around the globe.

Laura checked the nearest clock. "Prepare action memo," she commanded. Nearby administrative monitors lit. Voice activated software came online within seconds. Laura spoke carefully to dictate and send the memorandum that would authorize starport assets to be loaned the state.

A drink of coffee fortified her as she worked. She added a few paragraphs of legalese intended to minimize the company's liability. "Close and send."

Laura stood and was about to leave when she noticed another incoming call. A quick read of the desktop told her it was third-term governor Sheldon Wheeler. He was calling from the starport in New Mexico.

Laura sat. "Phone, scramble and pick up."

Sheldon's voice came through the tastefully hidden speakers around the room.

"Jim, what's the word?" he asked.

"It's Laura," she corrected.

The politician chuckled. "Sorry. I can't see this little screen very well. Everyone looks the same to me through one of these things. How're you doing?"

The woman relaxed in the big chair. "I'm fine. We're sending up another piece of the space station in a few hours. And yes, before you ask, I just authorized movement of our best transportation to Chignik, Dillingham, and a few places around Lake Iliamna."

Wheeler laughed to shed some stress and express his relief. "Once again, you are on the ball. Where's Jim and what's he doing?"

"Can't say," Laura replied cryptically.

Wheeler moved to an unoccupied area in the departure lounge he and his staff were standing in. "There may be some good news. I'm on my way back from Washington. The

Pentagon would like to give us a free hand so they can deal with China. DHS is backing their play. The military could be leaving your starport real soon."

Laura squirmed. "Don't tease me like that, Sheldon."

He looked around. "It's not a joke. They want their fighter jets, and...they're gonna take their troops. You'd still be stuck with TSA and a DHS oversight team. I'm pretty sure there's nothing we can do about that."

"When?" she pressed.

"That's the hang up."

Laura gathered her thoughts. Wheeler's reticence was justified. The terminal he and his traveling advisors were loitering in was monitored by the Transportation Safety Administration, an organization that had an infamous reputation for surveillance and intrusion.

TSA did more than screen passengers that came and went from the starport every day. Its small army of minders kept a watchful eye on the starport's public spaces. Everything they saw and heard was reported daily to an administrator from the Department of Homeland Security, who worked onsite. Some cameras, microphones, and sensors were posted out in the open, where they could be easily seen by anyone who cared to look. Other devices were camouflaged or tucked away in less obvious locations.

Federal law gave DHS considerable leeway to interpret their Congressional mandate to observe, inspect, and protect. These same statutes required all American starports to provide offices and resources to support federal officials, administrative civil service, and military personnel.

"I understand," Laura signaled.

The governor couldn't say any more without coming to the attention of federal law enforcement officers, who were not inclined to be hospitable to a state-level leader as the nation came closer to war.

"We're booking a charter flight," Sheldon prompted.

Laura knew how the game was played. "Our door is always open," she offered.

He checked his watch. "Days like this make we wish we hadn't sold the jet."

Laura used a touch screen to look at inbound cargo schedules. "We've got a shipment coming in from Pennsylvania. The carrier is hull down at your location right now. I'm looking at nine empty seats."

"Take off?" he asked.

"Flight plan says two hours," she relayed.

Wheeler looked over his shoulder. "I have media following me. Every hour I stay on the ground gives them a little more time to talk about how I'm slow to deal with Small Rock. Can you accelerate that flight?"

"What's a few million dollars?" she quipped.

Laura put the governor on hold and made her arrangements. She got back to him five minutes later. "Okay. Here it is. Industrial terminal. You're on the dock for loading in fifteen minutes. Launch in thirty."

"Anything else I should know?" he asked.

She smiled. "This load has two stops. First one is Fairbanks, to drop off industrial machine parts. We're building a new liquefied natural gas plant so the folks can stay warm and we can make better plastics. The rest is construction materials that come to the starport."

"Sounds like a party," he nodded.

Laura laughed. "You get off in Fairbanks. We'll have a limo for you at the ramp. The rest is up to you."

"How do I pay for this?" Sheldon began to sweat.

"Pay for what?" she asked sweetly and hung up.

Laura eyed the phone suspiciously and reached out to type in a three-digit code.

"Purge log. Erase call."

Chapter Four

The end of October ushered in another marathon cold snap. Temperatures on Kodiak Island plummeted to historic lows for the fifth year in a row. Climate change experts made notes and collected samples from air, land, and sea.

Experts had warned for decades that spawning grounds in the Pacific Ocean, Arctic Ocean, Bering Sea, and Gulf of Alaska were under assault by unregulated fishing fleets. These poorly supervised expeditions were said to be stripping the sea floor beyond all hopes of recovery, through the use of massive nets that were trawled through deep water or dragged across the sea floor, scraping up every last possible ounce of seafood. No sea creature of any kind was thrown back once it was captured. Exceptional effort was made by massive floating processors to turn every part of every aquatic organism into food for the starving masses on dry land.

Extinction of the bluefin tuna seven years earlier had been mourned by the scientific community as tragic proof that the entire global ecosystem was now in crisis. No group or faction of political leaders seemed capable of dealing with this catastrophe, which seemed to worsen with the passing of each year. Was this just a case of over fishing on a grand scale, or was it a matter of climate change that involved more factors that couldn't be so easily explained?

Every nation located on the Asia Pacific Rim that depended on food from the sea was feeling the strain from consecutively diminished annual aquatic harvests. Billions of men, women, and children, in overcrowded cities that rationed electricity and water, were starving as droughts turned fertile breadbaskets into dustbowls.

Radio, television, and Internet sources babbled about sporadic food riots as they broke out in every major city. Images of police and military units facing down throngs of dirty unarmed civilians were too common. Charities were overwhelmed. Suicide statistics in Third World countries climbed to rates that had never been tracked before.

Circumstances were no better in the Atlantic and Indian Oceans. Official estimates of the remaining fish stocks were grim. Governments mobilized their navies and began to patrol their sovereign territorial waters in defense of what little seafood they had.

Boundary disputes between the United States, Russia, and China worsened as lawyers wrangled over deep sea land masses associated with the Pacific Outer Continental Shelf. Fifteen hundred miles of Canadian coastline separated Alaska from the contiguous United States, affectionately known as "the Lower 48." That one fact forced these people to get along with each other and make do with what they had, whenever they could get it.

The "Alaskan way," a philosophy of self-reliance, had come into its own after the 1968 discovery of oil in the northern part of the state, near Prudhoe Bay. It matured into a populist mythology as new industries took root. That spirit remained alive and well in the wake of the ongoing ecological crisis.

* * *

Jim Cook stepped off the subterranean monorail. He was dressed in stained cold weather gear. A black stocking cap and heavy insulated boots completed his disguise. He shuffled off the dirty, garbage-strewn platform with the rest of the night shift.

Frigid air blasted through the subway tunnel as if it were being propelled by a giant fan. Icicles hung from exposed alloy girders as another train passed on the far side of the terminal. It screamed through the man-made cavern at 75 miles per hour, vanishing in a haze of icy grit.

Some of the shambling men and women were going to their jobs. Most were getting off work after a long day of manual labor and chemical handling. Tobacco haze filled the air as dozens ignored the very obvious "No Smoking" signs.

Jim carefully avoided eye contact with anyone who seemed boisterous or easily annoyed. Fuelers and loaders didn't think highly of starport management, whom they often ridiculed. Union shop stewards kept the angriest among them in line, but that didn't prevent the occasional "accident."

Jim wanted to avoid any such run-ins. He traveled through the most dilapidated and rundown part of the employee housing and entertainment sectors without bodyguards. He never went in or came out the same way twice, and he *never* showed anyone his real I.D.

Every effort to keep crime under control in the nonsensitive parts of the growing starport had failed decades ago. Essential facilities could be properly monitored and policed. Habitations and long-term storage sites proved to be much harder to protect.

This part of the complex was called "Boom Town." The joke among starport staff and visitors was that everyone and everything in that zone was for sale, if you knew who to ask and how to pay for it.

Cook made his way through nine city blocks using a series of covered walkways. His destination, the Bloody Bucket, was one of the oldest drinking establishments inside the starport's official perimeter.

Music thumped and throbbed from speakers mounted high on the interior walls of what had once been a warehouse. Thundering bass notes were so deep and powerful that the wrinkled aluminum siding on the outside of the structure shivered in time with the music being hammered out by a live band. Jim paid the cover charge at the door and let the bouncer frisk him.

"You're a little old for this crowd," the big man said.

"I know the owner," Jim responded flatly.

The big enforcer grunted and moved on to the next potential patron.

Jim elbowed his way across the crowded floor to the bar. He put one foot on a rusty boot rail and took off his hat. A bald bartender approached.

"How you doin' tonight, Mr. Smith?" he asked loudly, his eyes roaming the room. Starport administrators had started the sign and countersign decades ago.

Jim looked over his shoulder. He didn't see anyone or anything that looked like trouble. "All is well. How about you?"

The wary man smiled and poured a glass of cold beer from a nearby tap. "We're good. My wife wants you to know that she appreciated that thing you did."

Jim took the glass when it was offered. He drank slowly before raising his voice to be heard over the energetic band. "You're welcome," he said loudly.

His host reached under the bar to push a button. "Go on back," he nodded.

Jim took his glass and went to the back of the room, where another large guard allowed him to pass through a door labeled "Employees Only." Another sentinel sat on a stool in a short hallway. "What's the word?"

"It's all good, Mr. C," the bouncer said while holding the inner door open.

"Make it stay that way," Jim prompted as he went in.

Reinforced walls and a million dollars' worth of electronics protected the spacious back room. Its tasteful decor was accented by expensive furniture that included a full bar and wall-mounted display screens.

This lavish lair was inhabited by members of the starport's underworld. They used it as their official place of business, a neutral location where they could coordinate their activities just enough to prevent turf wars that would draw the unwanted attention of the authorities.

A dozen men and women sat around a large circular table. Jim smiled at them and placed his glass on the flat surface. "How you all?" he asked while taking off his coat.

A round of noncommittal grunts and jovial profanities answered his question.

"How's the wife?" Anthony Siggs inquired politely. His coat and tie made the middle-aged businessman look reasonable and successful. Though his penchant for larceny wasn't widely known, those who were aware of his ruthless temper respected it.

Wanda Ness nodded as she texted with a wireless device in each hand. Her ebony features displayed no hint of the violence of which she was capable.

The starport's criminal cartel was now run just as efficiently as any a publicly traded company. Years of internecine warfare, fought in the neglected corners of the starport, had pushed out many of the smaller gangs and theft rings. All that remained were the most cunning and well-financed organizations that had ties to larger entities throughout the state and around the world.

Siggs was the cartel's current board president because he controlled the largest number of shares. Wanda was the group's version of a senior administrator. Jim sat between the two because they usually did most of the talking at these meetings.

An old-fashioned birch chair creaked under his weight as he sat. He swept a quick glance over the group and the clutter that was on the wide table. "Mrs. Cook is convinced that I'm a figment of her imagination," he joked.

Some of the observers laughed. "That's what you get for being such an honest man," Wanda snipped.

"If only that were true," Jim brooded while sipping from his glass.

A few people snickered.

The starport boss sat his glass down. "Mm. Okay. Let's get busy. This business with China is getting out of hand. I don't see any way around it. We're gonna have to protect what's ours and leave it to the nationals to sort things out the hard way."

"I told you it would come to this," Siggs admonished.

"Let's hear him out," Wanda urged.

All eyes were on Jim. He fidgeted with his glass. "Some of you were here the last time we did this little dance with the nice people across the big water. Most of you weren't."

"Where were you?" somebody asked.

"I was in school," Jim replied.

"We don't have all night," Siggs prodded.

"Let him talk," Wanda commanded.

Jim raised his glass. "I didn't start out with S.F.E., but I'm damned sure gonna finish with it. Everything this company has built on this rock is at risk. One wrong move, and its gone." He threw his glass into an unoccupied corner, where it shattered on impact and fell to the floor in a dozen small pieces. "Being new doesn't make me stupid."

"It *is* getting late," Wanda warned.

"You're going to need spies," Siggs mentioned, speaking as if it were no big deal.

Jim nodded. "You guys are smart enough to know which side of the bread your butter is on. I'll expect any advanced warning you can give."

"Nothing's free," somebody grumbled.

A ripple of derision died half way around the room.

Jim rapped his bare knuckles harshly on the table and swept his gaze around. "This is your home, too," he reminded the group.

Siggs raised a hand to silence any further argument. "It's okay. You made your point. Fleets need fuel. I'll tell you if we hear anything from our counterparts in China. Ports and warehouses are their specialty."

Jim drew in a deep breath. "Common sense dictates that nothing starts between the U.S. and China on or near dry land until the weather improves. That gives us a few months. I want you mutts to start getting ready."

"What exactly are we getting ready for?" Siggs inquired.

Jim licked his lips. "We are bigger than a bread box and smaller than a country. In China, corporate and political interests are the same thing. We have spaceflight technology they might want. It stands to reason they might try to take it."

"I hope you're not expecting us to do anything about that," Wanda warned.

"Never crossed my mind," Jim countered nonchalantly.

Siggs leaned closer with a gleam in his eye. "Agreed. We start by moving money, perishables, and family to the mainland. Small shipments. All of it goes out through the starport's air freight subsidiary."

"Why would we be so generous?" Jim asked.

Siggs rubbed his index finger on the expensive table. "TSA is going to nail some of our product if it moves through the regular commercial airports."

"I won't pay for drugs," Jim stated flatly.

"Gimme an alternative," the wolfish man challenged.

Jim rubbed his itchy nose. "Operations like yours have been piggy-backing people and packages onto privately owned vessels for centuries. Move your crud out of here on hired boats. It's not like the Coast Guard will stop you, and it'll mean you can send bigger loads."

Siggs and Wanda looked at each other. An unspoken worry about modern piracy passed between them.

Wanda nodded to indicate that the risk was ultimately acceptable, given the fact that they had so much to lose. It was a fair compromise. She looked around the room.

Nobody spoke. It was their way of saying that all of them knew the rule. Being the starport's friend was a good thing. It was a bad thing to not be the starport's friend.

"Our fams don't know what we do," she explained.

"You have your problems and we have ours," Jim replied.

"How soon we gotta go?" somebody asked.

"Can you do it in three months?"

The boss whispered with a nearby man. Their debate lasted for a full minute.

Siggs straightened in his seat. "Moving our loot like cargo is one thing. We can do that. People are something else. Some of us are bound to be arrested if we try to leave the island."

"I have no control over the Feds," Jim argued.

"Get some," Wanda demanded.

Jim reached for a nearby bowl of peanuts to give himself a chance to think. He ate one of the salty nuts to stall for time.

"Don't go to the U.S.," he suggested.

A scruffy man in the group waved his hand. "Most of us have American rap sheets. Nobody knows who we are in Australia or New Zealand. It can't take more than a month to fudge those travel docs."

Wanda slapped her hand on the table to demand silence.

"What's your point?" Siggs replied indignantly.

She looked coldly at Jim. "He's telling us to leave the damned country!"

"They're gonna catch half of us," Siggs admitted.

Jim shrugged. "Fine. Stay and see what happens. We're gonna get bombed. Cruise missile strikes, to be sure. You'd better stock up on medical, because we won't be giving it to you."

"That ain't cool," somebody objected.

Siggs nudged Jim. "You've made your point. Now, let me deal with this."

The executive got to his feet and put on his coat. "Let me be very clear about this. Any hostile force that sets foot on this starport will come for what's on it and in it. That means technology, tools, and whatever they can take from the gift shop." He looked down at Siggs. "Good luck with this. I'll be back next month to talk about some big ticket items that we're going to need."

"Guns?" the crafty deal maker suggested dryly.

Jim shook his head. "I want you to steal from our most worthy competition."

"Another starport?" Siggs wondered.

Jim tugged on his coat zipper. "New Mexico. They've been hacking into our computers and diverting some of our less-than-legal acquisitions for the last ten years. It's their turn to cough up a few things none of us are supposed to have."

"Avionics?" Wanda inquired.

"Surveillance electronics and satellite parts, of the national security kind," Jim suggested.

"Very expensive," Siggs leered.

"Very," Jim acknowledged glibly and left the room.

CHAPTER FIVE

The first week of November passed in a muted frenzy as key players at the starport worked diligently behind the scenes to carry out routine operations while shouldering the extra workload to upgrade the vulnerable space launch complex's defensive capabilities. These efforts included new construction and new hires.

Older machine shops that had once sat dormant were quietly reactivated and used to fabricate whole systems and individual parts for every legal security measure that federal and state laws would permit a nonmilitary organization of this type to have.

Tensions between the U.S., China, and Russia increased when three privately owned fishing vessels based out of King Cove went missing ten days before most Americans celebrated the Thanksgiving holiday. Matters were complicated when several American and Japanese Coast Guard VTOLs went missing shortly after responding to incomplete distress calls from civilian container ships that were later found to have been sunk in various locations southwest of Dutch Harbor.

U.S. government officials stationed on the Kodiak Starport began to compare notes. They used every asset at their disposal to take a closer look at what the corporation's workforce was up to.

New reports were written to document the increased capabilities that were being fielded, including sightings of exotic space planes and other advanced aircraft. Some of this information was shared with Alaskan state officials. Most of the accumulated data was classified as either "sensitive" or "secret" and sent to the nation's capital for further evaluation.

*   *   *

Hundreds of guests converged on the Governor's Mansion in Juneau for an invitation-only banquet. Clear skies favored the seaside city with a halo of twinkling stars.

Sheldon Wheeler stood in front of a full-length mirror and put on his tie. He made the knot quickly while admiring the outdoor view. He went to the open door of the steamy master bath and stuck his head in. "I'm going down to the office," he told his wife.

"Okay!" she replied from inside the roaring shower.

He used the private carpeted stairwell to trot down to the ground level, across the dimly lit tiled hallway, and through the back door of his large office. The sounds of a large gathering in the main hall reached his ears as he closed the door.

Sensors in the ceiling detected his presence and turned on soft area lighting. "Work lights on," he commanded loudly. LED lamps winked on with full brightness as he slipped into the high backed chair behind his long desk. A phone display on his desk clattered with an old-fashioned ring tone

"Phyllis?" he asked after touching the screen.

The staff assistant was formal. "Yes, sir. One of your party guests wishes to speak with you. He claims this is a matter of some urgency."

"Who is it?" Sheldon inquired.

"Mr. Ivan Gallagher."

The politician opened his mouth and paused. Gallagher wasn't known for his social calls. He closed his mouth and thought.

"Sir?" the assistant prodded.

Sheldon looked at his watch. "The event doesn't start for an hour. We have time. Let him in."

"I believe he's been noticed by the media," the astute women observed.

Wheeler groaned. "I'm sure he tried to hide. Let him in, and then go tell the staff to begin seating. Serve the first course when ready and don't be stingy with the booze. Tell them I have a call that can't wait."

Phyllis was an old hand at political galas. She knew how to cover for her boss.

Ivan Gallagher shuffled slowly into Sheldon's office through a side door normally reserved for staff. His smooth, bald head glowed in the strong light. An expensive suit hung from his lean shoulders as if it were still on the rack.

"Sheldon," he hailed laconically.

The governor waved him over. "Have a seat," he invited.

Ivan walked slowly with a long, black cane in one steady hand. His orthopedic shoes thumped on the brown carpet like hollow logs. Rimless glasses framed the old man's gaunt face, giving him a studious look.

Sheldon braced himself. "We never have these little chats unless you want something."

Ivan lowered himself into the nearest chair with his cane still in one hand. "I'm here to collect on some of what you owe the company," he said casually.

"I should be having this talk with Laura or Jim." Wheeler nodded pensively.

Ivan shrugged. "They have things to do. I'm retired. Besides, I was gonna come here and drink your hooch, anyway. Might as well kill two birds with one stone."

Sheldon stroked his freshly shaved chin. "I don't think you know how to retire. Guys like you are always up to something. What does Alaska Aerospace Electronics want from the State of Alaska today?"

Ivan wiggled his cane and shook his head. "It's not my company anymore and this isn't about me. The first thing I want is a list of names."

"Context?" Sheldon requested.

Ivan laid the cane across his lap. "You want us to protect Alaskan interests when the spit hits the fan with China. We'd like to oblige, but we need a free hand."

"You've got all the leeway I can give."

Ivan shook his head. "The Feds have people inside our organization. Been there for at least ten years."

"I wouldn't know anything about that," Sheldon protested.

Ivan pressed on. "Everyone from the Department of Homeland Security on down through the Pentagon has undercover observers on, in, and around the starport. You may not know who they are, but you can find out."

"That's treason," Sheldon whispered.

Ivan placed one hand on each end of his cane. He rocked it back and forth over his knobby knees. "I'm not here to debate the nuts and bolts of citizenship and its responsibilities. You've asked us to defend state interests when the shooting war starts because you know the Feds will pull their troops out and leave us hanging."

Sheldon looked around his office. "I can't believe you'd come in here—into this *unsecured* office—and ask me for *that*. Have you lost your mind?"

Ivan smirked. "Nice try. Your people are better than that. This office gets a going over at random intervals every day, whether you are here or not. The last sweep was 58 minutes ago."

Sheldon simmered. "Okay. Fine. You've got big ears. Probably been having me watched for years. That doesn't change the fact that giving you those names would be treason. Besides, it's the Attorney General you want. He's got that information. Not me. Good luck getting it out of him."

Ivan shrugged. "I had to try," he admitted wryly.

Sheldon grimaced. He didn't like being toyed with.

Ivan steadied his cane. "Next item. I want a pardon for Sasha Xavier."

"Are you nuts?" The governor straightened in his seat, his face blanching.

"Probably," Ivan quipped.

Sheldon gripped the edge of his desk. "That woman is a menace. She's a high-tech terrorist. You saw what she did to the university campus in Fairbanks."

"They had it coming," Ivan insisted.

Sheldon took offense. "No! She had legal recourse for what they did to her, and she didn't use it. Two wrongs don't make a right. Two million dollars' worth of computers and fifty million dollars' worth of data!"

"That belonged to her!"

"That's not the point!" Sheldon shouted.

Ivan raised his chin. "Look, Sheldon. You don't just take eight years of somebody's life and expect them to let it go without a fight. The Feds made a big mistake with that one."

The younger man slumped. "So, what? I'm supposed to make it right by letting her go with a clean slate?"

Ivan shook his head again. "She's got a skill set we need. She won't work on a leash. I need you to let her go."

Sheldon racked his brain. "She's been in the clink for two years. She's got to be rusty. Why can't get you some cowboys for that kind of thing?"

Ivan sighed. "You really are a blockhead."

Sheldon bristled. "That's Governor Blockhead! I don't need a lecture on subtleties or the value of a unique mind. I know the value of unorthodox thinking. There has to be another creative problem solver out there who isn't serving a five-year hitch for cybercrimes."

Ivan lifted his cane and waved it around. "What do you think I've been doing for the last few months? I've been to Seattle, Las Vegas, Silicon Valley, and a few other places I'd rather not mention. I've interviewed more than a hundred candidates. Nobody else has her reputation, or her willingness to do certain things."

Sheldon shuddered. "What in the Hell does a reputation for being crazy have to do with any of this?"

"That's classified." Ivan smiled.

The frustrated man wagged a finger at his antagonist. "Not so fast. Sell me. Why do you need somebody like that? I'll grant you that we're running the biggest defensive play of all time, but we are, allegedly, acting on principle. That woman hasn't got a shred of moral fiber in her entire body."

"You're too judgmental," Ivan said with a pitying glance.

Sheldon made a fist and let it go. "I'm looking out for an entire state with 800,000 registered voters. I have to be judgmental."

Ivan lowered his cane and tapped it on the floor. "Come on. All of this will look really good in your memoir. It might even get you a fourth term."

The politician grimaced. "There won't be a fourth term. It's getting worse at the Small Rock mine. Their crud is going to reach Bristol Bay in the spring. The only thing stopping it now is the natural deep freeze."

Ivan played with his cane for a moment. "You *are* easily distracted, aren't you?"

"Millions of gallons of poisoned water from an arsenic lake is nothing to laugh at," Sheldon griped.

Ivan waved his hand dismissively at the younger man. "I'm not laughing at you. Fight your battles one at a time. That's what they do at the starport. One crisis at a time."

Sheldon stood up. "You're right. You've got your mission, and so do I. That pardon will go out by the end of this week."

Ivan struggled to his feet. He reached into his coat for a computer memory device. "Here. Take this. It's got circumstantial evidence on it that can be used to justify your reasoning behind the pardon."

Sheldon took the small object and put it in a desk drawer. "How do I make the A.G. go along with this when he finds out just how flimsy your fake evidence turns out to be? I did appoint him, but he isn't stupid."

Ivan cleared his throat. "There are also some funky bank statements in there that belong to Mr. Law-and-Order. Looks like he's been taking money from some interesting people for a long time."

Sheldon glanced down at his desk. He rapped his knuckles on the wood. "I don't need you to give me dirt on my own people."

"You didn't know about it?" Ivan replied with arched eyebrows.

Sheldon shook his head slowly. "That's not the point. I'll ask for it if and when I want it. Please. Don't ever do this again unless I ask for it. Are we clear?"

"Yeah," the old man grunted as he turned to leave.

"Who's being judgmental now?" Sheldon complained.

Ivan reached the door he'd come in through and opened it. "Judgment is nothing to be ashamed it. It's not something you leave on a shelf. It should be used. That's how you know if you're doing the right thing or not."

"You should've been governor," Sheldon muttered.

Ivan twirled his cane. "You're right. I should have been governor. You beat me to it. I'll just have to make do with my millionaire playboy lifestyle. At least I can afford therapy."

CHAPTER SIX

The first day of December dawned on Kodiak Island under a lead gray sky. Massive cloud banks blotted out the sun. Blowing snow formed a dense layer of ice that encased every above ground structure at the starport. All launches were cancelled. Every rocket, shuttle, and lifting body had been towed into wind-resistant hangars or subterranean machine shops.

Search and rescue aircraft at the Coast Guard station near Old Harbor waited inside their own warm hangars. Air crews and pararescue personnel hoped they wouldn't be needed.

The Bering Sea rose and fell as massive saltwater swells pushed tons of shattered ice on the shores of the Aleutian Islands. No one saw Billy Richter arrive on Unalaska Island. Nobody saw how he got into King Cove, either. The small, isolated fishing town was locked down to ride out the storm. Nobody wanted to think about the damage that was being done to the fishing boats in the modestly sheltered marina.

Billy's cold weather gear was soaked through as he approached a dilapidated structure near a cluster of warehouses close to the northwestern side of the docks. Big, red letters on the side of the building spelled out "Diner."

Billy's hands were numb when he reached for the door. Warm air and the small of fried food swirled around him and made his nose begin to run. He shut the door and sauntered in to find an empty chair at the counter.

An older Aleut woman in a blue sweater came over to take his order.

"Coffee, scrambled eggs, and toast," he requested.

"Home fries?"

Billy took off his knit cap and stuffed it in his coat. Yes, please." He smiled.

She went into the back as he sat down. His feet began to warm while his eyes started to adjust.

Old light fixtures and ancient incandescent bulbs cast a soothing yellow light over the tables, fixtures, and patrons. Faded photos on the walls gave silent testimony to fishermen and locals who were no longer among the living. Big grins. Stoic expressions. None of the people in those photos had given an inch or compromised in any way when it came to residing in this isolated community or making a living on the unforgiving sea.

Footsteps on the fractured linoleum warned Billy of an approaching person. He swiveled slowly with one hand on the counter. A tall man in plaid shirt and blue jeans, wearing a baseball cap with a logo on it belonging to the island's largest land-based employer, Ice Cycle Seafood, moved toward him.

"You must be new around here," the fisherman said when he got closer.

"That obvious?" Billy smiled.

The inquisitor stopped just three feet away. "You just came in. The rest of us have been here for a few hours. You're the only one ordering. Most of us can only afford coffee or tea."

"I've always been a big spender," Billy quipped, shrugging. He could see a dozen men and women in the back of the eatery, watching his every move. They sat in a loose group around a trio of wooden tables, on which their coats and hats were piled. An uncompromising lifestyle had made them unafraid to indulge their curiosity.

The spokesman for the group offered his calloused hand in a reluctant gesture of diplomacy. "Charlie Pike," he said without a smile.

Billy stood up to shake the man's hand. "Billy Richter."

Charlie eyed the starport logo on Billy's shirt. "What's a rocket jockey doing out here?" he asked after releasing his iron grip.

Billy paused when the waitress brought him a hot cup of coffee. "Thanks," he said, then sat to wait while she went back for the rest of his order.

Pike took a seat next to him at the counter. "Richter. I've head the name. Some guy out of Homer has been trying to farm salmon."

Billy took two sips of the hot brew to steady himself for what would come next. "That's my father you're talking about, and there's no trying to it. He's been doing it successfully for the last ten years."

Charlie frowned. "Fish farming is a waste of time and resources. We gotta do better with what God gave us. No amount of inbred fish can save this part of the ocean."

Billy hid his disagreement by taking another drink from the big, white mug. "The inbreeding problems have been licked. We need more fish farms than we've got, and we need to protect our fishing grounds."

Charlie snorted and turned to face the kitchen. "I'll agree with the second part of that. It'll be a cold day in Hell before I eat a farmed fish."

Billy put his cup down and looked at his antagonist. "Look, man. I'm not here to start a fight. The truth is, I want to buy some fish nets and some of your time."

"Fish nets?" Charlie asked incredulously.

"Fish nets. Synthetic weave. No electronics."

Charlie sat quietly while the waitress served Billy. The smell of hot food filled the dining room.

"Anything else?" the pleasant woman inquired.

Richter reached into his pocket to pull out a pair of large bills. He handed them to her. "Keep the change and buy my friends some breakfast."

The hostess beamed at the sudden windfall. "All of them?" she inquired, after a quick survey of her customers.

Billy slowed when he heard a murmur from the spectators. He laid more cash on the counter. "Everybody eats today, all day, courtesy of the Kodiak Starport."

The grateful woman gathered up the money and rushed off. "Everyone be patient!" she hollered before entering the kitchen.

Somebody took out a wireless phone to make a fast call. "Get on down here now. There's a mainlander in here and he's buying breakfast for everyone. How do I know? Yeah, bring the kids."

"That's mighty big of you," Charlie mumbled.

Billy picked up a fork. "I'm a big man. Now, why don't you introduce me to your pals and let's talk about fish nets."

"Why do you want our fish nets?" Charlie asked while reevaluating Billy.

"Can't say," the hungry man mumbled with his mouth full.

"You're not fishing. Are you?" Charlie probed.

Billy washed his food down with more coffee. "Nope. You fish. We fly. That's the way it is. Anything else would upset the natural order of things."

"What else can you do with fish nets?" Charlie wondered.

"Catch stuff," Billy assured.

"What's that supposed to mean?" Charlie growled.

"Can't say," Billy reiterated.

"Are you making fun of me?" Charlie grated.

Billy put his fork down. "I didn't come all the way out here just to pull your leg, Charlie. You see what's going on out there. This pot is about to boil over. A lot of good people are going to get hurt unless we do something."

"Who is 'we,' exactly?" somebody shouted.

Billy drained his coffee cup and put it down. "That's a good question. Let's wait until the food gets out here and then I'll tell you."

Charlie glared at Billy. "We're broke. We can't invest in anything."

Billy turned. His chair squeaked. "I'm the one who's here to invest. It's my boss's money, but they've sent me out here to make a deal with you guys."

"What do we have?" somebody questioned.

Billy grabbed a piece of toast off his plate. "Fish nets and eyeballs. That's all we want. Cash on the barrelhead for the nets. Weekly payments, just to let us rent your eyes, complete with tax records for Uncle Sam."

Charlie folded his arms. "We're listening," he stated flatly.

* * *

Norman Ahgupuk drove to the starport's V.I.P. terminal through dense falling snow just after midnight. His tense grip on the steering wheel guided the big, black squad carrier he was driving around slower vehicles. He fell in behind a diesel snow plow and slowed down. Glare from his own headlights reflected off a bright orange warning placard on the big machine's rear end. The lumbering duo turned the corner and started their long trek down a brightly lit access road secured on two sides by high chain link fencing.

Norman took one hand off the wheel to active the dashboard phone. His call rang three times, giving him a moment to study his reflection in a side mirror. Wrinkled uniform. Tired face. Two days' worth of stubble on his chin.

"What's up?" Jim's voice boomed through the speakers in the cab.

Norman turned down the volume. "Almost at the V.I.P. I was calling to ask why I have to be the one to do this. You're the boss around here. Why aren't you out in this crap to meet and greet?"

Jim laughed through his own fatigue. "Because I'm out in this crap doing something that she doesn't need to know about."

"I feel like I'm being used," Norman sighed.

"You can't tell her what you don't know," Jim counseled.

Norman thumped his fist on the steering wheel. "Come on. Throw me a bone! Why does she want to see my birds?"

Static filled the line for a moment. Jim coughed. "No. Put that over there. Look, Norm. She owns ten percent of our stock *and* she's the one who put money under the table to feed *my* birds. Give her a peek and send her home. That's all."

"What about our pilots?"

"You really think she's gonna ask?" Jim countered, sounding unsure.

"I would."

Jim thought for a moment. "Yeah. I suppose. Who's up at this time of night?"

"Should be just the mechanics," Norman recalled.

Jim grunted. "Play it cool. Take her to the nest. Show her what she came to see and call it good."

"You don't trust her," Norman observed as the plow ahead of him slowed.

Jim shook his head. "No, I don't. She's too reclusive. Almost no social profile to speak of. I like my privacy just as much as the next guy, but she's almost nonexistent. I have the impression she's into something very hush-hush. Never been able to prove it. Have you ever met anybody like that?"

Norman lowered his cruising speed. "The Air Force is full of espionage types. Been like that ever since the first Gulf War."

Jim snickered. "I don't want to know what she's into. She's done this kind of thing before. Don't give her any reason to call Laura. Trust your instincts and she'll be gone before the sun comes up."

"I'll get it done."

"I know you will."

"What's really got you out so late?" Norman asked.

Jim sighed and swore. "It's the space station. *Gold Rush* is our biggest investment. It's also a big, fat target."

"What's the view like?" Norman asked, following the plow through a wide turn.

"Wouldn't know. Never been up."

Norman reduced speed when he saw his turn coming up. "I've just arrived at V.I.P. parking. My dad says you owe him a ride into space."

Jim chuckled. "Everybody should go at least once."

"Too bad that'll never happen."

"Never say never," Jim quipped, then hung up.

Norman rolled to a stop at the parking lot's outer checkpoint. The driver's side window came down with the push of a button. He showed his I.D. to a pair of guards who came out of a heated booth dressed in full cold weather gear. They saluted as he drove away.

He passed through the inner checkpoint after asking for directions to his designated parking spot near the building. He guided the big truck into the wide spot and shut off the engine, then got out and shrugged into his parka.

"Be polite," the retired officer reminded himself.

Norman went into the isolated terminal, through three checkpoints, to the heated hangar where new arrivals could park their private jets. He arrived in the lounge just in time to see a wide-bodied passenger plane roll to a stop at the center of the cavernous enclosure. A dozen members of the blue-coated ground crew rushed out with wheeled ramps and stairways.

Norman turned to the smartly dressed protocol officer standing nearby. "What am I up against?" he asked while opening his coat.

She smiled and showed him a tablet display. "Tanya Arvold. Blue chip investor. Holds ten percent of our preferred stock."

Norman studied the picture on the display. "Tell me something I don't know," he said, frowning.

The coordinator was unperturbed. She touched the screen. "As you can see from this, she's quite accomplished. Very philanthropic, too."

Norman looked up when a cargo ramp on the back of the plane came down. "Look. What's that all about?" He pointed.

"She always brings her own transportation," the officer explained.

Norman moved closer to the tinted glass. "I should have expected that. Does she travel with an entourage?"

The polite woman came closer. "It's not a problem. You'll be riding with her."

"I will?" he scowled.

"Yes," the planner asserted. "It's a must-do."

He said nothing for several minutes. A dozen people exited the aircraft from two forward stairways. A long custom-built vehicle drove down the cargo ramp and headed for the lounge's loading ramp.

Ahgupuk pointed to the passengers who were going in through another entrance. All were expensively dressed, followed by assistants towing luggage carts.

"Where are they going?" he asked.

"Most are here to see family," the coordinator confirmed.

"Must be nice," Norman muttered.

The six-wheeled custom limousine came to a stop at the bottom of the ramp. A passenger door in the middle of the vehicle opened.

The observant woman touched his arm. "It's okay, Mr. Ahgupuk. That's your cue."

Norman searched for his phone and made a quick call to his lead mechanic. "Company is coming. Clear out. Send everyone home. Yes, that means you, too."

"Please don't keep her waiting," the coordinator insisted.

The pilot was annoyed. He hung up and stowed his phone. He took off his coat and folded it under one arm.

"First, I miss my cue. Now I'm makin' em' late," he kidded to blow off steam.

The social director watched him leave the lounge and enter the limo. "You'll get used to it," she whispered.

* * *

"This is nice," Tanya declared grandly an hour later, after the long drive to a very secure and unofficial location.

"We don't need state of the art," Norman assured.

The soft-spoken woman stood wrapped in exotic furs while the aviator finished his ad hoc presentation near one of the stripped down fighters.

"Why can't this be done with drones?" she countered.

Five of the big, all-weather air superiority fighters filled the massive underground chamber to capacity. Bright lights, stained floors, and scattered tools made the place look chaotic.

"Drones can be hijacked," Norman explained.

"Electronically?"

"Just so," he nodded.

The smell of fuel was comforting to him. Tanya's entourage was nowhere in sight, which helped to relax the irritated pilot even further.

"Everybody likes drones," he conceded. "They're cheap and they don't risk lives. That's good, but losing control of drones means they can be used against you."

"How often does this happen?"

Norman was glad they were alone. "The official answer is 'never.' It's happened at least twice that I know of."

The well-travelled woman observed his every move, looking for any hint of deception. "That's right. Twice. What is your assessment of the Chinese capability?"

"Formidable."

"Have you ever flown against enemy drones?"

"Not officially," he conceded.

"Stay here," she insisted.

Norman watched Tanya walk around the nearest airplane.

"Why F-15s?" she asked on returning to his side.

"Cheap," he speculated.

"Why not something more modern?" she asked critically, slipping her hands in her pockets.

The retired officer shrugged. "I had no say in this. Everybody's going to war over one resource or another. We're gonna fight the Chinese for fish. There aren't many choices left on the surplus arms market just now."

"That's not very efficient," she scolded.

Norman refused to take the bait. "I'm an old nationalist. You don't get much more patriotic than the F-15 Strike Eagle."

"Is it a question of more money?"

He shook head. "It all comes down to availability just now. We're lucky to have these. I know guys who salvage military aircraft for a living. They're all out of work. That means there's no more surplus of any kind to be had."

"What would you do with more of my money?" she demanded sharply.

"I'm the wrong guy to ask," he replied, squirming.

"Why?"

Norman hesitated. He reached out to touch the nearest toolbox. "Jim and the others are making this up as they go along. One half-baked starport versus a modern carrier battle group. That's what they're likely to throw at us. We know they're coming. It's just a matter of when."

"You have doubts?" she surmised.

Norman shuddered. "Alaska is my home. The Pacific Ocean is a big place and Washington is a long way off. Everybody from the governor on down thinks we might be left to fend for ourselves."

"You don't think the people here can do this?" she probed.

Norman tilted his head. "I'm no sucker for lost causes. We have the tools. We have the talent. All we need now is a bit of good luck."

The eccentric woman was satisfied. "I've seen enough. You'll have more money if you need it, for whatever the purchase might be."

"I'll tell them," Ahgupuk nodded.

"Talk to me directly," Tanya told him plainly, "I'll give you a way reach me. Facts. Figures. Tell me everything. I'm going to know if you don't. Let's go back to the airport."

Chapter Seven

Christmas Day was dominated by bad news around the world that soured what should have been a festive occasion for billions of hungry people. Tensions between East and West reached new heights.

Armed fishing vessels fought over catches that would've been pathetic just five years earlier. News networks around the globe spent millions to send their most daring correspondents out to sea in an effort to broadcast scenes of burning ships, gun fire, and hair-raising scenes of hand-to-hand combat.

Reports from California, Oregon, and Washington State kept viewers up late into the night as municipal law enforcement leaders held press conferences to announce a series of regional crackdowns intended to reduce instances of crop theft from privately owned farmland in rural districts. Officials from the Department of Homeland Security articulated unambiguous federal support for these measures. Alaskans went to bed knowing that they faced an uncertain future.

Recent construction of new oil refineries and liquefied natural gas plants crowned a decade of achievements for America's 49th state. Several of these facilities had been financed with money appropriated by the state legislature. Controversy swirled around these enterprises long after they'd become operational. Governor Wheeler, who lobbied long and hard for the projects during his first and second terms, was now being vindicated as shipments of consumer goods to Alaska were becoming more expensive and less frequent.

State-owned oil and gas refineries did more than provide jobs for the private sector and extra income for the legislature to squabble over. Local fuel prices were kept low enough to aggravate champions of capitalism. This corporate consternation was a source of humor for many Alaskans who enjoyed what little shelter they had from global economic chaos.

Frozen ground kept toxic runoff from the Small Rock mine from reaching Bristol Bay. Biologists predicted absolute mayhem in the spring, when local water supplies would become undrinkable. Mass evacuations, begun months before, would continue as an estimated 40,000 people fled from the contaminated region. Computer modeling suggested a complete obliteration of the salmon fishery within two years of arsenic slurry contamination.

Local governments in every corner of the state felt compelled to take increasingly desperate actions as the year came to a miserable end. Some boroughs filed for bankruptcy to avoid the total shutdown of all public services. Others sold assets in a cautious effort to get clear of their modest debts. Activity at the Kodiak Starport slowed as customers struggled to balance their accounts before the end of the federal tax year.

* * *

Governor Sheldon Wheeler spoke to the state legislature at the end of January as part of the annual "State of the State" address that was carried live to the citizens of Alaska through every form of multimedia. He did so without a teleprompter. Every fact he cited sprang from memory. Every judgment about these things came from his heart.

Sheldon finished his half-hour evaluation of the state's economic forecast. "Never before in the history of this great land have we been so involved in global commerce. We've been so vulnerable to the wants and desires of our neighbors. As much as we wish for neutrality, we will not get it."

He thumped his fist on the podium. "There are conflicts going on around us that we can't stay out of."

The crowd in the meeting hall remained quiet. Cameras turned. Eyes moved.

Wheeler felt the weight of history descend on him. The tie around his neck seemed to clutch harder. He pursed his lips. "We've developed more coal, oil, and natural gas in the last decade than anyone thought we could. As controversial as it is, we've been farming fish for the last three decades. And we're better at it than anyone else, in spite of what the environmentalists had to say."

He gestured grandly with one hand as the audience murmured. "All these innovations and prosperity are ours because *we* made them happen. We've bumped heads with the multinational corporations when they've threatened out way of life, but otherwise we've dealt fairly with them. Even when it was clear they didn't intend to show us he same courtesy."

He paused. "No progress is made without paying some kind of price. Every effort we can muster is being made to deal with the Small Rock mining disaster. That project was pushed through—by many of you in this legislative body who are here tonight—before I came to this office."

The audience murmured. Sheldon raised a hand to ward off rising protest. "I'm not here to place blame. My opinions on this fiasco are on record. I *am* here to tell you that every public and private resource is being used to prevent this crisis from getting any worse than it already is."

Wheeler's opponents in the legislature exchanged meaning glances with each other without saying a word. The Governor waited while dozens of remotely controlled cameras panned around the big room. Network news anchors and quick-witted pundits provided commentary on the sour faces that were being illuminated during this awkward moment. Some of it was clinically serious. Others were less forgiving in their caustic remarks.

Sheldon shrugged as if the anger of his opponents didn't matter. "We're stuck between rival nations that *are* eventually going to fight. We're Americans, so we already know which side of this thing we're going to be on. I want to conclude my remarks tonight by making one thing perfectly clear."

He looked directly into the nearest camera. "This is a new year, full of new possibilities. We are prepared, even if the leadership in Washington isn't. We are resolved, even if the way forward doesn't seem obvious to anyone just now. Know it. Believe it. God bless America."

* * *

Jim Cook turned off his media feed. Screens around the "birdcage" overlooking the starport's operations and administrative area went blank.

"He didn't mention us," Laura Andrewyuk sighed from her office in Anchorage.

The CEO's face looked up at him from a flat screen embedded in the big desk. The tired man rubbed his face. "That's because I asked him to keep us out of the spotlight this time."

"Why?"

Jim stared at the dark windows around him. "All I ever wanted as a kid was to be an astronaut. I couldn't have that, so I set my sights on this job. Now, all I want is to be a rocket jockey just so I have the smallest chance to die in a fiery explosion that won't leave anything for my wife to bury."

"Is it getting to you?"

He was about to swear when a chime sounded. The male voice of that evening's senior launch controller came through with enthusiasm. Ceiling mounted cameras closed in on his workstation as the white-shirted professional made a historic announcement. "Attention, all departments. Commercial payload 400 achieves lift-off in three…two…one…"

Jim did swear when the intercom went silent. "See that? Did you hear that? Four hundred!"

"Makes me want to celebrate," Laura replied.

"If I had time," he laughed.

"Make time," Laura chided.

The troubled man rubbed his brow. "I would if I could, but *Gold Rush* is behind schedule again and Her Holiness is being a pain in the butt."

"You mean Sasha?"

"Yes, I mean Sasha," Jim fumed.

Laura snickered. "Genius is always hard to deal with, especially when it's being stored in a female body. Take some time off. Delegate. Let your people do their jobs."

He relented. "We've got everybody who wants a pay check out in the cold working very hard. Okay. I'll take the rest of this week off, if it'll make you feel better. It's not like things can get any worse around here."

"That's the spirit," Laura nodded, hanging up.

Jim touched a screen to make the windows around his skybox transparent. He watched the men and women on the operations floor in an attempt to absorb some of their good cheer. "Enjoy it," he muttered with an approving whisper.

Jim observed his wrist watch for a full minute before activating the intercom. "Moment's over." Happy men and women reacted to his audiovisual presence by cheering. Cook used one finger to raise the intercom's volume. "I see all. I know mostly all. Get back to work. There are two hours left on this shift before you can hit the bars."

He watched the supervisors shoo the technician back to their workstations, then activated a phone control with one hand. The device came online with a chirp. Jim cleared his throat. "Phone, call my wife and tell her I'm coming home for a long weekend."

A green light on the phone told him his call was in progress. Jim reached for his coffee cup as the door to his office opened. Norman Ahgupuk stormed in wearing a snow covered parka and knee-high insulated boots.

"Did you just kill my staff assistant?" Jim asked while sitting up straight.

Normal tore off his snow-covered parka and threw in on a nearby chair. "There was nobody out there, otherwise I might have. *Who in the Hell do you think you are?"*

Jim picked up one of his business cards that lay scattered on his desk. He held it up. "See? That's my picture. That's my name. I'm *supposed* to be the senior administrator for this here plucky little starport."

Norman tugged at his uniform and sat in the closest chair. "Don't patronize me!" he growled.

Jim dropped his card. "Okay. Let's play. What's got you so riled up?"

Norman reigned in his temper. He hoisted both hands, as if to surrender. "I'm sorry. I must've broken at least three different kinds of protocol coming in here like this. I'm sorry."

"I can see that," Jim observed with a neutral tone.

Norman gathered his thoughts. "I just spent two hours being grilled by some jackhole from the Department of Homeland Security."

"Joshua Stringer," Jim nodded.

"You knew about this?"

The executive steepled his fingers. "There's so much that I could plead guilty to. Please be more specific so I can feel your pain or have you fired for insubordination."

The outraged man forced himself to back down. He slouched in his chair. "That little rat accused me of being involved with some cockeyed plan to hide gun and missile emplacements inside water towers. Then he hits me up about stolen satellite gear that was taken from the New Mexico starport."

"What did you tell him?" Jim asked.

"I didn't tell him a damned thing!" Norman exploded. "We're pilots! You know that. Just a bunch of old guys trying to fly some old birds. That weasel even accused us of being involved in a space plane project."

"What did you say that?"

Norman laughed. "Why on this green Earth would you waste your time rehabbing a dozen obsolete fighters if you have military-grade spacecraft? I may be past my prime, but I'm not stupid."

"Of course not."

Norman sensed the changed in the administrator's mood. He stiffened. "Oh man," he breathed.

Jim sat up and let his hands wander. "The important thing here is that you didn't give Stringer anything to go on. I'm sure he knows what you're doing, but he can't prove a lick of it. With any luck, he won't catch on until it's too late."

Norman had enough experience as an Air Force officer to know when he was out of the loop. "You *do* have space planes."

"That would be illegal," Jim protested softly.

"But you do have triple-A in those water towers," Norman recounted.

"What could make you say that?" Jim asked delicately.

Norman looked around the austere room for a moment. "Stringer had pictures of people working inside, and on top of, water towers that I've seen around the starport. They were taken last summer. Why do we have so many water towers, anyway?"

Jim shrugged. "Federal government. Environmental Protection Agency. Two years ago, some greenie in D.C. decided that all starports must have gravity-fed water distribution systems in place as a backup to normal fire suppression systems."

The former office cursed mildly when he realized what was happening. He moved to the edge of his seat. "Okay. I get it. I screwed up. Coming here tells Stringer that I'm guilty of hiding something. He's gonna poke at me even harder."

"Yes," Jim acknowledged.

Norman sighed. "The water tower thing is real. Makes sense. Elevated platforms at regular intervals in and around the complex could provide adequate fields of fire for a local air defense net."

"Which we officially do not have," Jim emphasized.

"Because that'd be illegal." He lowered his head. "You could've told me. You know my old man. What makes you think I wouldn't keep your secret?"

Jim tilted his head sympathetically. "It's in my contract. I'm not allowed to trust anyone. I knew Stringer would get to you, eventually. You're the new guy, doing the one thing that seems really out of place at the moment. Yes, you're still the bait intended to keep Homeland Security off my back."

Norman fell back in his seat. "Do we still get to fly?" he asked hesitantly.

Jim tapped a touch screen which caused a projection map to light up the ceiling. "We expect things to start in the spring. U.S. and Chinese naval elements will clash out here somewhere. Then they'll move towards Alaska."

Norman looked up. "Yeah. You're assuming that the Chinese win that battle. They've never fought carrier-on-carrier. We have."

"A hundred years go," Jim reminded the younger man.

The aviator conceded the point. "My money is on the U.S. of A. I haven't asked yet because we're still doing simulator time. How will you arrange for training? My pilots are good, but they'll need at least fifty hours each in both day and night conditions before they're airworthy. And we'll need to train with live ordnance."

The administrator shrugged. "Stringer is fixated. Might as well give him something to watch. You can start basic flight training next week. We've got an air strip near your hangars, with its own snowplows, that isn't being used."

"You *want* them to watch me?"

"I do now," Jim confirmed.

The disgruntled officer frowned. "My pilots won't like being your distraction."

"Don't tell them."

"I should say *something*," the officer protested.

"No, you shouldn't," Jim insisted.

"Can I at least confirm the air defense?"

"To the pilots? Yes," Cook replied, nodding.

Norman studied the projection. "Fine. We zoom around in local airspace. That doesn't solve the problem of ordnance training."

Jim turned off the map. "You've heard of the Small Rock mine?"

"Every day," Norman griped.

Jim made a wide gesture with his hands. "As the spring thaw hits, there will be more evacuations from the Aleutians. That includes King Cove and the airport at Cold Bay."

"The Air Force will want to base fighters out of Cold Bay," Norman observed.

Jim wagged a finger. "Not going to happen. I have connections in the FAA. They tell me the insurance companies have no taste for this fight. Every commercial airline that flies in that part of the world has had its coverage cancelled."

"That's cowardly."

"That's being realistic," the executive corrected.

Norman shifted in his seat, trying to get comfortable. "You've got a deal in the works to get Cold Bay? What about the locals?"

"I don't intend to pay rent," Jim quipped.

"What about the locals?" Norman repeated.

"All out by the first of April," Jim replied, as if he were parting with a secret.

Norman rubbed his chin. "Airlift in. Bring our own gear. Can you do that?"

Jim laughed in with real mirth. "We're the Kodiak Starport. We launch satellites and move tons of low-orbit freight every week. I hear a rumor that we build billion dollar space stations, too. Trust me; we can handle some old planes, old pilots, and old electronics. I've even got some old food and water lined up for you."

"How does any of that help me?" Norman retorted.

"Suppose the Chinese fight for King Cove or Cold Bay?"

Norman was astonished. "Why would you fight for King Cove in the first place?" he countered.

Cook grinned. "Think strategically. You get an out-of-the-way practice field if nobody fights. If they resist, we force their attention away from the starport."

Norman flinched. "I'm sure the folks in Washington will love you for that."

"All's fair in love and war," Jim joked.

"Are you nuts?" Norman asked, blanching.

The older man shook his head. "You wanted practice with guns and bombs. That would do it."

Norman bristled. "Flying a jet isn't like driving a car. You don't just get in, turn the key, and go. Even with upgraded avionics, we need a chance to make mistakes."

"You're all veteran pilots," Jim reminded.

"Trained on more recent systems," Norman countered.

"Which is why you should start making those mistakes now, even if Homeland is watching."

Norman thumped his knee with one fist. "We were hired to fly local combat air patrol. That's a defensive mission. Now you're saying we might do close air support. That's an offensive mission. Have you got the munitions for that?"

"Yes," Jim lied.

"When can I see them?" Norman demanded.

"Soon," Jim promised.

"Extra pay."

"Everybody gets double."

"Gunnery range," Norman challenged.

Jim rolled his eyes. "Can't you do that sort of thing far out at sea, where nobody can see it?"

"We could, but the FAA will see everything we do on radar. That's going to mean big fines. Unless you have permits?"

"We'll pay," Jim sighed.

"What about the space planes?"

Jim scowled. "We'd be breaking 50 different federal laws and a dozen international treaties if we had any such thing."

"You might be building them under government contract," Norman suggested.

Jim rolled his eyes again. "Can you imagine the bureaucratic specs on a military spacecraft? They'd be so ambiguous and paradoxical that any contractor who tried to follow through on them would go stark raving mad."

"Are you building them with your own money?" Norman inquired weakly.

Jim pushed his chair back. "Any space plane we did have under development would be very expensive and it wouldn't be ready for use during this crisis."

Norman got to his feet. "I'm sorry about the intrusion. Stringer got to me."

"He's good at his job," Jim admitted.

"I'll try to be better at mine," Norman promised.

"Keep one more thing in mind," Jim warned.

Norman reached for his coat. "Yeah? What's that?"

Jim walked around his desk. "Everybody gets to go off on me just once. You've had yours. Don't ever come into my office like that again. Don't ever make those kind of assumptions about me again. Push my buttons again and I'll have you fired."

Chapter Eight

International tensions escalated throughout the month of February. Winter grain harvests in many countries were bountiful, but they didn't come close to meeting the demands of an increasingly hungry global population.

Farms in the United States fared no better. Armed clashes were covered by the media. Activists, police officers, and National Guard troops squared off against large numbers of poor and homeless people who had nothing to lose by charging barricades in an attempt to reach food.

Illegal fishing operations around the world were located and disrupted by every available means. Governments harnessed intelligence-gathering assets, espionage resources, and military and naval units to crack down on seafood piracy.

The most well-known environmentalist groups officially reversed their positions on fish farming, backing away from more than six decades of formal opposition to the practice. Observers from these groups began "standing watch" at the more vulnerable privately operated fish farms and government-run hatcheries.

North Korean warships fired on Vietnamese fishing boats a few yards outside the internationally recognized 12-mile boundary as the month ended. The desperate fishermen, aware that such a fight was possible, had come armed with a mix of obsolete recoilless rifles, light machineguns, and assorted infantry weapons. Their wood-and-steel hulls, equipped with civilian radios, were no match for the low-silhouette frigates that used radar guided cannons against them. Electronic countermeasures prevented any of the distress calls from reaching friendly ears.

North Korea's state-run media was quick to announce the results of the battle. A straight-faced man read from the teleprompter with grim certainty. "We repelled this unjustified incursion into our sacred waters as passionately as we would defend our sovereign soil."

Reporters in the region scrambled to document the carnage six hours after the shooting stopped. Aircraft loaded with cameras and commentators flew over wreckage-strewn waters to review the loss of life.

"No survivors."

"We can't see any warships nearby."

"Clothing of all types, just floating."

A well-known defense analyst from New Zealand summarized international opinion while offering his own scathing assessment. "Everybody should calm down. This isn't the first time that this sort of thing has happened in the last 15 months, but it is the first time that anyone has bragged about it."

Three more high profile naval engagements occurred during the month of March in the eastern Indian Ocean. Japanese fishing fleets attempted to retain neutrality, though they were quickly drawn into a series of running battles that forced them back to port.

Maritime insurance companies revoked policies in an effort to minimize losses. Corporate frugality didn't prevent hungry people from setting sail in search of their next meal. Profiteers, who didn't care about insurance coverage or lawful permits, stepped up their efforts to find and exploit what little the seas still had to offer.

Alaskans braced for a difficult spring as federal, state, and local officials struggled to cope with renewed evacuations from the southwestern part of the State. The Alaska Peninsula was being deliberately depopulated in anticipation of the continued westward movement of toxic runoff from the Small Rock mine.

Climbing temperatures thawed the frozen slurry, which found its way into rivers and lakes that were commonly used for drinking water. Warm winds from Siberia accelerated the warming trend, which caused water bodies in the region to open up just enough to be vulnerable to the arsenic that had once been used to leach gold and copper from crushed rock taken from the Small Rock mine.

* * *

The first day of May dawned in the Arctic, full of bitter promise. High clouds moved over southwestern Alaska, propelled by warm winds form Japan. Southcentral Alaska was already experiencing breakup—a period of intense melting that would often cause a risk of flooding for some communities.

Beatrice Brown steadied herself in the shifting wind. Her customary trench coat felt thin and insufficient against the wind coming in from the sea. Some of her gear had been lost or taken away ahead of schedule. She felt unprepared.

Dillingham's waterfront was deserted. The massive fish processing plant was locked down and its windows were boarded shut. Evacuated residents, now scattered to other parts of the world, wondered if they'd ever be coming back.

The cameraman stood in the long, cold shadow of the last ship to leave the area. He waved to indicate that the video feed was streaming onto the Internet.

The finality of the moment made a lump rise in her throat. "I'm Beatrice Brown, reporting for Polar News," she croaked.

Keening seagulls overhead made her feel mocked. She took another breath before going on. "I'm the last one out. There is no one else left in Dillingham. Every town and village between here and King Cove is being…just…empty. They…the residents….have all been moved inland."

"D'you wanna stop?" the camera operator asked.

Beatrice knew the sound pickups on the camera weren't getting all of what she said. "Let's finish it."

The broad-shouldered man steadied his aim.

She turned. "The entire length of this pier has been the scene of intense activity for the last six months, as state and federal officials tried to get a handle on the Small Rock mining disaster. State hydrology experts have confirmed that the water table in this area is already contaminated. The entire region will be without clean water in just a few weeks."

She waited for the camera to be panned up and down the deserted wharf. "People in the Aleutians will be shielded from this for at least another month. Those islands, surrounded by all that salt water, may not notice any ill effects for a few years—five, maybe ten, at most. The truth is that we really don't know what comes next."

Beatrice focused her diminishing willpower on the camera. She took a step closer. "Bulldozers are working around the clock to stop the flow of toxic waste from the Small Rock containment zone. A spokesman from Governor Wheeler's office says the current estimate is that they will have the flow stopped by sometime in early June. Once that happens, natural filtration processes are projected to clean the waste from the region within five to ten years.

"I wish I could be more objective," she said pleadingly.

"You're doing fine," her colleague told her.

She coughed. "There's just so much going on in the world right now. So much bad news. We can't stop. We've got to pull together and figure a way out of these things. We can't just give up."

"Settle down," the big man warned.

"I don't care if I get fired!" she angrily replied. "It's killing me to report all of this that doesn't seem to be anyone's fault. We know who the corrupt politicians are. We also know which corporations are cutting corners. How much more do you need to see? When are you going to stand up and do something?"

The cathartic release of her rant left her speechless for several seconds. "Turn it off," she said quietly.

"They're gonna have your butt in a sling for that," the technician groaned.

Beatrice stomped away, heading for the ship. "I really don't care!" she shouted.

She received a call two hours later, while the ship was at sea. Alone in her cabin, she sat on the edge of her bunk and flipped the phone open. "Yeah?" the unhappy woman mumbled, expecting to be a harangued by a news bureau chief.

"Ms. Brown? This is James Cook at the Kodiak Starport."

Beatrice paused to read the phone's caller I.D. "What do you want?" she asked bluntly.

"I saw your last bit from Dillingham."

"So?"

"I'm going to do something about one of those problems you mentioned," he replied calmly. "I could use an experienced observer to act as a somewhat partial witness to what's about to happen."

"And you think that's me?"

"Your honesty was inspiring," he responded. "It made me think. We've never had a good relationship with the media. I'd like to change that."

"How?"

Jim chuckled, "How'd you like to work for us?"

"Why?" she wondered.

Jim paused to gather his thoughts. "I'd like somebody with your point of view to see what we do. You'll have as much access as I can afford to give without compromising vital activities."

"You're asking me to leave Polar News?"

"I am," Cook confirmed.

Beatrice's heart raced as she thought quickly. "Double my salary. I want unrestricted access to you. I also want an editor, video lab, tech support, and a publicist."

"Working on it now," Jim told her.

"I want stock," Beatrice added, "Enough to retire on when this is over."

"Agreed. We'll have a contract for you to sign when you arrive at your destination."

"Where am I going?" Beatrice probed.

Jim coughed. "That ship you're on is going to Anchorage. You'll be getting off at King Cove."

"There's nobody in King Cove," she argued.

"I didn't say there was."

Her curiosity was piqued. "What's going on there?"

"Go to King Cove and find out," he coaxed.

"You're asking for a lot," Beatrice complained.

"I was a demanding child. I still am," he joked.

"What are you expecting me to find?"

"The biggest thing since Felix Pedro struck gold."

* * *

Jim sat motionless for five seconds before opening a desk drawer. Inside sat an old, encrypted phone system that dated back to the earliest days of the starport. He used a plastic key to open a lid before typing an access code into a keypad. Picking up the handset, he pressed one more button before entering the number he wanted to call.

Old circuits hummed. Obsolete dial tones chirped and radio frequencies hissed. Electromagnetic interference distorted the voice on the other end of the line.

"This is Teflon Leader. What's you're authentication?" the male voice queried.

"Authentication is 'revolver,'" Jim quoted from memory.

"I accept. Pass your message."

"Make it happen."

The radio phone crackled. "Teflon is inbound. Are we cleared to engage?"

"Smoke 'em," Cook ordered, then hung up.

* * *

Search and rescue units from the starport arrived in King Cove minutes later by long-range VTOL. Six tilt-rotor aircraft, painted stark white with no other markings or visible identification numbers, hovered inches off the deck near the marina, close to the ground, while dozens of men and women in cold weather gear made short leaps to the soil from lowered ramps or open doors.

Everyone was dressed in the custom-made, striped, gray-tone camouflage that the starport was known for. Equipment bundles and cargo pallets were released from the droning aircraft before they departed.

The insertion was completed in just three minutes. Two-man teams fanned out to secure a 50-yard perimeter as technicians went to work unpacking all-terrain vehicles and communications hardware.

Billy Richter was the last person out before the air transport withdrew. He wore an integrated helmet with a multichannel radio whispering in his ear and a digital distance magnification system that shielded his eyes from the sun while acting as a virtual data display. He watched his people move before giving orders through the radio.

"Bravo Romeo is feet dry."

The pilot of what looked like a chartered executive jet circled high overhead. "Stand by for recon report." His aircraft, painted in civilian markings with obvious commercial logos belonging to a popular regional airline, had sensors of every type studding the belly.

"Recon Alpha is on station. No airborne threats detected," he relayed.

Billy stepped aside as two men on an ATV drove by. He glanced at the sky. "Transport, this airspace is clear. Move to loiter."

The VTOLs turned west and flew out to sea just feet above waves, where they would wait for their services to be needed.

Three specialists rode in the dark passenger compartment of the surveillance plane, surrounded by two million dollars' worth of electronics. They relayed their findings in causal shorthand to squad leaders on the ground as the defensive perimeter expanded.

"Moving thermals, 50 to 900 yards beyond your perimeter."

"Six teams. Pairs. Moving defensive. I think they intend to engage."

"Positive lock on local E.M. Military radios; multiple channels are in use."

"Computer classifies traffic as known configuration for PRC naval commandos."

Billy flagged down one of his officers. "How'd they get here so fast?" he asked, speaking into the radio.

"Helicopter, center of town," Recon explained.

"U.S. Coast Guard markings," a technician added.

Billy looked at the display on his tablet computer and showed to the approaching figure. "Somebody wants a fight. Recon, widen your search. Climb to 10,000. Redirect active systems out to sea."

"They're gonna see us," the pilot objected.

"Bad guys can see you right now," Billy snapped.

The pilot remained reluctant to obey Billy's commands. "That's easy for a man with his feet on dry land to say. Warships aren't in my contract."

"*If* they're out there," Billy chided.

The experienced aviator hesitated. "It's your call, FDR. That helo didn't come from Shangri-La. If there's a Chinese warship out there, me and the boys are gonna live just long enough tell you about it."

Billy used his magnifying visor to scan the nearby mountain tops. "Sorry. We have to know. Any hint of trouble out there means we go home, even if you don't."

The pilot conferred with his crew for a moment. "That chopper is a real strong hint. Looks like the right make and model, but it's not supposed to be here. I'm sure the folks from Beijing expect to be dancing with federal troops. U.S. Marines or, at the very least, Alaska National Guard."

"Instead, they get us," Billy snorted.

"We're done with ground scan in two minutes," the pilot relayed.

"Finish and then get up there," Billy snapped.

"You have company," a technician called out.

"What's their play?" Billy asked.

The system operator read his instruments carefully. "Holding. Looks like a three-way field of fire."

That made Billy stop abruptly. He rushed over to a pair of men carrying a large cylinder containing a crew-served weapon. "Unpack that thing and get ready to rake the high ground!" He didn't wait to see if they complied before galloping toward the place where his command post was supposed to be.

The use of dazzling lasers was now common on the world's many battlefields. The variable light wave patterns from portable emitters could be used to temporarily blind anyone who looked right at them. Two-man sniper teams carried them as standard equipment, to be used in defensive situations.

Billy slowed to a walk as his lungs heaved. He keyed his radio. "Perimeter units, hold at 100 yards from CP and report all I.R. contacts. Appropriate shelter as needed."

"Ground scan complete," the pilot reported.

"Contacts holding. Radio traffic reducing," a tech added laconically.

Billy knew what he was asking for. The reconnaissance plane would have to gain altitude to increase the range of its ship-detecting optics and radars. Anything they could "see" would also be able to mark and identify them. The non-stealth aircraft would be easy pickings for any warship that reacted to their presence.

"Peek quick and get back down here," Billy ordered.

"Okay, then," the pilot replied. "Civvie transponder on. Can't say it's been good to know you. You're gonna owe us big if we live to collect."

Billy muted his mike as the airplane gained airspeed and altitude. He turned to his officer. "Company's waiting for us to come further inland."

"Told you so," the Aleut man grinned.

Billy accepted his error with a nod. "So you did. Break out the heavy weapons. Tell me when you can put rounds on the slopes."

The security chief handed off his tablet without saying another word and went toward his rapidly assembling command post. The recon jet climbed. The roar of its engines could be hard over the driving wind.

"Laser threat detected," a worried co-pilot called out.

"Proximity is danger close!" somebody warned.

"He's on our five o'clock," a technician added.

"Why didn't we see him?" another voice lamented.

Billy didn't have to ask where it came from. A single soldier, wearing cold weather gear with a chambered respirator and sitting inside a thermal shelter, could hide on the ice-covered mountain overlooking the seaside community and never be seen by airborne heat sensors.

Richter reached the building that was his temporary command post just as a flash of yellow high on the mountainside gave away the missile operator's position.

"C.M. deployed," the co-pilot called out as chaff and flares fell from the plane.

The pilot of the converted executive jet realized that the ascending missile was below and behind him. The heat-seeker was faster than his aircraft. There was only one way he knew of to avoid being shot down. He'd have risk to flying past the missile, forcing it to miss him by mere inches. The antiaircraft weapon wouldn't have enough fuel to turn around. "Forcing the merge," he growled.

The desperate man put the nimble airplane through a snap roll that culminated in a sharp turn, heading toward the accelerating rocket. Loose objects inside the plane bounced around the cabin and cockpit. Load alarms sounded from the instrument panel as extreme g-forces threatened to snap the wings off the accelerating airframe.

"Now would be a good time to say mayday," the co-pilot huffed.

Billy looked up through his mag visor to see the jet twist and turn as it trailed white hot flares and shreds of sparkling aluminum designed to confuse radar-guided or heat-seeking missiles. "Get lucky," he whispered.

All three men in the back of the descending aircraft swore. Billy's mouth fell open when he saw that the jet was heading towards the wispy, gyrating track of the missile, as if the pilot were intending to ram the fin-stabilized projectile.

Billy screamed when he saw the jet disintegrate. He charged into the commandeered storefront to avoid seeing the wreckage hit the mountainside.

Conditions inside the boating supply store were chaotic. Shelves had been hastily pushed aside to make room for equipment as men and women tried to get in out of the cold.

The corporate officer stopped long enough to survey his surroundings before going the nearest satellite connection. He pushed his way past a soldier and tapped in his access code. The connection went through to the starport instantly.

"You're late," Jim heckled through Billy's headset.

The adrenaline-charged man didn't waste time with formalities. "Fight's on. We need air. Send the Eagles."

"Naval activity?" Jim pressed.

Billy wiped his sweaty face. "Didn't see anything on the way in. Not enough time to look once we landed. The Commies got here ahead of us. They had a shooter on high ground that popped our recon. What's *Gold Rush* say about ships in our area?"

Jim sighed. "*Gold Rush* is…not online."

Billy swore. "Oh, come on! We've got people dying down here! You said she had everything under control!"

Jim lowered his voice. "Sasha and that station have two things in common. They're both temperamental and they need constant attention. Everything was fine until about 15 minutes ago. We started getting alarms. Then, nothing."

"Nothing?"

"Dead air."

Billy looked around the room. "We're gonna spill a lot of blood in the next few hours. I can't justify—"

"Make it happen," Jim demanded.

A ball of ice formed in Billy's stomach. "Yeah. Sure. I was hoping it wouldn't come to this. How much air support can you give me?"

The administrator mumbled under his breath. "It was a risk worth taking. We lost. Iron up and cry about it later. The 15s are coming. Three of them will be talking to you in 10 minutes. Are you staying or leaving?"

Billy realized he'd given away his tablet. He looked at the nearest digital map that had just been plugged in. "Loss of recon is a setback. We know they're here. They certainly know we're on the scene. Probably know who we are, too."

Jim interrupted. "I see your feeds. Which is it? Stay or go?"

Billy loosened the chip strap on his helmet. "They let our transports go in favor of getting a shot at a more expensive asset. That tells me they intend to stay. We have to fight 'em. It's the only way to reach Cold Bay with any degree of safety."

"I agree," Jim replied.

Billy made up his mind. "We're gonna have to take the casualties. I'll send the transports back for reinforcements. We'll fix and fornicate these guys with air support. Should be over with by nightfall."

"I like it," Jim grinned.

"They'll fight harder for Cold Bay," Billy predicted.

"Let 'em," Jim snorted and signed off.

Chapter Nine

Billy Richter's mission to secure the abandoned community at King Cove took 51 hours. Minimal air support, difficult weather, and lightly armed troops had proven to be larger limitations than he'd been ready for.

Starport security forces, trained for antiterrorism duty, had mild success in their countersniper actions. The Special Forces unit that resisted their efforts played for time, exploiting logistical weakness when they could, giving ground when they had to.

Billy kept his heartache over troop casualties to himself. Norman Ahgupuk's estimation of his improvised squadron's effectiveness was accurate. No more than two of the old all-weather fighters were in orbit over the town at any given time. Their use of infrared and thermal imaging systems to spot unshielded ground targets did more good than their bombs or guns. Norman's pilots were rotated through the area of operations in three-hour shifts.

The commandos were driven out of King Cove at the cost of three lightly armored vehicles and seven starport soldiers. The last enemies were picked off by vehicle-mounted snipers as they tried to cross the barren wildlife preserve that separated King Cove from Cold Bay.

Billy watched with morbid interest as the last of his dead were collected and placed near his command post. In addition to the casualties the defenders had suffered, three men and two women had also been killed by air strikes that went wrong.

"Ten for sixteen," Billy lamented.

The sound of departing jets faded in the cold afternoon sky. The former soldier was lost in a moment of introspection when Jim's voice burst into his headset.

"It wasn't sixteen for ten," the distant man offered.

Billy adjusted the hood of his parka. "Too many mistakes," he said bitterly.

"Learn as we go. You're the master of King Cove now. That's all that matters."

Billy stepped closer the building to get out of the wind. "Stop it. Can the platitudes! I used to be a drill instructor. I know losses like this are bad for morale."

"You did outnumber them," Jim observed.

"After we brought in reinforcements," Billy argued.

"Good soldiers mourn their losses," Jim said plainly.

Billy wiped his nose. "Okay. Let's move on. Where's the baggage you were telling me about?"

Jim coughed through the radio. "Your combat correspondent arrives on the next big thing to reach King Cove. Should be there in four hours."

"Yay," Billy grunted.

Jim shrugged. "She's a big name in these parts. Please don't fold, spindle, or mutilate. We need her to see what you see so that we can all stay out of jail."

"What makes you think I won't commit any war crimes?"

"You're better than that," Jim replied with conviction.

Billy watched the nearest sentry walk away. "I'll meet her at the docks."

* * *

The freighter carrying Beatrice Brown arrived as the sun began to set. She was taken to the marina by a motor launch. The small, fiberglass hull rode the waves with just enough chop to send up a fine spray that blanketed the entire boat.

The reporter and the launch operator shared the sparse cabin without much conversation. The compact Filipino man who guided the boat was formal, though never quite polite, as they made the 20-minute run into the harbor.

Beatrice endured. She was the reason for the ship's detour, which didn't sit well with the crew. Everything they heard over commercial radio lead them to believe that war between the Americans and Chinese would begin any day.

Several reports had been heard over unscrambled shortwave radio from fishermen at sea. The few who were optimistic enough or desperate enough to risk deep water called in sightings of trawlers flying foreign flags. Partial sightings of what could have been warships put every civilian sailor in the region on edge. The lack of flag identifications made every cargo ship captain who was in transit feel uneasy.

There was nothing she could say. There was nothing else she could do. Beatrice zipped up her coat and collected her things, reaching dry land with a leap to the dock from the boat. She waved her thanks to the boatman as he departed.

Billy Richter and three of his subordinates arrived just in time to meet her. His driver parked an armored squad carrier at the end of the pier after letting Billy out. He walked out to meet the reporter with a calm wave.

"Did you have trouble finding us?" he asked.

Beatrice looked around. "I've been here before. Many times. Who are you, anyway?"

"Billy Richter," he replied, offering her his gloved hand.

"Kodiak Starport?" she guessed.

He took some of her luggage. "Starport security services. I have orders to let you see everything we do. That's going to include some violence."

Beatrice scanned her surroundings. "What exactly is going on here?" she asked.

Billy gestured at the waiting squad carrier. "Walk with me," he invited.

She looked over her shoulder at the retreating launch. "My ship made an unscheduled stop," she said in an effort to be friendly.

Billy guided her toward the waiting vehicle. "I'll bet you were popular with the captain and crew. Can we skip the pleasantries?"

"Please do," Beatrice consented, walking faster.

Billy grinned. "Okay. Here's the straight dope. We're here to gain access to the airfield at Cold Bay."

"Why?" she probed.

"Not for me to know."

"What's happening now?"

He coughed. "We came in three days ago. I was hoping to do this without bloodshed. We met resistance. There were casualties on both sides."

"Who were you fighting?"

"Chinese. Special naval troops."

The woman stopped, surprised. "Hold on. You're not the Army. You can't do this. Who gave you the authority to do this?"

Billy halted and turned. "Nobody official gave us the go-ahead. I'm sure the people who run the spy satellites know that we're out here."

"Why would you do anything so stupid?" she challenged.

Billy frowned. "It wasn't my call to make. None of us would be out here if it were left up to me. Your contract says I have to give you full access, so I am."

"You're just following orders?" she jeered.

"Something like that," Billy replied gruffly.

She pivoted. "How do you feel about all these people who have been killed?"

He blinked. "I'm not proud of it, if that's what you mean."

"Regrets?"

"You're just a ray of sunshine," he observed.

"This is an illegal action," Beatrice said.

Billy shifted the luggage he was carrying from one hand to the other. "That's technically correct. Just like all the people I have killed, and will kill, in the days ahead. Look around. This place has been abandoned. It's just us and a handful of dead guys." He speared her with an angry look. "I'm gonna regret what's happened here for the rest of my life. I don't know if this could've been avoided. I just know that we had to win, which means they…had to lose."

"You're dragging this country into war," she argued.

Billy swung the bag he was carrying. "Get real. This fight is going to happen whether we want it or not. I'd bet you a dollar that Chinese forces are all over the Aleutians. Everything from here on down to Attu is in enemy hands."

Beatrice wasn't entirely surprised by the revelation. She knew enough about military operations to grasp the importance of what Billy was implying.

She now understood why she'd been hired. "None of that explains why *you* are *here*. Why am I talking to you when I should be talking to the U.S. Marines?"

"My orders are to take the airfield—" he began.

"Why?" Beatrice gestured wildly when he didn't speak. "What does a high-tech starport need with some rinky-dink airport in the middle of nowhere?"

Billy pointed at the patch on his shoulder. "Invading Alaska means they go through us—the starport—whether we want them to or not. That means we get a piece of the action, whether we want it or not."

She walked in silence for several seconds. "I see. This is some kind of preemptive strike."

Billy shouldered her rucksack without comment and kept walking toward the squad carrier.

Beatrice looked at the equipment bag in his hand. "That's a $10,000 helmet-and-camera system. Please, be careful with that. Even with a contract, I lose my job if it gets lost or broken."

He stopped manhandling the pack. "It's not just a preemptive strike. We want to draw attention away from the starport."

The journalist thought she understood. "Too many large, expensive things that can't be moved. You're defending your investment."

"That's about the size of it," he acknowledged.

"What's next?" she inquired.

Billy pointed at the waiting vehicle. "Come with me and I'll show you."

* * *

There was no reaction from Washington. There was no response from Beijing. Richter's actions in Alaska appeared to go unnoticed by every government now teetering on the edge of financial ruin.

Beatrice was appalled by the destruction she saw in King Cove. She put on a lightweight camera headset and begin her walkthrough of the homes and businesses that had been abandoned in the wake of the Small Rock mining disaster. Twenty-three damaged or destroyed structures came to her attention. She worked late into the night, talking to starport soldiers about what they'd seen. Their short, simple observations only fueled her curiosity.

"As you can see from this pattern of craters, our bombs missed the target."

"Two of their men made a last stand in there. No, they didn't surrender."

"I gave the order to burn 'em out. There was no point wasting bullets."

The journalist took it all in. She was numb and unable to eat long after the sun went down. She'd never seen so much property damage or photographed so many dead bodies in one place. She picked at cold remixed rations for dinner.

A soldier led her to a cot in the living room of an abandoned house next to a warm portable space heater.

"We won't disrespect 'em by sleepin' in their beds," he explained before leaving her alone with a semi-automatic handgun. When she wouldn't take it, he admonished her. "Relax. You won't have to shoot anyone. We got patrols going all night. There's even a guard on your front porch. Keep the back door locked. Use this gun like a whistle. All you do is pull the trigger. We'll hear the noise and come running."

The idea that a privately run corporation could take this kind of action was outrageous. She fell asleep on her borrowed cot. The faces of deceased commandos disturbed her fertile imagination. Her dreams were vulgar and tortured.

* * *

The senior officer in Cold Bay assessed his losses and reported his findings to Elite Forces Command, located in mainland China. He spoke through an encrypted satellite connection late into the night, arguing for a withdrawal of his remaining forces.

Communist party officials were interrupted in meetings, summoned from social events, or woken from sleep to deliberate on the matter when the military chain of command refused to take action without approval from Beijing.

High-ranking intelligence officers debated the merits of the case vigorously. Their covert mission, to gather intelligence and secure forward operating bases, was being challenged by a nongovernmental entity. Paper and electronic records documenting the first clash between Chinese forces and the Kodiak Starport were eagerly sifted and reinterpreted. Private security units were common sights on modern battlefields. Nobody questioned their presence.

Politicians in the Politburo who governed the People's Republic of China *did* question the need for retreat in the face of civilian opposition. They saw no reason why the starport's glorified police force shouldn't be defeated.

Senior diplomats counseled discretion. There was no doubt in their minds that a fight with America was nearly at hand. Why give up any advantage? Those among them who had been to the continental United States suggested that the use of mercenaries to counter their special forces indicated that China held the upper hand in terms of raw military power.

The officer in Cold Bay didn't care about the relative strengths of either nation. The presence of his force had been detected. An entire detachment had been killed or captured. Martial wisdom strongly suggested that his enemy would reinforce his numbers and attack with overwhelming firepower at first light.

Party leaders in brightly lit map rooms argued while generals and admirals stood nearby. The lack of any force reaction from the U.S. military, or official reaction from the U.S. government, solidified the resolve of China's ruling elite.

Military preferences to retreat from Cold Bay were overruled. No reluctance should be shown in the presence of hired guns. Additional commandos would be brought in from the only special operations submarine they had in the region.

Career-minded analysts agreed with elected leadership. Past activity indicated that the corporation in control of the starport would fight to defend its own interests.

Officers and politicians forged an understanding. The lack of diplomatic repercussions presented PRC forces an ideal opportunity to knock out some or all of the starport's offensive capabilities, which could make the launch complex easier to attack in the future,

All known military and diplomatic risks were acceptable in the face of weak U.S. resolve. Additional orders were issued to move units in the Aleutian Islands to Cold Bay as quickly as local conditions would permit.

* * *

Beatrice slept in her clothes, though without boots. She was roused after just five hours of rest. She opened her eyes to find Billy Richter standing over her.

"I didn't hear you come in," she muttered.

"That'll change," he told her cheerfully.

The familiar setting of a darkened home kept her mind at ease. "I read your file. How does a former enlisted soldier get to run an operation like this? You weren't even an officer."

Billy opened his coat and sat on a nearby sofa. "That's a long story. You need to get up and get dressed."

"Do I have time for a bucket bath?" she inquired soberly.

"No point," he assured her.

"Why?" She yawned, rubbing her eyes.

He stood up. "Everything we're about to do involves getting hot and sweaty."

"I'm not that kind of girl," she groaned.

* * *

High, fast-moving clouds from Siberia threatened a mix of rain and sleet. The attack on Cold Bay began just as the sunrise streamed over the horizon. An overnight buildup of airlifted supplies and equipment from the starport provided Richter's troops with enough armored transports and weapon carriers to drive two dozen armed men and women through the wildlife refuge, on the road between King Cove and Cold Bay.

Richter's lead element approached from the landward side of the airport. The second group came in by air, onboard the same unmarked VTOLs they'd used to cross 400 miles of ocean from the starport on Kodiak Island.

Billy, his control team, and Beatrice Brown, trailed the VTOLs in the captured Coast Guard helicopter that the commandos had used to infiltrate King Cove. GPS and extremely accurate digital clocks kept everyone on schedule.

They flew low to the ground at just under a speed of 100 knots.

"This chopper looks real," Beatrice commented through her helmet intercom. The headgear she wore was different than those of the soldiers and air crew. Developed by Polar News Service, it contained cameras, computers, and satellite links. Nicknamed "the fish bowl," it was a source of pride for all reporters who worked for the company.

The pilot rapped his knuckles on a black instrument panel. "It is. Looks like they took this one off one of our cutters. Might've been the *Hammond*. I hear she went down without a trace six months ago. Probably hit them at sea, when the bird was still on deck. It's ours now."

Billy was in no mood for humor. The long-range helicopter droned on for several minutes.

Beatrice held several pieces of equipment in her lap. Borrowed cold weather camouflage kept her warm from head to toe. The word "Media" was stenciled in bright orange paint on the front of her vest, in both English and Chinese. "Still not sure how I feel about the color," she mumbled while examining her wardrobe.

The airport's runways loomed large in the long-range camera screen as they approached their destination. A control tower stood tall nearby. Beatrice waited. Computers and cameras in her helmet did their job, recording information from the radios and cameras on the helicopter.

Comms chat was confident. Efforts to sweep the small community that supported the airport were going well. Three dismounted SWAT teams were checking and clearing the area with stoic efficiency, using numbered maps and carefully prepared aerial photos.

"Structure Ten-One, clear. We have overwatch. Team Two is go Ten-Three."

"Perimeter set, open ground through A-One is clear to traverse."

"Come out, come out, wherever you are…"

Billy sat patiently with his eyes closed behind a lowered sun visor, taking it all in as the various aircraft got closer to their drop zones. He keyed his mike slowly. "Ghost Flight, terrain thermal check."

High overhead, Norman Ahgupuk cruised in one of the rebuilt F-15s with a wingman just a hundred yards off his right shoulder. The two-ship element orbited above the cloud cover, beyond the range of any known shoulder fired missiles.

Norman checked his instruments again. "I see what you see. Looks like their Alamo is the airport. Terminal buildings. Hangars. Your VTOLs ought to be in SAM range now."

Billy tried not to think about that. Shoulder-fired antiaircraft missiles were one thing. Bigger systems, of the type that could be set up on a tripod or towed behind a truck, would have longer ranges and be more accurate.

Mechanics at the starport had hastily upgraded two of his tilt-rotor troop carriers with better detection systems. That small effort was about to pay off.

An alarm sounded over the squadron frequency. "Call it out," Billy ordered while adjusting his helmet.

One of the pilots sounded off. "Hostile emissions detected. Computer says radar charging. Acquisition type. We are at seven miles and closing."

"Decoy. Give 'em a taste," Billy ordered.

"Located and locked," Norman announced.

"Wait your turn!" Billy scolded.

"Decoy going up," another pilot announced.

An empty transport broke away from the formation to gain altitude. External reflectors on the rising aircraft's wings and tail redirected the incoming radar emissions, scattering them in a strobe pattern that would be enough to frustrate or confuse any human radar operator within just a few seconds.

"Frequency change!" the monitor called out.

"It's acquiring," Norman added.

"Wait for the launch," Billy ordered.

The Chinese ground-based antiaircraft radar was positioned on top of an innocuous administrative building near the main terminal. It relayed what it "saw" through loosely strung fiber-optic cable to a portable display set up on the ground floor. A technician relayed the returns to a waiting officer. "Crude, but effective," the officer commented.

The officer was not impressed. He had six short-range missiles at his commend. All of them had autonomous radar and independent tracking systems built into their warheads, allowing them to seek out their own victims after launch. He doubted that his very smart airplane killers would be so easily fooled. "Continue acquiring the decoy," he told the technician.

The missile operator smiled.

The officer leaned in to see the readout for himself. "Designate their fighters as primary target and shoot. Full spread."

Three swipes of a finger on two different touch screens put everything in motion. Automated launch equipment on the roof pivoted as the missiles were programmed with targeting priorities. Electric motors pointed six canisters at the sky. Half a dozen rocket engines ignited at the same time.

"Launch detected," the decoy pilot called out. He cut back on air speed, dropping towards the frozen earth below, recovering at the last instant to skim the tree tops.

"Said they'd go for the fighters," somebody commented.

"Return the favor," Billy ordered.

Norman and his wingman were already busy with the intercept. In its day, the F-15 Strike Eagle had served as an air superiority fighter. That mission had changed in the age of stealth. The large airframe was now more commonly configured as a multirole platform.

The custom-built versions being flown by starport pilots had been rebuilt with contemporary avionics and upgraded engines. Ahgupuk and his partner increased their interval by 200 yards as wing-mounted pods on each speeding jet unmasked to reveal clusters of one-shot chemical lasers.

Sensors on and in each aircraft detected the rising missiles that were closing range very quickly. No active radars were needed. The computer-controlled pods aimed and fired a total of 12 laser bursts from each aircraft. Nine of 24 invisible beams struck their intended targets. All six heat seekers were destroyed in what looked like a single rolling fireball.

"Three seconds," Norman bragged.

"Formation, reduce speed," Billy barked.

"We're done, so we're gone," Norman announced.

"Gunships, go!" Billy shouted.

Three VTOLs with improvised gun mounts sprinted out ahead of the inbound aerial armada as the fighters withdrew. Billy had no time to congratulate the pilots. He knew the laser pods they carried were spent. He also knew that another pair of fighters configured for ground attack would be taking their place any second now.

"Insertion in 60 seconds," Billy advised.

The pre-positioned defenders braced themselves. Their squad nets buzzed with descriptions of the incoming aircraft and their apparent landing zones. Very little mention was made of their antiaircraft missiles.

Billy turned in his seat to look right at Beatrice. "You stick to me like glue."

She nodded.

The formation broke up as transports banked and descended on their designated targets. Starport forces already on the ground controlled perimeters around most of these landing locations. Sporadic shots rang out as snipers on both sides took shots of opportunity.

Billy's chopper dove for the broad flat roof of the main terminal building.

Machine gun fire raked the side of the helicopter. Several rounds punched through, into the cabin, spending themselves on the far side of the compartment. Beatrice screamed.

Billy jumped up and ripped the cargo door open. He leaped out with an assault rifle in both hands, looking left and right as troops boiled out around him. "Terminal breach in progress," he announced through his helmet radio.

Green lights on the reporter's helmet display told her that her equipment was functioning properly. She took a deep breath and scrambled out of the helicopter as it began to rise. More bullets struck the retreating aircraft as she rushed to keep up with the men who now ran for the nearest cover.

The sound of grenade explosions nearby made her stomach flutter. Multiple cameras in her big helmet took in the scene from several different angles that she'd be able to choose from later. She tucked in behind Billy as the man fired over the cowling of an air conditioning duct.

He pulled back when his magazine ran out. "Ever been in combat?" he asked her while releasing the empty clip.

"I reported on the drug wars in Fairbanks," she replied, her heart racing.

He dropped the empty mag and pulled another one from his vest. "How close did you get to the action?" he asked as he reloaded.

"Close enough to get blood on my clothes," she admitted uneasily.

Billy crouched to scan his surroundings. "Good. That means you won't be totally freaked by what comes next."

"I can hardly wait," Beatrice grumbled.

Shots rang out nearby. Billy motioned his squad forward with a hand signal. The assault continued.

Chapter Ten

Jim Cook was in his office overlooking the starport operations deck with the door closed. Every screen in his office was lit with launch status updates, space station construction reports, or fast-moving video of the battle unfolding at Cold Bay. Audio from Billy Richter's assault hissed and sputtered from speakers in the ceiling.

"Medic! Send stretcher and trauma kit."

"Incoming at two o'clock! RPG near the fuel hub."

"Thermal contact. Visual I.D. Sniper confirmed."

Cook snacked on fresh popcorn from a plastic bowl while listening to the fight traffic and typing responses to electronic memorandums and other in-house correspondence.

Billy's demeanor under fire was encouraging. Everything he said through his helmet radio was calmly spoken.

"Ghost Four, here's your next target."

"You sure about that?" the female pilot asked.

Richter said firmly, "This whole thing is for nothing if that fuel line cooks off. Put your bomb right *there*, and let's hope for the best."

Jim blinked when some of his screens went blank. Filters in each panel hid the flash. Automatic room lighting fluctuated in silent reaction to the sudden flash. He tried not to think about who might have died from bomb shrapnel in that instant. "Takes all the fun out of it," he muttered.

"APC hit and destroyed," the pilot cheered.

"It's about time," Jim grumped.

The cost of fuel for the old fighter planes was negligible when compared to what was being spent on ammunition, ordnance, and offensive energy weapon systems. Jim couldn't help himself. He imagined a large dollar figure that grew each time another bomb was dropped by one of the eager pilots. "Geezers, past their prime and having a second childhood," he moaned.

The door to his office slid open without warning. U.S. Army General Manika Sachdeva entered briskly with a military policeman not far behind.

"Wait outside," she ordered as the door closed.

Jim quickly turned off every screen in the room. The senior officer glanced through the nearest bay window at the operations area. "Hello, Jim. I'm sorry about the surprise visit. I just got off the jet from Seattle."

Jim straightened. "Excuse me. Is this my office? Was there *anyone* out there? I must need a new staff assistant."

The general stopped to scan the room. "There was nobody out there."

"Of course there wasn't," he sighed.

"I decided to come in."

"Of course you did," Jim replied dryly.

Manika sat in the nearest chair. "We know what you're doing," she stated flatly.

"I'm glad somebody does," he frowned insincerely.

She tapped his desk with one manicured finger. "No joking. I have it from a reliable source that the President himself is staying up-to-date on what you're doing in King Cove."

Jim laid his pen aside and folded his hands. "Are you here to arrest me?" he asked pointedly.

After a brief hesitation, she replied, "No."

Air conditioners whirred overheard.

"They wouldn't send a two-star just to say hello," he concluded after a moment of thought.

"I've been put in charge of the Arctic command," she told him confidently.

Jim knew General Sachdeva on a first-name basis. Her son worked at the starport as an attorney in the litigation department. "Go on," he urged.

Manika crossed her legs, striking a dignified pose. The medals and ribbons on her chest shifted. "There was quite a stir in Washington when your forces landed in King Cove. Some of my friends in the State Department nearly had heart attacks."

"I'm thinking about having one right now," Jim quipped with a nervous twitch.

She smiled. He was trying to respect her Indian composure by attempting to lighten the mood. "You've always been a gambler. That's what I told my superiors. They've decided to give you a free hand."

Jim nodded. "Nothing in this life is ever truly 'free.' Get to the point. What's the b-b-bad news?"

It was Manika's turn to frown. "A decision has been made to let them have the Aleutians. The whole chain. I'm to take the federal detachment here at the starport and relocate it to the mainland."

Jim looked out the nearest bay window at the men and women who did their jobs without any knowledge of what lay ahead. "I assume that choice was made to defend the port of Anchorage, which would be vital for any future operations."

The general made an affirmative gesture. "That's part of it. There are certain people and interest groups in Washington who don't like the Kodiak Starport. They'd like to see you take this one on the chin."

That made him laugh. "I'll bet the guys in New Mexico would love to see us go offline permanently."

"There is no love lost for you in Japan, either," she admonished softly.

Jim rubbed the stubble on his chin. "Yeah. Okay. Fine. Your masters can rest easy. You've delivered your message. Now, tell me. How much of a free hand do we have and how much immunity from post-war federal prosecution do I have?"

"Why?" she asked with real surprise.

He shook his head. "Let's not screw around here. Cards on the table?"

"Show me yours and I'll show you mine," she promised, nodding primly.

He slumped closer. "You must know about our arrangement with Governor Wheeler. Don't play coy with me. That man couldn't keep a secret if it was tattooed on his butt without his knowledge while he was asleep. I'm sure he said something over an unsecured line within the last year."

"Six months ago."

Jim accepted the confirmation with a grunt. "Okay. Here's how I see it. This contest between the U.S. and China plays out at sea. Win, lose, or draw, the whole thing is decided out there on the big water."

Manika brushed at the epaulet on her right shoulder like she was swatting a fly. "I've got two full Stryker brigades and half a million angry Alaskans that say they don't get very far on dry land."

Jim shook his head ruefully. "I'm not a soldier, but I've got a few of them on the payroll. They've done the math. The bad guys are coming with aircraft carriers. Just one of them off our coast means disaster."

She shifted in her seat, trying to get comfortable. "Air Force assets in this region have been reinforced with the coming conflict in mind. That includes airborne surveillance, command and control, antiship, antisubmarine, and air superiority capabilities."

"None of which will be tasked with protecting us," Jim emphasized with a sweeping gesture.

"You're inside our air defense!" Manika protested.

The aerospace manage manager nodded. "Yes, by just 300 miles. That won't be good enough to keep their cruise missiles out of our sky."

"You expect to be hit?" she queried dryly.

He gestured with his hands again to frame a picture. "They've made threats against Japan and they've got troops going ashore in places I've never heard of. Vietnam and Cambodia are asking for some kind of understanding, which means they're about enter this conflict as Chinese allies in order to get a piece of the action."

"You're not in this alone," Manika reproached.

He made a spiraling gesture with one hand. "We could be, right after they shoot down your fighters that come up to stop their bombers."

"You overestimate their capabilities," the strategy-minded officer rejoined.

Jim lowered his head. "My gut says they'll take us intact if they can."

"I would," Manika admitted.

He glared at her. "What would you do when you couldn't capture this little slice of high-tech heaven? Tell me. Be honest. What would come next?"

The career officer looked away.

"Necessity would dictate..." She paused.

"*That* is why I need a free hand," he insisted.

She tilted her head. "You win. I'll make the phone call. You want immunity from federal prosecution because of what you might have to do. Promise me you will not use anything nuclear, biological, or chemical."

"I swear," Jim professed with one raised hand.

She reached into a shirt pocket for a card and laid it on the desk. "That's an unlisted number and a nonserialized, auto-erasing, single-use command code. Understand?"

The agitated man picked up the card and scrutinized the handwriting. "Why so helpful?" he asked calmly.

Manika sat up. "I'm as expendable as you are."

"I doubt that very much."

"In what way do you doubt me?"

Jim turned slowly in his chair. "At the very least, you'll get a board of inquiry that'll take six months to ruin your life. You might even get a chance to say something to Congress before they toss you out with the trash. I, on the other hand, can be fired with just one phone call. It's in my 2,000-page contract."

"The media will hear what we say," Manika rejoined.

Jim laughed. "That and $5,000 will get you a ticket out of this starport on the next ballistic airliner."

"How crude. Do you even *like* your job?" she rasped.

He nodded. "I love my job. I'll do just about anything to keep this place open for business. Now, you've delivered your message, and I accept your terms. Show me something authentic from the Justice Department with a big presidential seal on it that'll keep me and mine out of jail, and I'll fill you in on what comes next."

"You've really thought this out, haven't you?"

Jim stood and opened the door to his office with a remote control. "This is a starport. We've got thousands of tons going up and down every month when times are good. Some of it moves pretty fast. We have to think ahead. Plan for every possible screw up. Then, we have to be ready to do something about it when those bad things happen," he said as the general left the room.

Cook placed the card he'd been given into his wallet and paused to think. He remained standing while making a call to the human resources department. "Transfer my staff assistant and get me a new one," he ordered impatiently.

Jim went back to work. He was interrupted two hours later when the encrypted data line to his secured printer announced an incoming transmission.

He got up and went to a black wall-mounted cabinet. Biometric sensors recognized him. The large outer door slid open to reveal a small inner door. He opened it using a nine-digit keypad and an old-fashioned metal key.

The dedicated printer was a recent addition. It hummed industriously while page after page of federal Department of Justice documentation slid into a collection tray. Jim picked up the growing stack and riffled through it as more pages kept coming. He refused to think about the lives that were being lost in and around Cold Bay. "Time enough to grieve later." he decided.

He glanced at his desk. "Phone, call the legal department. High priority. Tell them to send me a courier. Then, schedule a meeting with all senior litigators. I want somebody with a security clearance from public relations to sit in."

"Specify time of meeting," the phone insisted.

"Thirty minutes," he replied.

* * *

Beatrice was numb. Sounds of combat coming from all directions filled her ears. Four hours of fear and constant movement were taking their toll. The reporter's sweat-soaked clothing was now stained with blood from the soldiers around her, three of whom were no longer among the living.

The cameras in her oversized helmet captured everything she saw, and much more, in a 360-degree arc around her adrenaline-fueled body. Efforts to secure the terminal building her squad had landed on were being resisted tenaciously, floor by floor, room by room.

Wind from the Bering Sea buffeted every structure that starport and Chinese forces were fighting over. A perpetual aching chill slowed the movement of her extremities, even though she'd been inside for the last hour. Interior lights and heating were off. A combination of smoke and tear gas filled many of the corridors. Booby traps were constant dangers. Everyone on both sides of the battle relied on safety goggles, hearing protectors, and electronic vision devices.

Beatrice kept an eye on Billy Richter as the conflict raged. She was never more than a dozen feet away from the former army sergeant at any given moment. Billy walked and talked as if she wasn't there.

She watched him direct a grenade attack on the next room to be cleared. A controller in one hand allowed her to operate the equipment built into her helmet. Audio and video segments were identified, tagged, and archived for spontaneous use at a later date, when she'd have time to think and act more circumspectly.

Richter's men entered the room after their grenades went off. They signaled silently that there were no defenders.

"This time," Beatrice thought.

The men and women in Richter's squad weren't so distant from the reporter. They'd push her aside if she got in their way. Somebody would drag her down to the ground if she was being what they called "sniper bait." Beatrice didn't like being thought of as baggage. She focused on her work, verbalizing audio commentary inside her helmet that couldn't be heard by the people around here when she had the visor closed and sound baffles turned on.

A sudden commotion further down the wide hallway got her attention. A military robot rolled into view in the corridor junction on four small, very quiet, black wheels. The olive-drab Chinese-built remote controlled platform turned on the surprised starport troops with a combination of automatic weapons, rotary shotguns, and grenade launchers.

Beatrice rose up on one knee and gripped her controller. A shoulder-fired rocket flew from somewhere behind her. It roared down the high-ceilinged corridor as personnel scattered. The squad tasked with stopping the marauding machine was cut to pieces in a hail of bullets and explosives. The reporter's digital equipment recorded the slaughter.

Screams of pain and fear were momentarily blotted out as the small-diameter armor-defeating missile struck the robot.

Its shaped charge warhead obliterated the man-sized construct in an expanding fireball that incinerated nearby combatants.

Windows in all directions blew out. Doors were knocked off their hinges. Construction materials in the walls, floor, and ceiling caught fire as separated body parts began to fall around the shocked starport soldiers.

"Suck it up!" Billy commanded loudly.

Military robots were a fact of life on the modern battlefield. They were usually used prior to a counterattack, to confuse commanders and break enemy morale.

Troops held in reserve rushed past Beatrice as she tried to stop herself from vomiting. She swallowed rising bile, reaching out to touch the nearest wall with a gloved hand to keep her camera aim steady.

Billy directed his defense, which formed rapidly. He tasked two of his men to find fire extinguishers when the counterattack didn't come.

The reporter breathed a sigh of relief. Her satellite phone beeped for attention. "Check phone connection," she told her helmet's onboard assistant.

"No mistake. Valid incoming call," the device responded in a gender-neutral voice.

Beatrice was annoyed. She glanced at the phone readout and swore. Crawling on her hands and knees, the field journalist maneuvered into the nearest empty room. She hid under a desk and caught her breath before answering the unexpected and unwanted call.

"You've got a lot of nerve calling me at a time like this!" she snarled.

Jim's face popped up on her display. "Your contract says I call when I want."

"What in the bloody screaming Hell is so important?" Beatrice demanded.

"Start broadcasting," Jim told her.

"*Now*?"

The administrator nodded. "The folks over at Polar News are standing by, ready to go live with you. They've got an anchor, studio crew, and a full PR team just waiting to do what you tell them."

"Wow," Beatrice breathed, blushing.

Jim shook his head. "Not 'wow.' I kept my promise. Now it's time for you to keep yours. Get out there and show the world what we're doing."

Beatrice took a deep breath. "You can't expect me to do this *now*. Have you seen what's happening to your guys? That's not going to look good for either of us. Give them a few hours to get this under control—"

"No," Jim insisted. He forged ahead before she could reply. "It'll take you at least 15 minutes to work things out with your studio unit, and another five or ten to brief everyone else. That doesn't include whatever you have to tell the anchor. Who knows how long that'll take?"

Beatrice looked around the ravaged office. "I could use a few minutes to clean up my video clips. How do I break the news to Billy?"

"I'll tell him."

Beatrice closed her eyes for a moment. "Sounds like the fight is moving to the other side of the building. Okay. Fine. I'll get started, but I won't stay out of this. I'll make my reports and then go back to see what's happening."

"Billy, or one his team leaders will get whatever you need," Jim assured.

"Pulitzer Prize, here I come," she whispered.

Chapter Eleven

The operation to storm Cold Bay was a ratings bonanza for Polar News Service. Starport troops took possession of the airport after three days of brutal close quarters combat. More mistakes were made. New lessons were learned.

Publicly traded shares in PNS doubled their value as crowd-sourced fund managers rushed to buy in. A perpetually tired and dirty Beatrice Brown became the most frequently watched personalities on the World Wide Web.

International reaction to the skirmish was mixed. Spokespersons for the U.S. government downplayed what they called an "unofficial and unsanctioned event."

Chinese representatives made similar statements. Corporations no longer hesitated to use mercenaries to advance their own agendas. In this respect, Shadow Fusion Enterprises was no different than any other profit-driven player on the global stage. The fact that an aerospace conglomerate employed this privately funded security force generated some controversy among popular pundits.

"They can't finish building a space station. How are they gonna fight a war?"

"It's not like these guys are drilling for oil. What are they fighting for?"

"Has anyone told them that this kind of thing is massively illegal?"

Chinese government representatives wasted no time in decrying the motivations the starport's administration and the firm that backed it. "S.F.E. makes a big deal about being the gateway to the future. That's their official slogan. This interference in matters that don't concern them is unacceptable."

Billy Richter was blunt in his after-action assessment when he talked with his boss by encrypted satellite phone. "You've seen the body count. We can't do this again. I *won't* do this again. We needed better training."

Jim strolled through a secured hanger with a remote phone receiver clipped to one ear, watching a dozen technicians finish rebuilding four F-15s. "I hear you. This is a launch complex. Where am I going to put a boot camp?"

Billy's voice chirped and crackled through random interference. "I know some guys in Fairbanks. They can do it, for a price. They'll use their own land. We need better rehearsal."

Jim stepped back as an electric cart rolled by. His voice echoed off the high ceiling. "No time for that. You've have to hold your drills in and around the starport. It's what the guys from Homeland Security will be expecting, anyway. Might as well give them something to look at."

Richter wasn't satisfied. "Remind me to buy you a conscience. That's no good. We need privacy. Look, we'll do it out here. We've already got King Cove. Might as well use it. I still think they might hit us with cruise missiles."

"Nope," Jim replied, shaking his head.

"They have to retaliate somehow," Billy insisted.

"Nope," Jim repeated.

Billy took a deep breath. His boss might be right. His boss might also be in a wicked mood, intending to tease him. Billy decided to change the subject. "How soon can you have us resupplied?"

"End of the week," Jim assured.

"Gotta be sooner," Billy insisted.

Cook nodded to himself. "I'll scrape up what I have. You might be right about the cruise missile thing. I don't suppose they can be talked out of a counterattack?"

"I don't speak Chinese," Billy quipped.

Jim looked up at the nose of the nearest fighter jet. "Billy? Level with me. What's the mood out there?"

Richter coughed. "I think the technical term is 'crap.' Most of these people are ex-law enforcement. No more than a third have military experience. We bled too much. Not enough heavy weapons. It's all in my report."

Jim paused when a power tool howled. He went back toward the soundproofed offices. "You're not up to your ears in naval infantry, so I think it's a safe bet to say that they won't counterattack before the middle of May. Still no sign of warships?"

"None," Billy replied after checking his displays.

Jim smiled. "I'll bet you somebody in Beijing is watching our reporter in the field. Somebody with a degree in risk management must have told them it would be bad P.R. to strike American territory with strategic weapons on live television."

Billy's voice conveyed his skepticism. "Are you sure about that? She's not going to like being used as a missile shield. Wait one." He paused. "I've just been told that the first group of F-15s has landed.

"There's another matter I'd like to bring up. Will you increase my credit line?"

"If anyone asks, I was surprised. What do you want to buy now?" Jim asked apprehensively.

The ad hoc force commander grunted. "We need more manpower. We can't recruit mercs off the open market. It'd be too easy to accidentally pick up infiltrators. Hiring local would reduce that risk. I want to beat the bushes and see what turns up. Well, that, and I need three new VTOLs to replace the units we got chewed up in this attack."

Jim noticed that he was being observed by loitering mechanics. He walked into the nearest empty office and closed the door. He plopped into the only chair in the small room. "I didn't think it would be this difficult," he admitted.

"The OPFOR *was* made up of professional soldiers," Billy reminded him.

Jim didn't respond.

"More people are going to die before this is over," Billy observed.

"I know," Jim replied testily.

"Give me what I need to minimize the damage."

"I'll see what the bean counters will part with," Jim sighed. He hung up.

* * *

Chinese leaders interpreted what they learned about the fight for Cold Bay from overt and covert sources in a way that reflected their own self-interest. The improvised use of mercenaries by such a small company strongly implied American weakness.

American leaders in Washington, D.C., interpreted what they knew about starport activities and recent enemy actions in a similar way. Pentagon strategists predicted a counterattack within 24 hours that didn't happen. The apparent failure to react within 48 hours strongly implied Chinese weakness.

U.S. naval units in the Bering and Chukchi Seas were put on high alert and ordered to intercept Chinese reinforcements if they approached the Aleutian Island archipelago. American Coast Guard elements stationed at Dutch Harbor withdrew to mainland positions in anticipation of a shooting war.

Chinese squadrons sailed from Hong Kong in a deliberate effort to screen troop transports and supply ships entering Alaskan territorial waters. The presence of American frigates, destroyers, and observation aircraft set the stage for opening moves in a conflict that could escalate into a regional war.

Starport forces consolidated their improvised defenses in and around Cold Bay and King Cove as the mainstream media reported on the movements of every surface vessel they could see using civilian aircraft and real-time retail satellite imagery.

Every infotainment channel on the Internet predicted war with a dazzling array of interactive graphics as these forces came closer to each other. Commentators of every political persuasion had a lot to say about the naval posturing.

"Pentagon sources won't confirm how many U.S. warships are in the region."

"Too many recessions and too many fiscal cutbacks. Not enough foresight."

"American military strength in the Asia-Pacific region is notoriously depleted."

Government leaders and military planners weren't the only people using space-based platforms to watch what was happening in the Arctic. A constant stream of sensor data went to and from the space station *Gold Rush*, which flew high over the central Pacific Ocean in a geostationary orbit that allowed it to see Kodiak Island.

Frustrated engineers in space suits labored for months in airless vacuum to bring dozens of temperamental systems online. Sasha Xavier had been supervising this ordeal for the previous three months. Every successful installation or fix seemed to spawn two new equipment failures. Her frustration and tenacity was becoming the stuff of legend.

Born in the Alaskan bush somewhere near Nome, Sasha's flowing red hair and large green eyes accentuated a tall, lean physique that made her look more like a gymnast than a capricious genius who would one day hold multiple doctorates in subjects ranging from music to mathematics, as well as all forms of physics and engineering in between. At just 26 years of age, she'd already pioneered five new technologies, earned six patents, and amassed enough wealth to ensure perpetual stability for herself and future family members. She'd also been to prison for less honorable deeds.

"No!" she screamed from inside her white space suit.

She floated at the end of her tether near the ventral docking collar. "Don't do that! The station's rotation will tear out every fiber-optic line you've just installed. Put that damned thing in *this* socket, over here!"

Half a dozen engineers in orange vacc suits, working with thruster packs and remote control claws, stopped their movements. The prefabricated segment they were trying to connect floated on a leash between them. The moon was clearly visible far beyond the station.

Sasha looked up at the slowly spinning habitat ring that encircled the entire station. The star field visible beyond the moon never failed to inspire her. It was her favorite thing to look at before going to sleep.

She rolled her eyes. "C'mon, fellas. This is why I came out here two freakin' hours ago to mark the insertion point. Tab A into slot B. Connect the power cable and let the autowelder do its job."

Running lights flashed on a robot waiting nearby.

"Yes, I'm talking about you," she fumed.

The bulbous machine flashed its lights again.

She was just about to turn her attention to another chore when an encrypted channel opened on her helmet radio. A burst of static made her flinch.

A male voice spoke through her headset much too loudly. "*Gold Rush*, this ground station. How is the hen house?"

Sasha used a control on her wrist to reset the audio volume in her helmet. "Ground, we are online with all major systems. That includes plumbing. Weather monitoring radars have been reprogrammed and recalibrated. We see what you see."

"What's the status of mother hen?" the man asked.

Sasha didn't like thruster packs. She tugged on her tether to turn around for a better look at the station. "Henny Penny is…not quite ready."

"How long?"

Sasha watched the engineers work. "One more power coupling to go, then we can run some juice through the system. Call it two hours, if there are no shorts in the system *and* if all the computers play nice. If the software doesn't glitch, you'll have an improvised rod from God. I won't guarantee how many shots you get."

"We have a situation developing," the voice said.

Sasha cursed. "I don't care if Godzilla is wrecking Tokyo! You tell His Holiness that I've got my own situation. These working conditions are intolerable! No. Wait. Get him on this line. I'll tell him myself!"

Minutes passed. Sasha watched the engineers successfully connect the vital component. Jim Cook, somewhere deep inside the starport, finally came on the frequency with machinery rattling in the background.

He was direct. "Sasha? Chinese aircraft carriers and their battle groups are going to sea. We count six. Cloud cover could be hiding one more. We're going to need that package very soon. A matter of days at the most."

"Of course. Just like the Chinese to be ahead of schedule," she spluttered.

"Historians can decide who started it," Jim snorted.

"We've still got the final power test."

Jim bowed his head. "How good is the camouflage?"

Sasha beamed with pride. "Anyone who comes to have a look won't see anything that's incriminating. Everyone who built this thing will be off the station in three days. I only wish we had time to build the real thing instead of this improvised geegaw."

Jim shuddered. "It makes me sick to my stomach. I never thought I'd be the one to put this kind of thing in space. I want all trace of it to be gone when we're done."

"It will be," she promised.

"Back in twelve hours," he mumbled and hung up.

CHAPTER TWELVE

Elements of the U.S. Navy were ordered to the outer limits of American territorial waters along the chain of the Aleutian Islands in a deliberate effort to prevent the Chinese from reinforcing commandos and light infantry that were already known to be ashore. Chinese and American military satellites changed positions around the globe as intelligence experts on both sides attempted to gain a better understanding of the events that were unfolding around them.

Sasha Xavier watched the movements of satellites from other countries from her perch in *Gold Rush's* small, incomplete operations bay. The 24 full color, flat panel monitors suspended over partially assembled workstations showed her the tracks of more than 70 manmade platforms. She worked alone in the dimly lit compartment, dressed in an insulated jump suit, magnetic shoes, display glasses, and a multifunction headset. Her long, red hair hovered above and behind her head like a wrinkled cloth. The station's slow rotation provided her with just enough g-force to feel like she was in light gravity.

Sasha worked with small hand tools to quickly complete the electronic adjustments that would bring various instrument panels to life and immediate usefulness. Her entire body moved effortlessly and efficiently while a news feed played in her left glasses lens. Revolving part diagrams and status updates linked to the instrument boards she was building filled the other. Soft, artificially generated voices verbalized text from assembly diagrams, part descriptions, and user manuals in her ears. A bank of green lights winked on, making her smile.

"You're not a bad space station," she whispered compassionately. "You *were* designed by idiots," she added reproachfully as more systems activated.

Two of the green lights turned to red. "I know. I see it," she cooed softly. The red lights turned green after two new circuits were completed.

A chime sounded from the overhead intercom. A man's voice came through confidently. "Engineering shows all boards green. Auxiliary controls are responding."

Sasha parted her hands and backed away from the open instrument panel. "Integrate radar, lidar, and thermal imaging," she ordered with anticipation.

"Connection in five seconds," the engineer warned.

Sasha glanced around the small room. "Come on, baby. We've got people counting on us."

The unseen engineer ignored her ruminations. He knew better than to interrupt Sasha when she was talking to herself or the technology she held in such high regard. "Should be online now," he told her.

Unshielded systems around the room chirped. New displays appeared on every monitor. Sasha turned off her display glasses and strolled around the compartment that would eventually have more furniture in it. "I like it," she told the station.

Sasha closed one of the workstations and activated the look-down radar system. Custom-built computer programs quickly picked out the slowly moving surface naval units on the ocean far below.

"Sync up with ground?" the engineer asked.

"Do it," Sasha commanded.

* * *

A cheer went up throughout the whole space control wing in the starport administration complex. Jim Cook came down from his office to stand near the center of the cavernous control room.

He shouted to make himself heard over the jubilant crowd. "It's good news! But, it's only 8:05 in the a.m., so let's stay on task!"

Jim put on a wireless headset and keyed the intercom so he could be heard on every level of the complex. "Attention, all departments. We have eyes in the sky. *Gold Rush* is finally talking to us." He was conscious of the many gazes following his every move. "Department heads, update your evacuation plans."

Whispers went through the room faster than an unchecked arson fire. The possibility of a mass evacuation wasn't new, nor was it entirely unexpected.

Jim went to the nearest schedule of next launches to study it. "Everyone, lock down your inventories. Flight coordinators, close the launch schedule after midnight Alaska Standard Time tonight."

He looked directly at the nearest surveillance camera. "We're caught in the middle of something we didn't start. It's time for us to protect our own. We have to assume the Chinese will pay us a visit, much like they did 16 years ago."

"We'll be ready for 'em," somebody muttered.

Jim didn't bother to look for whoever had made the remark. "We will be ready for them. As ready as we can be."

Dozens of men and women became silent. The hum of air conditioning and the chatter of radios seemed louder than normal.

Jim turned to look at the people gathered nearby. "All nonessential personnel will begin packing *after you finish your shift*. You still owe me three hours and fifty-five minutes, and I want 'em!"

His words were met with snickers and giggles. He cleared his throat. "Everybody on the approved lists gets seat on the next company bird going back to Anchorage. Actual evacuation begins in five hours. Anyone not on the approved lists will find their own way off this island, or stay here with me to welcome our uninvited guests."

"Aren't you being a little premature?" one of the nearby specialists asked.

Jim pointed to a large display on the ceiling. "The shooting starts any time now. Even if the U.S. Navy falls back, which is quite likely, we're still going to see fighting in 24 hours."

"Sea conditions are bad," a meteorologist observed.

"This shouldn't happen until sometime in May!" somebody else protested.

Jim rapped his knuckles on the edge of a cluttered work surface. “Don’t let that distract you. Check your assignments and get back to work!”

A studious woman pointed at the master display projected on the ceiling. “Why can’t we see the U.S. carriers?” she asked.

Jim cringed. He turned slowly to face her. “I told certain people to screen out that data because we’ve all got enough to do just now.” He took a breath and let it out. “Look. Some of you independent contractors are Americans. Some of you are not. I don’t want to tempt anyone into trying to make a few extra bucks on the side by ratting on the U.S. Navy.”

A hush fell across the room. Movement ceased. Men and women looked at each other with open suspicion. Somebody coughed.

“Knock it off!” Jim bellowed.

* * *

Climatic changes in the Arctic region over the previous two decades had resulted in worsening sea conditions during seasonally warm periods. Reductions in sea ice meant that there were no windbreaks or atmospheric thermal barriers to slow storm fronts.

Military and civilian vessels just south of Dutch Harbor were buffeted by high winds and fierce waves that came at alarmingly short intervals. Commercial operations in the northern Aleutian region were limited to necessary shipping by order the U.S. government through its maritime agencies.

Internet services around the world reached maximum capacity as news and entertainment corporations fed fears in an effort to generate higher ratings.

“—Americans may have withdrawn the few aircraft carriers they still have.”

“Traditional doctrine would call for the first attacks to come from submarines.”

“—have not been able to confirm the exact nature of the U.S. response…”

“U.S., Japan, and China have closed their northern airspace to civilian traffic.”

The first clash happened just after 10:15 in the morning, Alaska Standard Time. Six Chinese Type 99 attack submarines, pre-positioned north of the Aleutian Islands, unexpectedly moved through the archipelago.

American satellite recognition occurred as underwater sonar nets detected the shallow water transits. Each of the hunter-killers relied on satellite uplinks to aim and launch a barrage of cruise missiles configured to seek out any surface contact within their individually assigned flight paths.

Two foreign-flagged fishing boats, one U.S.-registered floating fish processor, and nine U.S. Navy warships were sunk within eight minutes. The closest stricken vessel went down 100 miles from its nearest attacker.

Media outlets around the world reacted to the bleat of distress calls that sounded, repeated, and went silent within just a few desperate minutes.

"—no question that we're hearing the last transmission from a dying ship."

"—reports that two more submarines have just sailed from Honolulu."

"We can confirm that the nuclear powered aircraft carrier *George H.W. Bush*, CVN 77, has joined its battle group after an extensive refit..."

Five hours passed as orders from the Pentagon in Washington, D.C., were transmitted through encrypted satellites. National defense postures in the United States and China increased to wartime levels of readiness. Land-based bombers took off from their coastal bases in southeastern China on a course intended to put them within the air defense envelopes of their slowly advancing carrier battle groups.

Activity at the starport became frenzied as a trio of *Seawolf*-class submarines lurking on the surface of a choppy sea several hundred miles northwest of Dutch Harbor began to move westward. The old boats produced long, white wakes as their propellers worked up to full rpms. Most of the men and women aboard these Cold War relics were third-generation sailors whose grandparents had served with pride on nuclear powered attack submarines.

Captain Allen Brester, commanding SSN 21 *Seawolf*, stood atop the conning tower with mixed feelings while he used an infrared lamp to signal, “Good luck and good hunting,” to his two trailing counterparts. Knowing that the quirks and capabilities of their superseded subs would at last be put to the test didn’t make him feel any better about saying goodbye to old friends.

* * *

Jim fretted and went to find the shift supervisor. He turned, moving toward the operations area with determination, and stepped over to the raised dais near the center of the room.

“Keep a tight lid on this,” he told the tense man, once he found him.

“Got it, Boss.”

Jim grunted. “Raise our internal security level to soft blue. I want every uniform that’s not on leave to be in plain sight when the spit hits the fan.”

“Riots?” the controller guessed.

Jim lowered his voice. “*Gold Rush* will see the cruise missile launches when they happen. Some of those will be for us.”

“I could suppress the air raid sirens…” the worried supervisor whispered.

“Don’t. It’s better for morale if they have a chance to duck and cover.”

“Sure wish we could hit back.”

“Not until they throw the first punch.”

“What? Cruise missiles aren’t enough for you?” The man glared, open ridiculing Cook’s apparent effort at propriety.

“We’re not the only ones who are going to get a taste of Chinese manufacturing. We save our best for the main event.”

“Which is…?”

“Classified,” Jim replied emphatically.

The senior controller rose from the big chair at the center of the platform and stepped aside. Heads turned. The controller touched a screen on the arm of the chair. A chime sounded through the intercom. “Change of command,” he informed the workforce.

Jim touched the same screen to adapt his headset to the control interface. A wave of mild applause circled the room.

"Administrator One-One is on the net," he announced to all channels. He sat and looked up at the man he'd just relieved, then muted his microphone.

"Are you on the essential personnel list?" Jim asked the supervisor.

"No, sir."

"Are you married?"

"Yes," the younger man admitted uncomfortably.

"Kids?"

"Four." He gave Jim a nervous smile.

Cook rubbed his chin. "It's going to be a long night. Go to your family. They'll start boarding the evac flights at 1 a.m. Get to the terminal early and keep your mouth shut. No loose talk. Just get on the plane and go to Anchorage."

"Thank you," the grateful employee whispered. He fled rapidly, without looking back.

Jim watched the man leave. He reactivated his microphone. "Phone, scrambled line, call the skiff."

Dial tones chirped in his ear. The call went through instantly.

A stern male voice answered. "Skiff. We are secure. Send your authentication."

Jim entered his nine-digit authorization code on a hooded touch screen.

The intelligence officer waited for the code to be verified. "Mr. Cook. I thought we might be hearing from you any time now."

Jim adjusted his chair. "Be ready to disconnect the entire starport from all external data sources. We're not hacker proof. I just don't want to make it easy for them. You know what I mean?"

"On your command," the officer confirmed.

"How long to activate the Fish Net?" Jim requested.

The specialist consulted his operations plan. "Four to six hours."

Jim adjusted his chair and lowered his voice. "Call Dutch. Release the doves."

"On it," the coordinator affirmed and hung up.

* * *

Every bar in Dutch Harbor was filled with anxious customers who couldn't take their eyes off the televisions that were placed in every corner. Charlie Pike and several of his fellow unemployed fishermen were seated around rustic tables at the Dirty Plank, when the phone in his pocket buzzed for attention.

He emptied his beer glass in one long swallow and leaned back. The old salt looked around the dimly lit room, noticing that men and women suddenly hunched over with phones in their ears. He reached for his phone and flipped it open.

"Pike."

A slightly accented female voice greeted him. "Hello, Mr. Pike. I'm calling from the Fish Net service that you've subscribed to."

Charlie's blood ran cold. His mind flashed back to the encounter he and others had had with Billy Richter just a few months ago. "Fish Net" was the starport's illegal surveillance program. It paid civilian fishing boat operators to call in anything that might be considered suspicious to an unlisted radio telephone exchange.

Pike was a military veteran. He knew what the corporate folks on Kodiak Island wanted. The Chinese navy would tend to overlook civilian shipping that rode high in the water without too many radio antennas, such as fishing boats without cargo.

Billy's first remuneration to the individual boat captains had been made in cash. The payments that followed were doled out each week as electronic bank transfers from a fisherman's charity created to keep unemployed nautical workers on the job as the world's economy continued to worsen.

"Time to pay for our sins," the old man grumbled.

The operator continued. "Mr. Pike, we'd like you to head out immediately."

Charlie noticed GPS coordinates appearing in the text window on his phone. He looked at the men gathered around his table. "Round 'em up," he whispered.

Real intelligence-gathering ships would be spotted by American or Chinese observers. Those snoopers would have equipment and electromagnetic signatures that could be sniffed out. They'd be sunk as fast as they were found.

Charlie cleared his throat. "I know these numbers. I haven't got fuel in my tanks for that kind of cruise."

The operator remained cordial. "An account has been set up for you at the fuel depot. Charge it to Fish Net."

Charlie scratched the back of his head as the men around him got up to leave. "Gonna need groceries," he proffered uneasily.

"Charge them to Fish Net."

Charlie realized that everyone with an open phone had the same idea. They knew what was at stake for Alaskans on the mainland if the Chinese came ashore with armed intent. Governor Wheeler's recent televised speeches left no doubt in anyone's mind about what was to come as the weather got warmer.

Charlie's wandering eye stopped when it reached the nearest TV screen. "Say, this is looking pretty serious. I got family on this island, relocated from King Cove. I don't suppose you have airline tickets in your back pocket, do you?"

"Already waiting for your wife at the airport Mr. Pike," the woman on the other end of the line said compassionately.

Charlie smiled. "Alright then. Let's go find us some trouble."

CHAPTER THIRTEEN

Sasha Xavier was jarred awake from a sound sleep in her private quarters four hours later when alarms went off throughout the space station.

"That better mean war," she cursed.

The pressurized compartments that she and the members of her work shift slept in were all dark as the alert sounded. The slow rotation of the habitat ring provided a microgravity just good enough for everyone to sleep in without side effects.

She wiggled loose from her safety harness and closed up her jumpsuit using sticky tabs. "Intercom, Operations. What now?" she demanded.

Computers put her call through to the man on duty in the command module. "Whole lotta shakin' goin' on," he replied.

Sasha pressed both feet into her mag boots. "Explain."

Sounds of nearby activity made it clear that everyone was reacting to the alarm. "Go to your stations!" she shouted through the walls.

The technician on duty remained calm. "Our computers have tagged more than 50 missile launches form the Chinese and a dozen launches from the Americans. Looks like war."

"What's the ship count?" she asked while putting on a headset.

The engineer paused to count. "Computer says seven ChiCom aircraft carrier battle groups, one carrier per group. Five lesser surface groups. Four American carrier battle groups, similar configuration. Computer also says 19 U.S. Navy vessels in the region."

"All 19 are operating independently," Sasha surmised while adjusting her clothes.

"Satellite movement!" the man warned.

Sasha cursed and hurried to her locker. Along the way, she patched into the station's intercom. "All hands! Rig for combat. Suit up and check your air. Everyone knows their place. Go there now!"

Red lights transformed *Gold Rush*'s interior into a sinister environment. Sasha put on her space suit as the staff manning the station's various command-and-control positions relayed new details.

"Launch detections confirmed. Intermediate packages. Source is northeastern China."

"I read about this online. Those *should* be conventional payload ICBMs."

"Oh, man! They'd better not be nukes or this'll be a short fight."

Sasha pulled on a portable air bottle and slapped her helmet on. It fell into place with a metallic click. "Satellite movement?" she asked as she rushed through the nearest crawlspace.

"Trouble with the side-scan radars," an unidentified voice mumbled.

The frantic woman pulled herself toward the command module, through cold, dark parts of the station that had no gravity. "Okay, fine. Let's assume their birds are moving. Everyone seal up. Reverse the air circulation in 60 seconds. Vent whatever we can't store. Let's avoid explosive decompression before they start shooting at us."

"Venting in 60," somebody confirmed.

Sasha popped into the command module and headed for her chair as fast as she could. "Do we still have contact with UAF?" she asked.

"Nerd net is online," somebody joked.

Sasha rearranged her air supply and buckled her seat belt. "Pass the word while we still can. Send text only. Tell them to turn everything off. I mean *everything*. Water, sewer, electrical, and cable TV. Make sure they get this message in Juneau. That means all the government computers, too."

The man next to her shrugged. "What are you so worried about?"

"The end of the world," Sasha stated melodramatically.

"They wouldn't!" a voice from behind her gasped.

Sasha plugged her suit's umbilical hose into the station's air supply. "Keep your pants on. I'm not worried about nukes. I'm worried about what happens when they start killing all those unprotected satellites."

"Loss of comms," a woman sobbed.

"The Chinese will hack us," another woman added.

Sasha grinned. "I hope they try."

"Not afraid of anything, eh?" somebody snickered.

Sasha raised a fist to knock on her helmet. "I don't like the idea of being hit by all those little specs of wreckage that'll be passing through our neighborhood."

* * *

Worldwide media fascination was focused on the Asia Pacific Rim. Government-initiated secrecy prevented most civilian newsmakers from effectively monitoring the actions of either faction as they occurred in space.

A limited number of privately owned satellites provided partial coverage of the carnage. American and Chinese antisatellite weapons and electronic counter measures took a swift toll on more than 60 previously targeted platforms.

Images of flaring rocket thrusters and exploding satellites caused a sensation and spiked the ratings of every infotainment program with access to those premium feeds.

All of those video and sensor data sources were destroyed in the first 30 minutes of action. Commentators were horrified when their expensive orbital infrastructure went offline. Fifty news channels shut down at the same time.

"I think half the planet just went blind."

"Are we still on? Can anybody see us?"

"Please be patient while we switch to—"

Governments around the world had solemnly proclaimed for the last century that space would be always be neutral territory. That alleged nonaligned status evaporated as military systems from a dozen nations fired on U.S. and Chinese targets in an effort to defend their own telecommunications capabilities.

The destruction of military and civilian systems, in both high and low orbits, set off a chain reaction of unintended consequences as nonaligned nations invoked the right to defend their own space-based assets. Seventy-five percent of global communications failed as the vacuum around Earth filled with expanding clouds of hot gas and wreckage.

Civilian global positioning technologies became useless as their corresponding satellites were vaporized.

* * *

Carefully coordinated cyberattacks made things worse. Eighty percent of all regionally controlled power generation utilities in the U.S., Canada, and Mexico were infiltrated and shut down by malicious programmers who evaded detection. Half the world's Internet bandwidth collapsed as satellites from more than 50 countries were destroyed or disabled by ground-based antisatellite, or ASAT, weapons. Efforts to reroute traffic through civil telecom hubs failed when enemy cyberattacks shut them off.

Preprogrammed military satellites, or MILSATs, were ordered into action by more than a dozen nations in an effort to defend their airspace. These MILSATs hunted for soft civilian targets using a variety of sensors. Guided missiles, fast moving projectiles, and shrapnel shot through expanding clouds of hot gas and wreckage to create a storm of metal and plastic that crippled or destroyed every structure it impaled.

Land-based data backups kept most national militaries from losing their all of command-and-control capabilities. Billions of wireless phone calls dropped in the same instant, leaving millions patients and health care providers in the dark.

American and Chinese commanders lost control of their deepwater navies. Vessels far out to sea, suddenly bereft of satellite connections, resorted to carefully rehearsed wartime operating procedures. Civilian air traffic controllers around the world panicked as network failures mounted, forcing them to rely on verbal pattern management techniques.

"Radio check. Can anyone hear me?"

"Don't wait for approval! Find somebody to manually reset the damned thing!"

"Attention all inbound traffic, slow down. Execute published holding protocols."

* * *

Sasha squirmed inside her suit, which was getting hotter by the minute. Displays around the compartment glowed with brightly tagged icons that noted the known or suspected locations of American and Chinese aircraft and ships.

"Side-scan is online," a technician reported from another compartment.

Sasha turned on her chair to watch the new data fill her workstation displays. Alarms began to sound as computer software reacted to the fast-moving debris that approached the station from various angles and elevations.

A genderless synthetic voice called out, "Crash warning," in a tone that was devoid of feeling.

A five-second study of the new radar tracks made it clear to Sasha that *Gold Rush* would be torn apart as the debris clouds collided. She cursed. "We've got to get out of low orbit!"

Another chime sounded in the dimly lit compartment. "Decompression cycle is complete," a female voice announced soberly.

Sasha looked over her shoulder at the only military radar display in the cabin. Red light from the overheard illuminators gleamed off her helmet. "We have two or three minutes before the neighbor's trash arrives."

"Liquid fuel preheat takes eight minutes," an engineer cautioned.

Sasha checked her own display. "No time for that. We'll have to do this the hard way. Light the candles."

The veteran space workers around Sasha went to work. There was no need for elaboration. All of them knew the importance of rapid action.

"Lock down all compartments. All hands, brace for high-speed station break!"

"NATO-friendly GPS is offline!" a technician shouted through the din.

The military global positioning system, a century-old staple in navigation, was a vital backup to anyone who moved on air, land, or sea. This extremely precise direction-finding technology was also used by vehicles and platforms in space to maintain orbits and prevent collisions.

Sasha began to sweat. Destruction of the American network of course-plotting satellites meant one thing. She leaned out of her chair, into the flight officer's workspace to stab a touch screen with two gloved fingers. "Forget the automated reference points! Fly this beast manually! You drive, I'll shut the rockets off before things get out of hand."

"We don't have a procedure for this!" the flight control officer choked.

Everyone in the compartment looked at Sasha. Sudden starts and stops using variable thrust rockets were incredibly unsafe. Their fuel burn would be grossly inefficient under emergency conditions, such as the circumstance they were now experiencing.

"Do it like this!" she bellowed while striking the main panel with her fist.

A dry horn sounded three times, followed by an apathetic automated response. "Override accepted."

Curses flooded the intercom from all parts of the space station as *Gold Rush* began to shudder. Vibrations went through all of the compartments as every solid rocket fixed to the ventral superstructure flared to life.

"What's the burn time?" the nervous pilot asked.

Sasha pointed at his vector panel. "We are 'up.' The earth is 'down.' *That* was our orbital path. *Those* are the tracks from incoming debris. Work it out. Do your damned math and don't get me killed!"

Gold Rush began to pick up speed as it moved from low orbit, further away from Earth. Seven more satellites above the Arctic region were destroyed by a combination of air and ground launched antisatellite weapons. Focused energy beans and fast-moving missiles took out more slow moving targets over Europe, Africa, and the Indian Ocean.

The venerable International Space Station, located 15,000 miles away from *Gold Rush*, came under attack while restoration crews were attempting to abandon the old platform.

Six of the thirty men and women employed to refit the station were left behind in the frantic scramble to reach the escape pod. The marooned workers perished anonymously as the station was hit by more than a dozen guided missiles in less than 60 seconds. Directional radio receivers on the ground heard their last angry words faintly through a curtain of manmade electronic jamming.

* * *

Jim Cook leaped out of his chair when the first air raid siren went off. The starport's Regional Defense Command, located in a deep underground bunker, sprang into action. Intercoms crackled on every level of the big operations center.

"RDC calls airborne threat warning."

"Airborne source confirmed."

Jim wiped sweat from his face with a handkerchief. "Everybody stay cool. It's up to the computers now. Traffic check, report?"

"Clear skies," a shrill voice called out.

The administrator knew that all eyes were on him. He straightened his posture and reached for a computer pad. He typed while he talked. "Ops, lock your boards and get the Hell out of here. Go to your assigned shelters. Essential personnel, stay with me."

The brightly lit room erupted in a frenzy of activity as men and women in white shirts rushed through their chores and fled. The few wearing red shirts went to their damage control stations.

Jim changed channels to speak with the skiff.

"First strike in eight minutes," the expert relayed.

Jim lowered his voice. "Charge the grid and unmask all batteries. Time to see if we got what we paid for."

Text messages scrolled past at eye level on a nearby screen, telling Jim that starport forces dug in around King Cove and Cold Bay were being hit with conventional warheads from ICBMs.

"Gonna be a long night," he mumbled.

"I've got an extra seat down here, if you want it," the officer offered.

Jim glanced at the departing men and women around him. "This is the first chance I've had to get myself killed in quite a few years. Seems a shame to waste it."

An approaching guard in camouflage flagged Jim down with a long slow wave.

"Gotta go," Jim sighed and closed his call.

The motivated sentinel came to a precise stop at the bottom of the dais. Stripes on his sleeve indicated he was an officer. He didn't salute. "Liaison from Homeland Security wants into the building."

Jim swore. "For cryin' out loud! Why can't he leave me alone for just one more day?"

"Sir?" the guard inquired carefully.

Jim came down off the dais. "Do you see what's happening?" he asked.

"Yes," the observant man nodded.

Jim clapped him on the shoulder. "Do you understand that I don't have time for DHS?"

"No time for DHS," the man nodded.

Jim raised his voice to be heard over the growing riot that burst our around him. "Lock this building. Lose Mr. Stringer's security clearance. Tow his car. Do whatever it takes to keep him away from me for the next two days. No, make that three days."

"I'd like to have that in writing," the sentry countered.

A man running from the room jostled Jim. Cook ignored the bump. "I can't seem to keep a secretary and we're going to be hit by incoming missiles. There's no time to for a memo. I will *personally* owe you for this, *if we live.* Is that good enough?"

The guard risked another look around at the worsening chaos. He adjusted the beret on his head. "I…will take this to my captain and we'll see what happens to Mr. Stringer."

The guard trotted away.

Jim ran back up the dais, muttering, "'Give it to me in writing'…" as he ascended.

CHAPTER FOURTEEN

Gray clouds dropped cold rain on the fog-shrouded starport. Aboveground sirens wailed. Belowground alarms warbled. Streetlights blazed in the predusk gloom. Roads became clogged with ice-covered vehicles as people rushed to airports and ferry terminals in an effort to escape the violence.

Very few of the panicked evacuees paid any attention to the water towers located in and around the sprawling space launch complex. Each water tank stood 90 feet high, supported by four massive legs. All of these elevated water depositories were, in fact, part of a government mandated fire suppression system that doubled as potable water storage.

Structural modifications made a year earlier added 20 feet to the height of each tower. Thousands of people queued to leave Kodiak Island, unaware that all the steel gray water towers were transforming. Massive electric motors hummed. Ice shattered and fell from clamshell doors that formed each tower's crown. Door segments turned like flower petals to form inverted oval shrapnel barriers that wrapped around the waist of each 100,000-gallon water tank – that did actually contain clean water.

Small dishes and thin whip antennas sprouted from the top of each tower and reached for the sky as missile launchers and Miniguns were exposed to the driving rain. Computer-driven radars and thermal imaging devices activated automatically.

Jim Cook and his skeleton crew remained in the operations building. He disconnected his headset and let it rest around his neck. On his orders, they retreated to an engineering workshop two stories underground.

Crimson strobe lights flashed in the corridor. Each sentinel, armed and wearing body armor, held a heavy door open for the group as they rushed in. There was a pause when the technicians saw what awaited them. Row upon row of obsolete instrumentation, flanked by clean work benches stacked with gleaming tools, hissed, hummed, or purred under the harsh white glare of equally outdated fluorescent lights.

"Yes, these things are old," Jim warned.

The dozen men and women milled around uncertainly before pulling plastic dust covers off the refurbished equipment. Forlorn whispers echoed off the concrete ceiling.

"I've never seen so many buttons and keyboards."

"Check this. Liquid crystal digital monitors."

"What? No touch screens? How do we…?"

A pair of guards closed double doors leading to the workshop and waited for what would come next.

Jim rushed over to a bank of switches on a nearby wall, toggling all of them into the "on" position. "Don't panic! All of this was top of the line gear in its day. The software interfaces are a bit limited, but you'll get used to that. All we really need to do here is stay in contact with *Gold Rush*."

"The communications hub should be up to that," somebody suggested.

Jim took off his suit coat and laid it on an empty console. "The comm hub is going to have a bad accident any minute now. We'll pick up the slack if the interlinks are still working."

"What if they don't work?" somebody whined.

Jim strode to a high backed chair and sat. "No interlink means we're dead from a cruise missile attack or in the dark until electricity gets restored. Take your pick. Neither one is going to be very much fun."

The administrator's nervous ground control team took their places with some hesitation before starting the verbal procedure of an old-fashioned checklist to activate and synchronize their workstations.

Chaos continued to unfold outdoors. Armed security guards in rain gear took up positions to surround the administration building.

"Does anyone on this rock still have Internet or satellite?" Jim asked.

"Federal government uplinks are the only thing still online," he was told.

"Turn 'em off," Jim demanded spontaneously.

All nonessential personnel were being allowed to exit the structure before it was locked and sealed by even more anxious men and armed guards.

* * *

Joshua Stringer and other federal officials were forcefully escorted back to their waiting automobiles. Outrage crept through their ranks when all of their networked devices suddenly stopped working.

"You can't do this!" Stringer shouted.

The officer charged with keeping him at bay pointed at the sky. "Sir, we have more than rain coming our way. You should get to a safer location."

The starport's DHS liaison waved his credentials at the unaffected man. "Everything you're doing here is in direct violation of federal law. Take me to Mr. Cook, or get a working phone, *right now*!"

Stringer and his subordinates argued with protective personnel for several minutes before going back to their own vehicles.

"Looks like evacuation," Stringer guessed out loud.

His aides kept trying to find a working wireless network as their small convoy returned to their assigned office space. They rolled into a parking lot filled with frantic bystanders and moving cars.

Joshua got out of his SUV. His necktie flapped in the breeze while tried to make sense of the situation. "What's going on? Where's everyone going and where's our security?" he demanded.

"Checking," somebody assured him.

Screams of terror rippled through the crowded parking lot as the night sky lit with long streams of green tracer bullets that reached into the low-hanging clouds. "Where are those coming from?" Stringer asked, pointing.

Fiery detonations above the clouds went unseen as computer-controlled radars guided defending guns and heat-seeking rockets to fill the sky with fast-moving bullets and metal fragments. Six of 18 inbound cruise missiles were hit at supersonic speeds by "flak," or fast-moving shrapnel. The impacted missiles disintegrated five miles from the starport.

Fourteen independently targeted reentry vehicles, borne aloft by ICBMs, were three minutes behind schedule, though still inbound. Defensive systems analyzed, tracked, and waited with digital patience to engage these new threats.

Seven of 12 remaining cruise missiles unsuccessfully deployed their onboard countermeasures. They were destroyed by rotary gun fire just two miles from the starport in spectacular showers of flaming wreckage. Five strategic weapons passed through long smoking tendrils of debris that corkscrewed through the night air.

Joshua and his staffers fought their way into the nearest office building as scalding debris began to fall. Security guards made an effort to direct traffic away from the area as more hot metal crashed to the ground. Some of it landed with a sizzle in the cold ocean. Other segments fell like shooting stars on cars, rooftops, and exposed human flesh.

"Who gave the order to leave?" he shouted.

A uniformed Federal Protective Service elbowed his way closer to the DHS representative. "Everyone started getting phone calls and text messages about five minutes ago saying that company staff were heading for the airports. Turns out they've been leaving for the last five or six hours."

Joshua pulled one of his aides closer. "Work with FPS to get this under control. Close the building. Send everyone home. Get my staff back here by 9 a.m. Sort this out."

"Nothing left to sort," the aide quipped.

Joshua glanced at his watch. "It's almost 4. Sun'll be up by the time we get back. Let's hope the people who run this place know what they're doing."

Five of the Chinese launched cruise missiles dove on their preprogrammed targets. Each of the supersonic computer-guided missiles delivered their conventional explosive payloads to the rooftop aim points of U.S. government buildings located in and around the starport.

U.S. Army garrison and Department of Homeland Security installations in and around the starport erupted in flames as thousand-pound shaped charges tore through them, killing hundreds of confused men and women who were reacting to mixed messages from their superiors.

Stringer and members of his entourage were killed in a matter of seconds as the five-story building they were in collapsed on top of them in a cloud of smoke and fire.

Collateral damage to the power grid caused local blackouts within a city block radius of each ground-shaking impact. Computer-controlled utilities owned by the starport shut off broken water mains and rerouted the flow of electricity.

Fourteen independently targeted warheads, delivered by just one intercontinental ballistic missile, screamed down from the stratosphere at supersonic velocities to strike at starport fueling facilities, communications arrays, and electrical generation sites. The improvised air defense grid picked off nine of these weapons. The five remaining warheads found their targets. The ground shook for a distance of two and a half miles in every direction, causing already panicked employees and dependents to speed up the pace of their evacuation.

* * *

Jim Cook and his red-shirted staff cringed when the upper stories of the building they were beneath began to sway. Overhead lights flickered. Dust fell from the unpainted concrete ceiling. Unutilized equipment around the room wobbled on legs, pegs, and struts that weren't bolted to the concrete floor.

Somebody pointed at a large screen. "Look at what they're hitting. Government buildings are obvious targets. Our comms and power plants, too. Nothing aimed at the airports. Not even the helipads. Why are they being so nice?"

Jim looked for a plug-in to activate his headset. "Nothing nice about it. Military necessity. They're being practical. Somebody might want those locations for, I dunno, a helicopter assault landing or some such."

Displays near him flickered with explosions. The administrator watched a pair of satellite dishes go up in flames. "Very practical. We have launch sites and rocket fuel. They have spacecraft and ICBMs. Never mind all that proprietary technology that we got laying around. They'll take our stuff, if we let 'em."

"You expect troop landings?" a nearby woman asked.

Jim gave up on his headset and took it off. "Eventually. Both sides will have to shoot it out at sea before anyone can get a troopship close enough to unload hovercraft."

Somebody held up a microphone. "I have local comms on shortwave. Civil authorities are going nuts."

"Don't say anything to them!" Jim shouted. "We've got our own problems," he muttered.

A multiline telephone on Jim's desk startled everyone when it rang. He picked up the receiver.

"Where have you been?" Sasha demanded from inside her sweaty vacc suit.

Jim eyed the phone in his hand with real surprise.

"How are you talking to me through a land line?" he asked in open-mouthed awe.

She snickered. "It's a little something I did to a certain hotel after they screwed up my bill. Just my way of getting even."

"I begin to see why you went to prison."

"We weren't getting anything through the usual radio frequencies. I thought, why not give you a call? How are things?"

Jim's voice came to her through a static-filled connection peppered with pops and squeals. "No big deal. We've just been hit with strategic ordnance. Radars are down. Most of our wireless is on fire and I can't get a decent cup of coffee. How are you?"

The volatile genius looked around her compartment and all its red lights. "Sorry to hear about the coffee. It's getting hot up here. Had to move the station. We're using an old microwave link to reach you."

Jim sighed. "We're blind. How is *Gold Rush*?"

"Mostly good," Sasha obfuscated.

"Reserve comms?" Jim asked.

"You're talking to me, aren't you?" she gloated.

He coughed. "It'll take our ground stations a minute to reacquire your position. Keep your wireless—"

"I know how to run a phone company!" she snapped.

"Can you operate the package?" Jim asked seriously.

"Still sorting that out," she admitted.

He watched his own staff fumble around with their old systems for a moment. "Everybody's having to make do just now. We can provide you with software support. Don't expect fast build times. And let me know how the ground station synchronizations are tracking. We can make some adjustments from out end."

"You still want me to shoot a Chinese aircraft carrier?" she inquired.

"Last resort. Yes," he affirmed.

"Cool," she replied, her voice laced with anticipation.

Jim recovered what was left of his composure. "Anything else on your mind?"

Sasha took a moment to confer with her own crew. "The I.S.S. is gone, along with every satellite we had on track. It's only a matter of time until those guys in Peking figure out that we're still up here."

"Beijing," Jim corrected.

Sasha took a deep breath. "Okay. Whatever. We'll do what we came up here to do. Expect us to be ready 72 hours…or whenever I feel like it."

Jim coughed. "Stick to the plan. Don't do anything that makes them go nuclear."

Sasha laid a gloved hand on her communications interface. "I'm not sure I heard that last part. Get back to me when you have a better connection to talk through."

"You called me!" he protested loudly.

CHAPTER FIFTEEN

Deepwater navies around the world struggled to cope with a sudden lack of accurate global positioning information. Backup systems relying on centuries-old celestial navigation techniques failed with alarming frequency. Fewer than five percent of ships at sea had astrolabes or crewmembers qualified to use them.

Strategic and tactical air forces weren't spared from the technological backslide. American and Chinese long-range bomber crews flew their missions using maps, compasses, and stopwatches once it became obvious that their touch screen autopilots were no longer able to do the work for them.

Battlespace blindness and global communications deafness resulting from combat in space and the terrestrial targeting of high-tech infrastructure forced the Sino-American conflict to slow down. Military leaders on both sides were unable to locate or redirect many of their naval units. Confusion set in as politicians berated their martial subordinates. Attempts by the mainstream media to exploit the hysteria injected a sense of helplessness that spread through the corridors of power.

* * *

Billy Richter reached the starport using one of the conventional radios in the VTOL assigned for his personal use.

"How are you holding up?" Jim asked.

Billy sniffed. "Haven't slept in two days."

"How's the airport?" Jim asked, nudging Richter away from a sermon on guilt.

"Major buildings have been hit. Runways have been cratered." Billy paused and looked around at the interior of his aircraft. He was alone. "Strange. They didn't hit the fuel tanks."

"I was counting on that," Jim replied, nodding from the comfort of his swivel chair. He looked around the improvised operations area. "I took your advice. The red shirts and I are tucked away in an alternate location. It's not doing us much good, but we're still alive."

Billy thought about the parts of the airport that were still burning. "You're doing better than we are. I'm sending a flight back to you this evening with more casualties."

"How many?" Jim couldn't help asking.

Billy looked at the illuminated pad in his hand. "Seventeen dead, another forty wounded. It's been quiet in our skies for the last ten hours. I think they're done with us, for the moment."

Jim could imagine what Billy wasn't telling him. "How are the Eagles?"

Billy put down his pad and unzipped his coat. "Norman is supervising the runway clearance. Jim, they hit us with all the birds on the ground. I'll take full responsibility for that. We lost one, but the rest are fueled and ready to go."

"Pilots?" Jim inquired calmly.

"Swarski," Billy explained.

Jim paused. He could tell that Billy was at the end of his metaphorical rope. Common sense dictated that he ease up. "Sorry to hear that. We all knew it could happen. I don't know those guys as well as you do—"

"No, you don't," Billy snapped.

Jim laid his own microphone down for a moment, forcing himself to remain silent for a respectful minute. He picked up the handset and spoke slowly. "I hear you. Just tie a knot in it and hang on. This is going to get worse before it gets better. How is Beatrice holding up?"

Billy shifted in his seat. "She hasn't had a nervous breakdown, if that's what you mean. Right now, I think, she's interviewing our prisoners."

"Interesting. How many of those do you have?" Jim asked with real curiosity.

"These guys were tough. Twelve out of what we think is a possible of 74."

"Whoa," Jim mumbled to himself. He keyed his microphone slowly. "How many VTOLs are you sending home?"

Billy used his pad to look up the planned flight schedule. "Six. Lightly loaded, so they have enough fuel to reach Kodiak."

Jim didn't hesitate. "Don't say any more over this frequency. Send a subordinate to tell me what you want. We'll send it if we have it."

"I've got non-wounded I want to send home. They're done," Billy added.

Jim didn't have to ask for clarification. Two-thirds of the starport's security force was recruited from civilian sources. Their lack of military experience made them vulnerable to the stress they'd just endured. They'd have to be replaced.

Jim smiled at his team and flashed them a positive hand gesture when a piece of equipment they were working on suddenly came to life. "Send them with my blessing. We'll swap them out. One more thing. I want Beatrice. Got some work for her."

Billy wasn't surprised. "Yeah, sure. I expect our neighbors to be back at some point, if the battle turns in their favor. It's better if she isn't here."

Jim wasn't thinking about the reporter's safety. He wanted her at the starport to broadcast her commentary during the next phase of this conflict, which would be over very quickly if U.S. naval units in the Arctic Ocean were defeated.

The administrator paused to consider Billy's potential state of mind. "Don't forget why you are there. Make sure things are set up just like we planned, and then get back here fast as you can. I expect to see you in my office three days from now."

"Beatrice and my prisoners leave in two hours," Billy said and switched off.

* * *

Necessity gave birth to creativity as the hours passed. Elected leaders and career officers resorted to old-fashioned methods of regional observation in vain attempts to learn more about what was happening beyond their vulnerable borders. Human observers were placed in remote locations with landline telephones to increase the speed of their reporting.

Spy planes and observation aircraft took off, in spite of the risks associated with manually controlled flight in hostile airspace. Every government that could afford them mobilized ground-based military units in an effort to improvise useful radio networks. Short-range multichannel radio traffic began to pick up within 16 hours of the space-based blackout.

Chinese and American warships reduced speed as they continued to look for each other on the high seas. Ship-directed aerial reconnaissance was reduced in both scope and scale, in an effort to conserve precious fuel.

Submarine commanders on both sides had an average of 25 years of experience. Decades of training for just this kind of combat improved the morale of their crews. Sealed orders were opened. Prescribed actions were taken. Automated systems were reset for manual control. Hunter-killers for both nations began to act with greater autonomy and confidence. Subs engaged surface vessels using older periscope sighting methods, increasing the effectiveness of torpedoes and missiles that were normally capable of operating at much greater ranges.

Battles were over within minutes. Outcomes hinged on who found whom first. Six Chinese warships and two of their submarines went down within eight hours. Three times as many American assets were sunk in the Arctic Ocean.

Evacuations continued from the starport, even as hostile forces sailed further into U.S. territorial waters. Officials from the State of Alaska coordinated with National Guard representatives and their federal counterparts to assess the damage to military and civilian locations around the state.

The first official day of the war ended in fear and uncertainty for both sides. The unclaimed bodies of more than 700 men and women sank into the ocean's icy depths, burdened by growing layers of arctic ice that slowly overcame the inflated buoyancy of their cold weather floatation suits.

Strategic attacks by Chinese ICBMs and cruise missiles released from far flying bombers had found their marks only because sophisticated software backups allows their guidance systems to overcome the loss of GPS. Civilian and military facilities on Alaskan soil were in disarray. Nobody in the civilian chain of command could be sure of what the federal response to this aggression would be.

The second day of the war passed in a disjointed blur of frenzied activity for many Alaskans. Fear and uncertainty at the local level resulted in runs on banks and grocery stores as they opened.

The limited telecommunications resources provided by *Gold Rush* helped Governor Wheeler maintain control of the state's chaotic bureaucracy. Undamaged radio and wireless systems maintained by the University of Alaska played their own vital role in restoring some sense of order.

Regional media outlets began transmitting again shortly after official sunset. Anyone with a working AM/FM radio receiver, or a traversable satellite dish, was popular with his less fortunate neighbors. Alaskans watched or listened with keen interest as reports were broadcast with very few commercial breaks.

* * *

Beatrice Brown arrived, hot and sweaty, at the starport 48 hours after the battle at Cold Bay. She rushed off the VTOL just after midnight, carrying little more than her oversized helmet with all its miniaturized broadcast equipment and a shoulder bag as she dashed through the rain.

A recently bathed and casually dressed Jim Cook met her on the executive landing pad near his office. "What took you so long?"

She noticed that two armed guards flanked the administrator and his bloodshot eyes. She pointed at her own red-rimmed eyes with one finger. "That's quite the fashion statement."

"Copycat," he retorted.

They walked quickly out of the prop wash and into a warm lounge filled with people in transit. He held the door open for her. "You might find this interesting. The Chinese tried to shoot down *Gold Rush*."

"Tried?" Beatrice asked while shouldering her load through the crowd.

Jim waited for his guards to file in before closing the door. "We got lucky. Seems there's too much wreckage in the area. Antisatellite missiles can't get through the debris fields."

"You must be thrilled," the reporter responded.

He nodded vigorously, aware that he wasn't the only one suffering from a lack of sleep. "Yes. Yes, I am. There have been unforeseen technical problems with a certain package on the station, and—"

Beatrice set her bag on the floor as they waited for an elevator. "Billy told me. Your rail gun doesn't work."

"How many times have *you* put a rail gun in space?" Jim shot back in mock indignation.

The elevator opened. Beatrice pushed her bag in with a sweep of her foot. "I wouldn't," she rebuked before shuffling into the rear of the waiting lift.

Jim rushed in. His guards followed, pressing buttons to send the elevator down to the garage level. The doors closed. The ride took 30 seconds.

"I should have Billy shot and fired for spilling the beans," Jim mumbled.

Beatrice stood silently until they were out of the elevator and into a waiting SUV that would take them to the administrative annex. "Where are all the bomb craters?"

Jim pointed to the blackened remains of a U.S. government office building as they passed. "It's called selective targeting. They hit our power plants, telecoms, and administrative control centers. They even managed to get some of our deep bunkers that had people and things that I won't talk about in them."

"You're lucky to have anything left at all," Beatrice observed.

Jim fidgeted with his seatbelt in an effort to get comfortable. "I can see how you might think that. War is Hell. Billy said that Cold Bay will never be the same again. Hundreds will never go back."

The journalist held on to her kit bag. "It's one thing to bomb on live television as a presenter. It's a totally different thing to be bombed on live television as a target. And the fighting was…hard. It was bad."

"I can imagine," Jim nodded sympathetically.

Beatrice withdrew into herself for a long moment. "We heard some radio traffic on the flight over. Sounded like fishermen at sea, calling in sightings of American and Chinese warships. Who would they be telling?"

"Us."

Beatrice squirmed in her seat. The guard next to her tried to move over. "You, as in *you*?" she emphasized.

Jim shook his head as the vehicle shuddered over a bump in the road. "Not me, specifically. We have people who are handling that."

"When do I get to meet them?" the reported probed.

Jim shook his head emphatically. "These aren't the kind of people who want to be met. They need anonymity like you need high ratings. You can talk about what they do after the fact, but you'll never get to see their faces or know their names."

Beatrice knocked on the window as they passed a pair of armed men who were directing traffic through a busy intersection. "How much of this story are you actually going to let me tell?"

"As much as I can," Jim replied.

"I hate censorship."

Jim pointed to the ruins of the administrative complex. "My office used to be on the top floor, when there was a top floor. Nobody died, but the place burned because of two follow-on attacks that got through."

"You're changing the subject!" Beatrice argued.

Jim got out of the SUV after it came to a stop near an underground ramp. "Yes," he acknowledged, "I am changing the subject. You can say anything you want about what you see, hear, taste, touch, and smell around here, but you will *not* breathe one word about how we gather our intelligence."

* * *

Charlie Pike straddled the pilot's chair inside the wheelhouse of his 130-foot-long fishing boat, *Bering Sea*

Bonanza. The 250-ton vessel rode high in the water, its holds empty, as it cut through the frigid waves at 12 knots, 400 miles southwest of Shemya Island.

Instruments around the darkened bridge beeped, blinked, and chirped as the old fisherman minded his course. He wasn't entirely alone. Two members of his crew kept a roaming watch around the boat while the rest of the crew slept.

Pike had no illusions about what he was doing. He, and everyone else like him who was at sea as part of Operation Fish Net, was taking a big risk by reporting what they saw using old-fashioned radios.

The promise of a payday from the starport sounded good to the unemployed owners. Dozens had gone to sea with fatter wallets. Would the Chinese respect the fact that these were unarmed civilian fishing boats?

Charlie quietly cursed himself for being foolish enough to fumble around the dark in search of enemy warships. He adjusted his dirty cap and tried not to think about all the screens over his head that read "no satellite connection."

Both of his GPS terminals flashed warnings in red, "no signal."

"Just a harmless little crab boat," he mumbled.

Every outboard floodlight was turned on, making the vessel's superstructure visible through the night for more than five miles.

"See? I'm right here. No sneaking for me. No, sir."

The civilian transponder located on the top of *Bonanza's* tallest antenna broadcast his position to any vessel capable of receiving the unencrypted signal. Multichannel radios popped and hissed. Bold Alaskans chatted using an improvised code.

"*Beauregard*, this is *Laurence*. See your beacon. Why so far south?"

"Still trying to fix our radar. Thought we heard something on the shortwave."

"Stay in your assigned grid space. Do not deviate."

Charlie chuckled at the controlled pandemonium and reset his own surface radar with the touch of a button.

The civilian-grade surface radars that were routinely installed on most commercial fishing vessels lacked any substantial software-discrimination capability. Contacts displayed on the shipboard monitors were large, medium, or small. Any contact that didn't have a civilian locator beacon associated with it was assumed to be of interest to the military intelligence experts being employed by the starport. Charlie and his fellows would broadcast what they saw, when they saw it, without ever knowing if the starport got their messages or not.

Pike waved at the two-man patrol as they shuffled by his closed cabin window. Each sailor, clad in a bright orange deepwater survival suit, stopped at regular intervals to remove and reattach the safety lines that would prevent them from being tossed overboard in a sudden sea change.

Charlie was about to use the intercom to chat with them when his radar display began to beep. His bushy eyebrows went up when he counted three contacts. He kept one hand on the steering panel while using the radio. "*Bonanza*, Fish Net, position check, over. I have no GPS."

Charlie looked at a map on the wall behind him. He read off the coordinates of latitude and longitude that described his position as best he could guess. "I count three little ones, moving south-southeast."

He was surprised when the radio came to life with a female voice.

"*Bonanza*, this is Fish Net. Hold your course. Reduce speed," she ordered.

Charlie glanced at his instruments before easing back on his throttles. Any well-armed ship he could see on his limited radar was more than close enough to fire on him with a missile or gun. He reached for a tall steel mug and thought about waking the rest of his crew while watching his engine rpms drop.

"Dead is dead," he reasoned out loud.

"Let 'em sleep for one more hour," he decided after a swig of cold coffee.

CHAPTER SIXTEEN

Chinese and American leaders adapted to their loss of surveillance and communications platforms by implementing of long-standing disaster management procedures. Many of these reduced-communication protocols had originated during the Cold War, when nuclear annihilation seemed possible. Thousands scrambled in Washington and in Beijing to follow what they hoped were still good instructions.

Orders flowed from these capitals to other parts of their respective countries, through various departments, agencies, and bureaus. Civil servants and military personnel with access to stockpiled equipment, or the legal authority to assume control over privately owned facilities, urgently followed their instructions. Forgotten manuals were hastily read by young professionals whose parents hadn't been alive when they were written. In some cases, the curling yellow pages were hurriedly scanned and converted to digital images for distribution through e-mail. People with very little first-hand knowledge of such obsolete systems were rushed to remote locations, where they took dust covers off control boards at inactive radio transmitters or antenna receiver stations.

These adaptations slowed the pace of combat at sea over the next 24 hours. Naval engagements became localized within regions of just a few hundred square miles as formations of ships used airplanes, helicopters, and drones to locate and follow their opponents. Many pursuits proved unsuccessful when bad weather moved in.

Chinese submarine commanders, operating boats of the new *Shang V* class, were specifically tasked with the protection of aircraft carrier battle groups. Party leaders in Beijing chatted confidentially with members of the state-sponsored media in secluded surroundings, elaborating on the correctness of this conservative decision, vindicated by the fact that no American submarines were getting close enough to harm any of China's powerful aircraft carriers.

U.S. submarine warfare rules had few restrictions, in spite of the fact that Congressionally-approved military budgets had been shrinking for three decades. Spending for new ships wasn't politically popular in districts where unemployment and starvation threatened millions of insecure voters.

American sailors were aware of the odds they faced, even if the citizens they defended were not. Half a dozen *Virginia*-class submarines went to sea, equipped to carry U.S. Navy SEAL teams. The country's two remaining *Ohio*-class "boomers" continued their traditional role as strategic deterrents. Four *Los Angeles*-class attack boats were expected to hunt independently in the central Pacific.

A lopsided game of chess was now underway. CVN 78 *Gerald R. Ford* and its escorts, under the command of Admiral Rex Reynolds, probed 600 nautical miles southwest of, and parallel to, the Aleutian Islands, looking for the *Strong Prosperity* (*Qiángdà de shǔxìng*), under the flag of Admiral Chen Lang. All other American formations in the Arctic and western Pacific regions were assigned to keep the bulk of China's fleet from breaking out into the Central Pacific.

Three American destroyers, two guided missile frigates, and one Japanese *Soryu*-class submarine were lost near the Taiwan Strait, leading many to suspect that an invasion of the island was imminent. American air patrols flew out of bases in Japan to interdict opposing reconnaissance.

Chinese cryptanalysts eventually tumbled to the existence of Fish Net and began to follow it with considerable interest.

The first of many short-lived carrier-on-carrier battles to be fought since the Second World War occurred 72 hours later, just 365 miles southwest of Okinawa.

* * *

Chinese naval infantry arrived without opposition in the Aleutian Islands and requested air support after spotting overflights on their positions from what they assumed were U.S. Navy reconnaissance units. Military planners in Beijing interpreted this request for assistance as proof that an American carrier battle group was operating nearby. This presented an opportunity for decisive action.

The planes observed by the invaders were actually Norman Ahgupuk's training flights, which were widening their patrol radius on orders from the starport. Degraded intelligence-gathering capabilities, combined with human error, prevented proper identification of this force as it left the area.

Fighters from the Chinese aircraft carrier *Strong Prosperity* scrambled in search of the threat. They engaged the long-range combat air patrol from *Gerald R. Ford*'s battle group without ever knowing how accidental the encounter really was.

Modern Chinese fighters, built entirely from domestic designs and refined materials, engaged the *Ford*'s aging American F-35 naval variants that had been created by a consortium of contractors, using parts and materials processed around the world. Stealth features common to the aircraft on both sides made first-strike instrument lock harder to achieve than most preconflict training scenarios had suggested.

Admiral Reynolds opted to maneuver, rather than engage in what would surely be a knock-down, drag-out fight. He suspected that Chinese air and reconnaissance units could be operating from some of the remote islands. They might endanger the survivability of the ships under his command.

Officers aboard *Strong Prosperity* expected the *Ford*'s course alteration to evade the intervention of land-based aviation. Admiral Chen ordered his vessels to steer accordingly. The fight would take place further out to sea. There would be no hope of rescue for American sailors and airmen who ended up in the frigid Arctic waters.

Severed data links prevented both sides from making the most of their electronics. Pilots relied on their extensive training and well-practiced backup plans to form local networks within their squadrons. Leaders on land, feeling safe inside comfortable bunkers, relied on relayed transmissions from ships at sea to make sense of what happened.

Once-crisp video became grainy as it was processed at slower bit rates. Digital audio became choppy as it was fed through jumpy microwave links that didn't always line up properly. Computers on warships throughout the region quickly decoded English and Mandarin transmissions as they flowed through encrypted radio channels.

"Climbing through 40,000..."

"Tígāo nǐ de shíjiān jiàngé!"

"Almost there..."

Additional aircraft quickly reinforced *Ford's* combat air patrol as the distance between the carriers decreased. American and Chinese squadrons, operating from similar time-tested air combat plans, attempted to gain dominance by accelerating as they climbed.

Pilots on both sides realized the futility of ejecting at high speeds over the frigid sea. The cold polar jet stream would kill them on the way down or they would freeze to death in the icy water long before search and rescue teams could reach them.

Time passed quickly. Missile lock was hard to achieve by conventional means for either side as they closed range on each other. Computer-aided firing solutions reduced the fear factor for all of the pilots as they watched their displays. Long-range missiles leaped from rotary launchers concealed inside sleek airframes traveling at more than 600 miles per hour. Dozens of smart weapons broke the sound barrier in just a few seconds.

"Formation, break and merge!" leaders on both sides called out during high-g turns. Flares, chaff, and electronic jamming filled the air as pilots pulled their best high speed fly-by maneuvers in an effort to avoid being shot down.

Three American and two Chinese aircraft were destroyed by direct hits. Four American and five Chinese fighters went down as a result of devastating near-misses that tore their aircraft apart.

The rapid loss of hard-to-replace pilots and hardware provoked an immediate reaction from the civilian leadership in both camps. Veteran aviators in each armed force argued for a swift follow up.

Heated arguments in Washington, D.C., lasted only a few minutes before the order was given for the *Ford* and its escorts to withdraw.

"We are engaged!" Admiral Reynolds protested.

Chinese leaders, with similar worries, ordered the *Strong Prosperity* to take a similar course of action.

"I have the upper hand!" Admiral Chen insisted.

Both officers were tactfully encouraged to comply. This knee-jerk reaction wouldn't be repeated. The political fallout from alleged weakness on both sides of the Pacific caused rapid changes in official policy, ensuring that both governments would more aggressively pursue their goals.

None of the returning pilots wanted to think about the single white parachute they saw descending slowly towards certain death as they went back to their respective carriers.

* * *

"It's my fault," Billy Richter told Jim Cook through a secured radio channel.

Jim looked around his improvised operations room. "Don't let this get to you. I was the one who ordered Norman to extend the range of his combat air patrol."

"We led them to one of our own carriers," Billy griped bitterly.

"They would've found each other."

"Where's that magic bullet?" Billy asked.

Jim sighed and rolled his eyes. "They tell me there's too much debris in low orbit to get a clear shot. They'll have to make a hole. That's gonna take time."

The day shift was servicing their equipment while Jim talked on the radio. The poor working conditions and improvised sleeping arrangements were merely something to be tolerated. Nobody complained as they worked to coax more life out of the old monitors and obsolete computers.

"Sunset in two hours," Billy mentioned.

"Tell me about the training accidents."

A display behind him blinked on and off. The woman working on it flinched after being shocked by a sudden surge of electricity from an open panel.

"One. Mechanical failure," Billy admitted.

The starport administrator nodded to himself. The loss of just one of his F-15s at this point in the conflict was acceptable. He coughed to clear his throat. "No new incursions?" he asked.

"Nothing in the last 24 hours," Billy replied.

Jim craned his neck to see a monitor on the far side of his underground lair. "The battle is moving away from you. Further out to sea."

"Is that confirmed?"

"It's not safe to light a radar," Jim huffed.

"Any word from the machine shop?"

Jim smiled at the prospect of revealing good news. "Three more birds with pilots are on the way tonight."

"That brings us to seven," Billy brightened.

Jim didn't want to dwell on the details. "Step up your training flights. Burn as much fuel as you want."

Billy paused to read a note that was handed to him. "Norm says they'll be 'acceptably proficient' in five days. Whatever that means."

Jim sipped from a cold cup of coffee before responding. "Okay, then. This was the easy part. Tell Mr. Flyboy to be ready in two days."

"I heard you lost the skiff," Billy commented.

The administrator sighed. "Not an actual loss. We shut it down because most of what they did relied on satellite uplinks. The rest is tied in to things that that we can handle from other locations."

"How is the air defense holding up?" Billy asked through a stifled yawn.

Jim thought about the nightly cruise missile attacks that pounded the starport. Emergency evacuations, carried out chaotically, had been completed two days previously with just 200 civilians killed and another 500 wounded.

He sighed. "No more ICBMs. Just cruise missiles. A few get through. They're guessing. Nobody can get an accurate damage assessment because the satellites are gone. It's cool. We can take this degree of punishment for a few more weeks."

Billy thought about what the fighter pilots might say. "How do they fly in that?" he asked.

Jim rubbed his tired eyes. "Got it taken care of. We have enough underground manufacturing sites to hide them. Got three covered trenches that are used to boost shuttles to takeoff speed on rocket sleds, if it should come to that. Each one is two miles long. More than enough for these old birds to get airborne."

Billy laughed as he imagined the obsolete airplanes being launched using systems meant to hold 50 times their weight. "That's a kick in the pants for somebody," he snickered.

Jim ended the conversation and hung up the microphone. He stood up to stretch his aching back. One of six phones on his desk rang for attention, causing him to flop down again.

"Yeah?" he growled into the old land line.

The male voice on the other end of the cable connection snickered. "Siggs here. Man, you sound wrung out. Sorry to bother you, but I have a real problem."

Jim cupped his hand over the receiver for a moment to gather his thoughts. Anthony Siggs was still the mouthpiece for the starport's organized criminal element.

Jim eyed the phone number that popped up on his handset. "Why are you still here?"

Siggs laughed more deeply. "Some of us took your offer of an easy exit."

"They got caught?" Jim guessed.

"A few of them are doing some pretty hard time," the boss admitted.

Jim turned his back on the room. "I don't care if they've all been shot by a North Korean firing squad. You have no reason to call me!"

"I got business now," Siggs cajoled.

Jim straightened. "I'm listening," he replied dryly.

The old fixer softened his tone as static crackled through the line. "My people have mouths to feed and bodies to bury. We're taking what we need from the civilian sectors."

"So?" Jim sniffed.

"We need medical."

"You need a doctor?"

The stylish rogue smiled through the phone. "Paramedics and a good cutter who can put people back together. Lead poisoning, if you know what I'm saying."

Jim uttered a silent curse. "I told you—" he started.

"Hear me out!" Siggs pled.

"Talk fast."

Siggs mumbled. There was no point in hiding this truth from the one person who could help him. "The larger gangs have been settling old scores. A few of the smaller outfits are trying to hustle some new turf out of the independents."

Jim glanced over his shoulder. He hunched over in his chair and lowered his voice. "You know what butters our bread around here. I'll get what you need, but you'll have to give me your word that nothing goes missing from the professional sectors. That includes the contractors. Leave them alone, or I'll show you a whole new kind of pain."

Siggs put Jim on hold for a minute to discuss the offer with his committee. "Your sacred ground has already been violated. There's only one way I can give an order like that. Somebody dies to make it stick. Know what I'm saying?"

"You really want to call out a hit in my starport?" Jim complained cantankerously.

"Why do you even care?" Siggs protested, his voice rising.

Jim shrugged. "No. I don't suppose I really do. Kill 'em all if you have to. Whatever it takes to limit the damage. You're out of work if we're out of business."

"When do I get my doctors?" the irritated man asked in a softer tone.

Jim turned in his chair to peck at a computer keyboard with his tired fingers. "I'll have three medics from our security force go to the Bloody Bucket in plain clothes. Should be there in a few hours."

"I'll make sure it's open for business."

Jim typed his orders slowly as he talked. "I'm giving them instructions to verify your situation before handing over supplies. The senior medic will have authority to requisition as needed. He also gets my say-so to shoot anyone who makes his job hard."

"Very cool," Siggs said gratefully.

"Did you hear me? They'll be armed," Jim warned.

"Wouldn't have it any other way," Siggs acknowledged.

Jim changed his grip on the phone. "Rob them or kill them, or even mess up their hair, and I'll go out of my way to find new and exciting ways to hurt you."

"Yeah, yeah. I heard you the first time. You don't like spending your limited resources on stuff like this. They'll be under my personal protection."

"Last thing. Call me again and you'll be the one who needs a doctor," Jim snapped.

CHAPTER SEVENTEEN

Charlie Pike was jolted from a sound sleep when one of his crew banged a boot on the edge of his bunk. "Fish Net," the bearded man mumbled.

Pike slept fully clothed, like many fishermen in rough seas. He stumbled into his boots and rushed for the bridge of the *Bearing Sea Bonanza.* He arrived in the cabin to sounds of an alert chime coming over the radio.

The dispatcher's voice was urgent as she activated the chime again. "*Bonanza*! Come on. Fish Net control calling *Bearing Sea Bonanza.* Alert Able is in effect. Squawk ident before responding, over."

He waited for his first mate to move out of the way before sitting at the helm. He struggled to think of the codes and phrases he was supposed to have memorized. "Right!" he grinned, suddenly recalling the necessary information.

Touching the nearest screen, he shut off the boat's identification transponder. He turned it on and off several times before activating his radio. "*Bonanza*, squawking ident," he confirmed.

The procedure was intended to let starport controllers know if one of the boats they'd hired was no longer under friendly control.

The dispatcher's voice responded, its urgency unabated. "Good job, *Bonanza.* Change course due north, best speed. Look for a parachute."

Charlie's heart skipped a beat. "One of ours?" he asked.

"Wouldn't send you if it was one of theirs," the dispatcher replied dispassionately.

Pike signed off and found his old binoculars. He went out to the rail for a quick scan of the horizon. Several deckhands were already pointing up and away.

"You are one lucky duck," Charlie whispered as he sighted the descending pilot.

The aviator seesawed back and forth between the risers of the parachute, protected from head-to-toe in a thermal flight suit that would double as a cold water survival system.

Thoughts of what it might be like to die in the swirling ocean without any hope of rescue filled Charlie's head. Recalling the dispatcher's voice made him scowl.

"Is he one of ours?" somebody asked.

Pike lowered his scarred binoculars and spat. "That's not the point. It *shouldn't* be the point. We're fishermen. We know what's about to happen."

"So?" another man chimed in.

Charlie tapped his foot on the deck. "That poor soul must think there's no help on the way. What would you do in his situation?"

Nobody spoke.

"We're all thinking the same thing. Let's hope we get there in time," the captain brooded.

* * *

SSN-21 *Seawolf* scored its third, fourth, and fifth kills of the conflict with Tomahawk cruise missiles that targeted the destroyer screen supporting *Strong Prosperity*. The devastation wrought by these missile attacks didn't deter the admiral commanding the Chinese battle group. Years of contingency training had prepared the entire chain of command for this moment.

A trio of Type 63 *Jiangkai* guided missile frigates inside the formation raced ahead while surviving destroyers spread out to maintain the carrier's air defense envelope.

The American submarine reduced speed, moving deeper into the icy undercurrents of the Arctic Ocean, turning wide to approach the Chinese aircraft carrier from astern.

* * *

Naval analysts in Beijing got word of the ambush ten minutes after the fact. They made their recommendations after just three minutes of consultation. Politburo members overseeing operations in the Arctic demanded further analysis, which took another five minutes to develop.

Computer projections, based on Western combat models, determined a 65 percent probability that *Strong Prosperity* would be sunk within a matter of hours, in spite of all efforts to the contrary.

Senior Communist party leaders were now resigned to further escalation. Any attempt to restrain their forces would only result in needless casualties. New orders were given as fast as the compromised telecom networks could transmit them.

U.S. Navy doctrine presumed immediate escalation after one or more of an opponent's major naval assets went to the bottom. Encrypted traffic, captured and decoded by American installations in Hawaii, confirmed the validity of this assumption as Pike's *Bering Sea Bonanza* got close enough to retrieve the hypothermic pilot who would be flown to Anchorage 12 hours later.

* * *

Sporadic communications between American submarines and the surface vessels they protected were encrypted and passed on to shore based installations for transmission to Washington, D.C. The comparatively slow pace of information retrieval reduced the reliability of computer-generated intelligence assessments, forcing human analysts to pass along their best-guess estimates of enemy locations, intentions, and logistical impairments.

Commercial news and entertainment corporations continued operating in the dark as engineers around the world struggled to improvise a hasty network of overland microwave transmitters and fiber optic cables that would reestablish content feeds to their paying customers. Freelance technicians made easy money by quickly constructing unmanned remote controlled drones with civilian markings, network logos, and full-spectrum camera arrays modified to work with obsolete directional microwave transceivers.

Politicians and war planners on both sides of the Arctic Ocean began experiencing increasing lag times in their situational awareness over the next 48 hours as American and Chinese ships were sunk, creating gaps in each nation's slowly shrinking zone of control.

Sluggish responses from their leaders didn't prevent Chinese admirals from pressing their advantages. Fighters from *Strong Prosperity's* battle group probed aggressively in search of the American task force protecting the carrier *Gerald R. Ford*.

Due to an unintentional blackout, Captain Brewster and the crew of SSN 21 *Seawolf* remained unaware of casualties in the region that included the other two hulls in their class, SSN-22 *Connecticut* and SSN-23 *Jimmy Carter*.

* * *

Over the next 72 hours, reports reached Washington that painted a grim picture. Efforts to prevent large-scale enemy fleet movements through the East China Sea were failing, slowly.

Japanese surface warfare squadrons, already decimated by losses sustained in a series of hit-and-run battles with Chinese vessels north of the Ryukyu Islands, fell back to a location due east of those islands to merge with a heavily reinforced American task force containing CVN 79 *John F. Kennedy* and CVN 81 *Enterprise*.

A series of tropical storms moving through the region were being used as cover by at least three Chinese battle groups as they forced their way into the deep water of the South Pacific. The same storms that hid surface ships from aerial view also interfered with communications between aircraft, vessels, and shore-based installations. Early hesitations associated with air combat losses evaporated as pilots in each air arm carried out their missions with fierce determination.

Carrier flight decks remained busy, even when they were soaked in the full force of a windy squall. Pilots loitered in mess halls or napped in ready rooms. Ship crews remained on edge as they performed their duties wearing life jackets.

Idle gossip below decks turned to complaints about no news from home. Every Chinese and American at sea had grown up in a world made more enjoyable by satellite-driven data transmission. The sudden failure of that convenience, and the bitterness its loss fostered, made it easier for sailors on both sides to hate the enemy.

Combat information centers deep inside the mobile multitude of moving warships bustled with activity around the clock. Each new watch section of specialists that came on duty settled in to operate dozens of instrument panels flanked by a combination of flat panel and holographic displays.

PRC battle groups, centered on the nuclear powered aircraft carriers *Glorious Destiny* (*Guāngróng de Mìngyùn*), *Celebrated Fortune* (*Zhùmíng de Cáifù*), and *Noble Dragon* (*Gāoguì de Lóng zú*), began their attack on the blocking coalition force at a range of 650 nautical miles. Hundreds of aircraft roared off the opposing flight decks in the region under the cover of rain-cloaked predawn darkness. Vigilant combat air patrols on both sides alerted the fleets they defended by VHF radio before being shot down. Fleet-level coordinators used their own integrated and encrypted radio networks to send and receive data as they gave verbal orders to form squadrons, stack altitude patterns, and set directions of attack.

Civilian media outposts around the world, hungry for anything to report, tried to eavesdrop on what they knew would be a furious battle. Unmanned drones were sent far out to sea in vain attempts to record or photograph anything of interest. Most of those vehicles ran out of fuel before they spied anything worth the expense of their launch. Radio and television technicians looked at and listened to frequency after frequency of meaningless clutter sent back by these drones as thousands of combatants died in the shark-infested waters of a turbulent East China Sea.

The fight was on. Clashes between hostile air wings began at high speed and long range with very smart, very expensive missiles. Sorties devolved into maneuvering contests at moderate speeds as pilots unleashed faster, cheaper, medium-range missiles, culminating in a short-range, low-speed brawl, with the remaining combatants firing guns through optical sights.

The largest carrier-versus-carrier battle since Midway in 1942 played out with no big budget media resources on-hand to bear witness. American aircrews and sailors went about their duties with an energetic, rebellious attitude that blended jingoism, jocularity, and jet fuel to form a mix of wry humor that helped them cope with their situation.

For the second time in their comparatively short history, career sailors of the United States Navy were being forced to square off against an aggressor made bold by flawed foreign policy instigated by short-sighted politicians who'd come into office on flimsy promises.

Computer projections promised leaders in Washington, D.C., bunkers that their very expensive warships and highly trained sailors would soon be littering the bottom of a fished-out ocean. A decision was quickly made, for purely biased reasons, to devolve control of the situation to commanders on the scene.

Admiral Thurmond Carlisle, whose flag flew from the bridge of the *Enterprise*, didn't care who got the blame for this turkey shoot. Planes were falling out of the sky. Every life in his task force was in peril as surviving enemy aircraft strove got within range to launch their payloads of antiship missiles at his zigzagging ships.

Chapter Eighteen

Norman Ahgupuk, still wearing his flight gear, paused at the entrance of the improvised operations center to present his I.D. A pair of seated guards working from the comfort of a hastily built bench and countertop used a laptop computer to verify his credentials and log his entry. He was approved and entered the building.

The retired air force officer gawked as he walked. He observed the state of equipment disrepair with mild amusement as he looked for Jim Cook amidst all the activity.

Most of the surrounding monitors were showcasing familiar imagery depicting enemy ship locations and projected destination calculations. Radios blared with sounds of air combat in faraway locations, with which he was all too well-acquainted. Thoughts of what was happening to those pilots, and the sharks that were feeding on some of them, did little to calm his nerves.

The deteriorating state of affairs at sea left him further unsettled as he stopped a passerby to ask for directions near the center of the bustling, brightly lit room. A busy woman pointed while wisps of dust fell on her from overhead.

Norman stifled a yawn. He didn't have much to complain about. His pilots and planes were safely transitioned back to the starport, where it appeared they would be needed. His empty stomach rumbled. He detoured to a table with refreshments to grab half a peanut butter sandwich and a hot cup of coffee before striding off to find the chief administrator.

He paused to eat and drink while everyone around him stayed busy. His trained eye noticed that many of the old monitors displayed solemn notifications that read "no data" or "offline," sometimes in flashing red letters. These were indications of just how reliant they'd become on satellite-driven data transmission.

Norman finished his food and beverage while pondering what air combat would be like for the carrier-based pilots who were now deprived of their spaced based assistance.

He located Jim, huddled with four other people. "You wanted to see me?" he said loudly, barging in on the group.

Cook looked up from his desk. "There you are. Everybody, go. I have business with this man."

The crowd dispersed. Jim pointed to a folding chair.

Norman sat. "I'm sorry about the delay—"

"Couldn't be helped." Jim interrupted.

Norman brushed dry crumbs from his calloused hands. "Give it to me straight."

Cook pointed to the nearest trio of monitors. "That's our look-down from *Gold Rush.* Their new position lets us see most of the northern and central Pacific. The other guys have seven flattops that we know about."

Norman turned to look. "I'm with you so far."

Jim cleared his throat with a swig of cold coffee. "The kids on our side brawl had just four carriers in the Pacific when the shooting started. The count is now three."

Norman coughed. "Those 'kids' you are referring to happen to be Americans."

"What's your point?"

"We are Americans," Norman observed passionately.

"True, but I'm not feeling very patriotic right now," Jim remarked sourly.

The aviator bridled at the comment. "I saw some of the damage to the starport as we flew in. Looks really bad from the air. I can image how you must feel."

Jim sat up. "The assumption has always been that China would move to take us intact because we have so much one-of-a-kind stuff that can't be moved, all in one place."

"You're unhappy because you guessed wrong?"

The insomniac administrator swiveled in his chair. "Wrong has cost me more lives than I have time to count, plus something like four billion dollars. Yes. I'm not happy."

Norman saw that Jim was miserable. "Take it from an old stick-and-rudder man who's had to fly after-action recon. Some things never change. Post-mission damage assessments have been guesswork ever since they started putting cameras in airplanes."

Jim stroked the stubble on his chin. "They don't know how bad they've hurt us, so they just keep on hurting us?"

"That's it, right there," Norman confirmed coldly.

"Would they stop pounding us if we let their recon flights come through unmolested?" Jim asked after a moment of brooding.

Norman considered the question. "Unlikely."

"Why?"

Ahgupuk hunched over. "How much of this place is underground?"

"Half."

Norman nodded. "There's your answer, right there. They're just being thorough, because they know that half your assets are underground."

Jim swore. "We get missile attacks every day. Sometimes every 12 hours. They've knocked down two out of three launch towers and collapsed two out of three sled trenches. And yes, before you ask, we can still support your planes."

"Are you out of business?"

Jim rubbed his fingers together. "There's more to it than that. Some of their ordnance has hit machine shops and fabrication plants. I don't know how much of that was deliberate and how much was accidental."

Norman frowned. "Neither do they. That's why they'll keep coming."

"Is that how they play this stupid game?" Jim blurted.

"Yes."

The edgy executive scanned the room for more real-time information. "I get what you're saying. We don't win this game with the rules as they're currently written." The physical movement around him was distracting. "I'm sure all of this would make more sense to me after a decent night's sleep."

Norman sat silently as Jim collapsed back into his chair with both eyes closed. It took a moment for the executive's tired mind to comprehend what he'd seen and heard. "It's not enough to kill their carrier," he reasoned.

"Excuse me?" Norman blinked.

Jim opened his bloodshot eyes. "We need to make a statement. Something very loud that gets their attention."

"What are you talking about?" Norman exclaimed.

"One minute!" Adrenaline jumpstarted Jim's heart as he leaped from his chair. He went quickly to the cluster of cluttered workstations being used to monitor what was left of the starport's radar arrays.

Norman ate candy from a dish on Jim's desk while he watched the animated man huddle with two men and a woman over a video table. Their discussion quickly deteriorated into an argument.

The pilot watched with growing interest as images of the approaching Chinese carrier battle group and engineering schematics of the *Gold Rush* space station flashed on and off the table's large display.

Jim left the trio with a grin. He returned to his chair with renewed vigor. "Okay. Here's the plan so far," he began with a gleam in his eye.

Norman pulled his chair in closer and took another piece of candy.

Jim picked up a tablet computer and used his index finger to sketch on the screen as he talked. "First, let me tell you that there *is* a rail gun onboard *Gold Rush*."

"It's real," Norman responded, his surprise evident.

Jim fidgeted. "Yeah. Why would we make up something like that?"

Norman spit his unfinished candy into a nearby garbage can. "It's illegal. There are no military systems in space! How many treaties did you break to do this?"

"All of them," Jim conceded.

"Why?" Norman exclaimed.

The enthusiastic man made an expansive gesture. "Look around! We're on the verge of going out of business. Hundreds dead. Thousands wounded. Billions lost that won't be covered by insurance. That's why!"

Norman raised a hand in an effort to arrest the anger he felt. "The ends don't always justify the means. Please, think about what you're saying. Think about what you might be doing here in the next few hours." He shook with frustration.

"This is a fight between sovereign governments—which this company is not—and here you sit, making big picture decisions that'll have unforeseen consequences for the next hundred years."

"Yes," Jim stubbornly replied.

Norman, who was no stranger to politics, forced himself to slow down. "Does Washington know?" he asked slowly.

"Not specifically," Jim replied with a leisurely swing of his arms.

"Nobody at the Pentagon would let you do this," Norman huffed contrarily.

Jim thought about the papers he'd received from the federal Justice Department, which were now stored in his personal safe. They might not stand up to politically motivated challenges after the fact, but they were the closest thing he and his subordinates had to a shield under the present circumstances.

He dropped the tablet on his desk. "Norman, please. Calm down. I'm reading you in because you need to know. Now you do."

"All of it."

"All of it," the administrator assured him.

Norman sat back and folded his arms.

Jim took that as his cue to continue. He turned a monitor on his desk toward the suspicious man. "We've been using *Gold Rush* to keep an eye on what's going on out there. As you can see, this fellow right here is coming to pay us a visit."

"*Strong Prosperity*," Norman read from the display.

Jim nodded. "Exactly. We're going to shoot that nice, big, fat capital warship with our oh-so-illegal space gun. All the other, less expensive, warships traveling with said target, soon to be a victim, will feel naked without their air cover and go home."

Norman sighed. "You've really got this figured out."

Jim straightened his necktie. "Absolutely. Your planes and your pilots are a precaution, just in case the aforementioned space gun doesn't work."

"Explain that," Norman said insistently.

Jim rolled his eyes. "It is what it sounds like. See these? This, this, and this. Those are amphibious landing ships full of naval infantry. It's their version of marines. We learned the hard way at King Cove and Cold Bay that we can't go toe-to-toe with those guys, so we've got to make 'em go away."

Norman thought he understood. "Launch on them before they launch on you."

"Right the first time," Jim replied, his tone congratulatory.

The veteran rocked back and forth in his chair. "I follow. No joy from the rail gun means Plan B. Send up the Eagles and slow dance inside the air defense envelope if things go wrong, just to keep their bombs off your targets? Risky, even under good conditions."

"Then, rearm and go kill their landing craft if you have to," the exhausted administrator concluded.

Norman rose slowly to his feet. "Not bad. It would've been good to know about the rail gun ahead of time. We've wasted a lot of time planning for other missions that are now irrelevant."

"Operational security," Jim replied blandly.

Norman studied all the screens he could see. "The laser-based interception system we tested over Cold Bay seems to work well enough. Is there any chance we can get some help from the Air Force units that are still flying out of Anchorage?"

Jim stood and moved around his desk. "Let me worry about the catering. Go talk to your pilots. Get them off to bed or whatever it is you guys do before combat."

Norman rubbed his face. "Based on what little I can see from here, if your projections are accurate, they can throw their birds at you in roughly four hours."

Jim put a hand on the officer's shoulder and steered him to the nearest exit. "I read on the Internet that fuel is a prime consideration in sustained deepwater combat scenarios. They can fly in four hours, but they won't when they don't have to."

The agitated aviator strained to see the projection.

Jim pointed. "The center icon means the carrier. The colored circles indicate three different possible areas of attack, based on fuel and payload they might assign to their aircraft."

"Short, medium, and long range," Norman nodded.

Jim was momentarily distracted by someone who handed him a pad. He signed the document without reading it. "Get lost," he commanded the intruder.

"When do you give the order to fire?" Norman yawned.

Jim stepped around the retreating man. "If all goes well, I plan to unleash our crime against humanity just before they come within long distance strike range. Three hours and fifty-odd minutes from now."

"Hm. Yeah. No point in letting them get closer," Norman concluded.

"None at all," Jim agreed.

The fatigued officer massaged his aching elbow. "I'm going to go stick my head in a bucket of ice water to freshen up, then I'm going to have that nap. You might want to do the same."

"See that door?" Jim pointed at the nearest exit.

"I'm going," the pilot muttered. "We'll be ready to go in two hours!" he shouted as he went out the door.

"Good to know," Jim growled.

He stormed across the low-ceilinged room, through a flurry of activity and radio chatter punctuated by the high-pitched modem squeal of data transmissions, toward a newly created communications hub.

"*Gold Rush*, now!" Jim commanded imperiously, stepping over tangled cables. Everyone in his path scattered to avoid his wrath.

A chubby technician, who'd seen him coming, had guessed his intent. The disheveled man held up an old-fashioned red phone receiver with a push-to-talk lever built into the handset.

Jim stepped away from an open panel that radiated static electricity before raising the handset and pressing the button to talk.

"Administrator One-One to *Gold Rush*," he signaled.

Sasha Xavier answered the call through a haze of static. Everyone in the room could hear the conversation from both sides through speakers mounted on the ceiling.

"*Gold Rush* here. I thought we might be hearing from you," she quipped.

"Company's coming real soon!" he replied urgently.

"Well, now. I can see that, and I have good news!" she offered, her high spirits evident.

"Thrill me," Jim urged while lowering his volume.

The eccentric engineer laughed. "You've been reading about me on the Internet again, haven't you?"

"I only look at the pictures," he replied stonily.

"The package is ready to go. That rod will fly even if I have to go out there and throw the damned thing myself."

"I would pay money to see that," Jim smirked.

"As if your heart could take that kind of strain," she mocked insincerely.

Jim looked over his shoulder at the gathering crowd of anxious men and women. He took his finger off the transmit button and laid the receiver flat on his chest.

"Don't you people have work to do?" he bellowed.

Sasha, unaware of the reason for the delay, assumed that she was being allowed to speak. "Radar mapping shows us that holes are starting to open up in the low orbit debris fields."

The ground control staff scattered. Jim raised the phone to his ear. "How long?" he asked apprehensively.

She took a deep breath that was audible through the static. "We're going to drop garbage canisters of netting into the debris to soak up some of the larger, faster moving parts that seem to be interfering with our target acquisition accuracy. The artificial fibers in those nets will take quite a beating and stop lot of wreckage."

Jim sighed. "Weeks? Months? Years?" he asked plaintively.

Sasha peeked at the station's lookdown radar display. "The cans have slow burn rockets on them…"

"I know how they dump the trash," Jim groaned.

Her mood darkened. "You're asking me to shoot at a moving target through a moving debris field. Have you ever done the math for something like this? And we have to move the station again. It'll be hours."

"Should I stop the planet?" he asked brazenly.

She accepted the sarcasm. "It's good that you called. I wanted to talk to you about targets. We've been testing out some of my new decryption software, and I think the U.S. Navy is getting its butt kicked near Japan."

"When did you find time to do this?"

"We can't hear *all* of their traffic!" she protested.

Jim took a deep breath. "The Navy has their problems. We have ours. We've got our eye on the *Strong Prosperity*. They'll be within aircraft striking range of Kodiak in just about four hours, give or take."

"We see it!" Sasha exclaimed.

After a moment of consideration, Jim asked, "How long to clean up your line of fire?"

"Why are there so many fishing boats headed your way?" she asked.

"Fish Net is redirecting them in case we need pilot pickup."

Sasha glanced at the lookdown radar map again. "Speaking of pilot pickup, I really think you should you make a phone call to somebody who can help those guys. That naval radio traffic near Japan sounds quite serious."

"Hey!" Jim barked.

Sasha sputtered into silence.

He cleared his throat. "Those are ships! They can move. This is a starport! We're stuck right where we are! Now, answer the question. How long to clean up your line of fire? It's important. I've got pilots and mechanics who need to know."

She responded quickly. "Two hours to send the refuse canisters through the debris field."

"Plus one more hour to fix the next thing that breaks," Jim added.

Sasha gritted her teeth. "And fifty minutes to track and shoot. That would be three hours and fifty minutes, which gives us ten minutes of fudge. Those are round numbers, by the way. Just for you. So you don't have to think so hard."

"How did you know about my plan?"

"Spies," she confided impishly.

Jim dragged his phone line to a point where he could see the largest screen with a course plot of the approaching carrier. "Have you double checked your firing solution calcs on the debris field? And what about evacuation?"

"Evacuation, as in bathroom?" Sasha retorted.

Jim wiped a line of sweat off his face. "You can shoot through a hole in the debris. That means they can do the same thing. Please. Just figure it out. The escape plan is up to you."

"Nice to know you care," Sasha sneered.

Jim struggled with the hot, sweaty phone cable in his hand. "Move the station. Clear your line of fire and call me when it's done. Try to give your people time to sleep. I need a few hours to arrange media coverage before you take the shot."

"Hold on there. You want me to do this on a live feed?" she protested.

"I do," he replied.

Jim waited while sounds of a muffled conversation came through the receiver in his perspiring hand.

"We don't like that idea," Sasha replied candidly.

"It's not a suggestion," Jim told her.

She *harrumphed* loudly before lowering her voice. "I agreed to do this on the condition of absolute secrecy. That same condition applies to everyone up here. You can't guarantee my anonymity, or anyone else's, if we do this on camera!"

He swore. "All right. Look. Disassemble every camera and microphone in every compartment and erase the data storage information for those things. We can fake the construction reports to show they haven't been installed."

"Already been done," Sasha admitted.

Jim took a deep breath. "What else would put your mind at ease?"

"That would a first, but you go ahead and try anyway," Sasha quipped.

He forced himself to continue. "All I want to see on the feed you send to us—and nobody else—is the observational data, *before you throw the switch.* That means video, thermal, radar, optical telescopes, anything else we've got installed that points down at the ground."

"All you're doing is proving where the shot came from," Sasha argued.

"Verifying for a stone cold fact what they will already know!" he maintained.

"Suppose federal authorities decide to come up here?" she inquired frostily.

Jim thumped the phone on his forehead. "You and everyone else who took part in this 'event' be long gone before they ever get there. I promise."

Sasha recovered her composure while the people around her argued. "That does make me feel better," she replied with mixed feelings.

"No, it doesn't," Jim sighed.

"I'd love to take credit for this," she reflected with quiet melancholy.

Jim scratched the back of his neck. "We'll violate the neutrality of space, break international treaties, and kill thousands, if that thing works."

The morality of what she was about to do was beginning to intrude on Sasha's conscience, thought she wasn't ready to admit it. "What will you do if the rail gun doesn't work?" Sasha asked artlessly.

Jim looked over his shoulder at the plot of the approaching aircraft carrier.

"Probably spend some unpleasant years behind barbed wire," he guessed.

* * *

SSN-21 *Seawolf* prowled deep in the Bering Sea, slowly approaching *Strong Prosperity's* battle group on a parabolic course that the sub's navigators promised would achieve interception within seven hours. The enemy formation's last known escorting submarine was identified. *Seawolf* fired a pair of torpedoes from a distance of 29 miles.

Captain Brewster and his exhausted crew had every reason to be cautious. Deprived of both satellite surveillance capability, as well as computer and data support from friendly surface vessels, the submariners were unwilling to use their antiship missiles. The unsupported weapons might miss their targets or be shot down if they failed to dodge point defense interception.

Lights were dimmed throughout the boat to simulate nighttime conditions. First watch rested while second watch went about their duties. The atmosphere was calm on the shadowy bridge as the captain conferred with his second-in-command. Executive Officer Jeffery James put his finger on a holographic projection of Kodiak Island. "Sound analysis indicates the guys upstairs are still sending cruise missiles in this direction. Regular intervals."

"What's on that rock worth shooting at?" the captain pondered out loud.

The X.O. tapped the projection to make new icons light up. "Civilian airport. Coast Guard station. Power generation facilities. Fish processing plant. Wind farms. And, of course, the starport."

"They've been thumping that island for two weeks," Brewster commented.

"Gotta be the starport," James guessed.

The skipper reached for his coffee mug. "They've got their problems and we have ours. Antiship is unreliable without satellite assist. That means we do it the old-fashioned way, with torpedoes."

"It'll be a one-way ride if we mess up," Jeffery warned.

The captain drank from his cup. "Gotta think big picture. Anything we do provokes a lethal response. Evade their escorts because we can. Smoking those fat cruisers limits their land attack options. Sink the big prize and we force all those vulnerable surface targets to turn for home because they lost their air cover."

James handed his superior a pad. "I've been talking this over with the staff. We've been looking for ways to change the equation. Alter the random factors. Know what I mean?"

Allen adjusted his glasses and took the pad. "I sure would like to give somebody a big surprise," he wished out loud.

He studied the proposal for several seconds, flicking through the pages with quick hand gestures that the device was easily able to interpret.

"This is what I had in mind."

"Decoy release?" Jeffery asked.

Brewster returned the electronic device. "This is your watch. You've got the con. I'm here because you asked to see me. Execute parts one and two of what you've got outlined here. Leave the rest to me, for the sake of accountability."

James took the pad. "You should get some sleep," he urged.

"Send somebody for me in two hours," the captain replied before leaving the bridge.

CHAPTER NINETEEN

Events in the northernmost portion of the East China Sea continued to unfold in their own frantic microcosm over the next six hours. The numbers of aircraft involved in each clash rapidly dwindled. The frequency of probes and intercepts by either side also began to diminish.

Chinese formations reduced speed and closed ranks, their pilots conscious of the fact that daylight would soon be upon them. The nocturnal advantage, which favored the American pilots, would soon be gone.

Naval strategists in Beijing had reason to be pleased. Their breakout into the central Pacific seemed to be a foregone conclusion. The depleted American task force, formidable as it was, would be routed or ruined when daylight restored high visibility flying conditions.

Surface vessels on the outskirts of American and Chinese formations were damaged or sunk by air launched antiship missiles as the action continued. Guided missile frigates preyed on any surface contact they could find. Destroyers and their ASW helicopters picked off enemy submarines.

Civilian analysts based out of Japan and South Korea, tasked with observing the conflict, were increasingly aggravated by the ineffectiveness of their unmanned aircraft in local nighttime conditions. Television personalities around the world echoed that frustration.

"...biggest thing since Midway and we've got nothing!"

"Who in their right mind doesn't want this coverage?"

"How are we supposed to know who is winning?"

Conditions at sea worsened by the hour for the American-led formation. Every U.S. sailor in uniform aboard those ships knew what was at stake. Aggressive tactics propelled Chinese forces closer to their goal of entry into the central Pacific, where their superior numbers could further tip the balance of power.

The atmosphere onboard *Enterprise* and *Kennedy* was electric as their combined surface groups turned. Electronic warfare systems probed the darkness for any weakness in the enemy's pattern of movement. Encrypted short-range communications flowed between ships of the beleaguered fleet as aircraft continued to come and go in the rain.

Admiral Carlisle, nestled deep in the combat information center aboard *Enterprise*, tried not to think about what was happening to the pilots overhead, 600 miles out. He turned to his helmsman. "Order the formation to make the next turn. What's our screen integrity?"

The officer in charge of monitoring the formation's antisubmarine capability held up a pad. "Destroyers are reporting intermittent sonar contacts west and south."

"Just enough sub shadow to let us know they care," the admiral exhaled.

He was playing for time, trading ocean for hours, hoping the opposition would make a mistake that he could exploit with his limited resources. No mistakes on their part would mean the loss of his entire task force if it couldn't withdraw to safer waters. That end would come for both U.S. carriers, in the form of air strikes or submarine attacks. Either method would mean the destruction of their screening vessels in a disjointed ship-to-ship slugging match with guided missiles that would further pollute the already contaminated sea.

Enterprise's air boss signaled from the flag bridge to the combat information center as he began to move models on a status table while radio traffic flowed.

"The last of our combat intercept relief group is landing now," he explained.

"How many made it back?" Thurmond asked.

"Two."

The answer provoked a muted response from everyone within earshot. It meant that at least a dozen pilots were dead or in the water. Numbers changed on displays. Available aircraft totals were downgraded. All digits suddenly changed color, from yellow to red. The new development caused a murmur to ripple through the large compartment. Anyone with a working knowledge of carrier air wing organizations could see that the combined taskforce was now desperately short of reliable pilots and aircraft.

A senior surface warfare officer approached the admiral's workstation. He saluted. "We must withdraw."

"Your opinion is duly noted," the older man acknowledged with a nod.

Heads turned as the flotilla changed course.

"We're not much better off than *Kennedy*," the circumspect officer insisted.

"How many subs are still making radio checks?" Carlisle asked out of habit.

"None."

"*Seawolf* chimed in 21 hours ago," somebody mentioned.

"No good to us. That's 2,000 miles north of here," another voice dissented.

"Doesn't prove anything," a third person responded.

The admiral sat up. The unseen pessimists could be wrong. Losing coordination with friendly submarines in a live fire situation wasn't unexpected. The boats assigned to protect his formation might have been sunk or they might be hunting.

He eyed the swivel-mounted monitor on the arm of his chair. "We have no air combat just now and we have no sign of inbound threats."

Nobody replied to such a direct statement of the obvious.

The admiral sat quietly while the tired and troubled men and women got back work. He cleared his throat and tried for something more inspiring. "It's not our job to die. It is our job to make them die. Using our cruisers and destroyers to slug it out with Harpoons and Tomahawks under these conditions, at these odds, means that none of our ships—and none of our sailors—would make it home."

A dozen eager faces looked in his direction.

Carlisle traced his finger over a navigation map on his terminal. "Helm, redirect the task force to the track I am sending you now."

* * *

Beatrice Brown turned up at Billy Richter's apartment with two uniformed guards in tow. She knocked loudly on the door. Cold wind blew here hair astray as dawn broke, lighting the clouds overhead.

The tired man opened his door after squinting through the peep hole. "We've got to stop meeting like this."

"Stop making me come out here," the journalist grunted. She wasn't a morning person.

Billy, dressed in green sweats, motioned for everyone to come inside. "What is it this time?" he asked.

"I want answers," she stated flatly.

"I keep them in the closet. Come in," he beckoned.

Billy closed the door once everyone was inside.

Beatrice pulled off her rain-slick coat and tossed it onto a wall hook in the foyer. "They won't let me interview the pilots!" she exclaimed loudly.

The guards unzipped their jackets and hung them neatly in the coat closet before following their charge into the living area.

Billy shrugged and squirmed into a pair of slippers to keep his feet warm. He turned on a lamp. "You're on thin ice," he cautioned.

She flopped on to the worn couch. "I don't care if I make them angry. I've got a letter from Cook that says I can go anywhere that's nonsensitive. That includes my camera, too. I want to speak with those pilots. Now, before this thing heats up."

One of the guards sat quietly. The other asked for the restroom.

"Down the hall and to the left," Billy told him. The security chief focused his attention on the reporter as the man walked away. "Did it ever occur to you that those pilots don't *want* to be seen?" he suggested.

Beatrice tried to sit up on the squishy couch. "I don't care about what they want. This is journalism and it's for the historical record."

"Hey!" Billy protested.

The reporter jumped to the edge of the couch. "No way, soldier! I checked, and none of them are officially off-limits to me. So, I want to see them and talk to them before they get killed."

Billy rubbed his face and took a deep breath. "I've learned enough about you in the last few weeks to know that your network is pushing for this stuff."

"Nobody pushes me," Beatrice replied assertively.

He looked up as the second guard returned and took a seat on the far side of the room. "Yeah. That's not encouraging. Look, I'm going to back Norman's lockout. And I'm going to tell you why."

The meticulous reporter didn't have many friends on Kodiak Island. "I'm listening," she responded, bristling.

Billy made eye contact with each guard. "Would the two of you please take a walk? Go start the truck or something. I'll send her out in a few minutes."

The men got their coats and went outside.

"I want my recorder," Beatrice announced.

Billy turned in his chair when he heard the front door close. "No recorder. This is entirely off the record. You'll understand when I tell you why those pilots are avoiding you."

The irate woman eased back on the couch. She'd known Billy long enough to know that he wouldn't be so candid with just anyone. His trust had to be earned.

"I'm listening."

He rested one arm on his chair and looked right at her. "We don't have permits for these planes. All of these pilots are past their prime, which means they have no legal certification to be in the cockpit."

"Go on," she urged.

He sighed and rolled his tired neck. "We're gonna have to answer for a lot of what we've done when this is all over. You know that."

"That's why I'm here."

Billy shrugged. "You wouldn't be here at all, if it was up to me. Norm and his people have skills that we need and we're not going to get them any other way. He knows it, and so do his pilots."

Beatrice frowned. "You're not selling me. Where's the down side to my story? Old aviators operate obsolete airplanes to fight off the invaders. That kind of thing is downright inspirational. Straight outta Hollywood."

"Yeah, right. That would be the first half of your two-part exposé," he chided.

"What's the second?" she asked skeptically.

"Surviving war heroes go to prison," Billy pronounced morbidly.

"You're joking," Beatrice scoffed.

Richter pointed at himself. "How do you know the Feds don't take me away for what I've done?"

The question made her think. "You've mentioned that before. Would our government really be that callous? You guys are on the front lines. They'd have to cut you some slack."

Billy shook his head. "Not necessarily. Our country's defense budget has been gutted. It's not cool to be patriotic anymore. Our leaders are pushing a new foreign policy line that assures everyone around us that we're just one of many in a community of equals. That kind of attitude doesn't promise justice for anyone who breaks the law to save the nation."

"*You* are paranoid," she accused.

Billy chuckled. "Norm is the one who won't let you near his pilots."

"Then he's out of his damned mind," she blurted.

Billy rested his chin on one fist. "Suppose I tell you that some of those pilots are in this country illegally and more than one has a criminal past."

"You couldn't get Americans to fly these planes?" Beatrice breathed.

Billy laughed. "We couldn't get very many American airplanes! They've all been sold for scrap or exported to other countries for quick cash when we downsized."

"How many Americans do you have in those cockpits?" she asked directly.

"Less than half," he admitted.

"How many have combat experience?"

"All of them."

"How many have criminal records?" she probed.

"Half," he confessed.

Beatrice sat up and swore. "Hold on. How do experienced combat pilots have criminal records? How's that even possible?"

Billy smirked. "Look around the world right now and what do you see? How many governments with air forces have defaulted on their debts? How many pilots do you think that puts out of work?"

"Criminal records?" Beatrice repeated in amazement.

He nodded. "One or two are just retired afterburner addicts looking for one last thrill. A couple of them just retired and have only meager pensions to live on. That's really all you need to know."

The reporter looked around the sparsely furnished apartment to stall for time while she gathered her thoughts. "Tell me something. How many of the people that work for you in security have criminal records?"

Billy stretched and yawned. "Depends on what you mean. A few have rap sheets. Nobody can wear our uniform with an outstanding warrant hanging over their head, if that's what you're asking."

She blinked. "How many of you can get in trouble based on what I've reported?"

He stood up. "Don't—"

"Be straight with me," she said insistently.

Billy paced back and forth, trying to decide how to parse his answer. "Yeah. It's possible. We've broken our fair share of laws. Don't be surprised if somebody from the World Court wants to have a few words with me."

She rested both hands in her lap. "You're the first person around here to admit that. I suppose—"

"*Nothing*," he said loudly. He took one step closer. "You suppose nothing and stay away from Norman's pilots because he asked you to. Please. I'm asking, not telling. The rest is up to you."

His tone of voice forced her to be silent. There was no attraction between then, but he'd always been sympathetic to her professional needs and generous when it came to matters of personal accommodation. She privately feared that he resented being her minder. Those worries resurfaced as he loomed over her. The look in his eyes communicated total sincerity.

"No pilots," she promised primly.

Billy took two steps back. His usual calm fell into place. "No talking to the pilots is one thing. Looking at them is something else. Has anyone from public relations taken you to our new television studio?"

Beatrice lowered her head. "It's been promised but I haven't seen it yet."

He went into his kitchen. "Go outside and wait with the guards. Give me a few minutes to take some vitamins and get dressed. We'll get some breakfast and go there. You'll have the place all to yourself, with a crew of six to help you."

She waited for him to draw a glass of water from the tap and return. "How does that help me see?" she inquired.

He swallowed a fistful of pills and chugged down half the water from a big purple plastic cup. "You'll have access to some of the data that each fighter sends back to us. Cockpit cameras and some of the radio chatter. Stuff like that. Just enough to see what's going on."

"It's been promised," she repeated.

He pointed at the front door. "Get out of here and have the men take you to the executive dining room. I'll be there in 20 minutes. I'll have the studio manager join us so the two of you can get acquainted."

CHAPTER TWENTY

Officials in Beijing were satisfied. They felt certain that aerial reconnaissance aviation, electronic emissions triangulation, and the occasional submarine contact, had determined the approximate locations of all three remaining U.S. aircraft carriers that were blocking their advance into the Pacific.

Ford and its surviving escort had turned during the night. They were now heading southwest, away from Kodiak Island, giving up any pretense of halting *Strong Prosperity's* advance towards mainland Alaska. *Enterprise* and *Kennedy* were traveling with what was left of the Japanese surface warfare group in a westerly direction at modest speed. *Glorious Destiny*, *Celebrated Fortune*, and *Noble Dragon* and their supporting vessels were poised to range unopposed once the coalition force was scattered. Operations in other theaters were going just as well.

Excitement grew when word leaked among senior analysts that *Strong Prosperity* traveled with a brigade of Chinese Marines, reinforced by two companies of engineers and a provisional reconstruction team. Enthusiastic speculation ran wild, in spite of supervisory admonitions, when interoffice communications and water cooler gossip revealed that the amphibious landing element had enough hovercraft, barges, and transport helicopters to land the entire offensive force in one effort.

Why was such a valued portion of the *Zhōngguó Rénmín Jiěfàngjūn Hǎijūnlùzhànduì* being sent to Alaska? Casual examination of nonclassified regional geographic and commercial references turned up a lot to laugh about. Fish canneries, the Kodiak Starport, and the port of Anchorage, topped the list of potential targets that seemed worth joking about.

* * *

Gold Rush changed orbit effortlessly, thanks to careful calculations and a slow thrust-and-coast sequence of preplanned maneuvers. The incomplete space station was moved a just a short distance, with a minor change in aspect to the debris fields now circling the Earth.

Sasha Xavier, snug in her vacc suit, ensconced in the softly lighted operations compartment, supervised the transition while eating yogurt from a flexible plastic tube through an open helmet visor.

"Nice driving," she told the man next to her.

Civilian and military observatories logged the event without any consideration of what that change in attitude and altitude might be leading up to. Radio traffic from around the world filled helmets and work spaces as the engineers and technicians went about their duties for the next two hours.

"State-run media now reports on all channels new criteria for food rationing."

"The commission's findings are disputed by more than a dozen countries."

"Fishermen throughout the Baltic States are demanding higher quotas."

Sasha finished off the yogurt with a long, slow pull before depositing the limp wrapper in a nearby trash receptacle.

"Keep an eye on the orbital plane," she admonished.

"I always thought there would be space planes by this stage of the fight," somebody behind her commented.

"Don't know and don't care," she dismissed.

The sudden pollution of the low orbit gravity well may have had something to do with a decision to keep military space planes on the ground. She reconsidered that possibility while watching a bank of monitors that were patched in to dozens of external multispectrum cameras.

Three different EVA crews unlocked the refuse canisters on the lower spinal column of the space station. Every clock she looked at seemed to be moving unnaturally fast.

Each of these manned operations was necessary for several reasons. Repeated equipment failures prevented the garbage containers from being launched remotely. Anatomical and software limitations prevented the robots normally used for heavy lifting and welding chores around the station from releasing each canister in a timely manner.

The chore was nerve-wracking for the people who had to do it, but only because they had to contend with Sasha as she watched the clock at every step of the process. She called out the order and intervals without mercy.

"Release number one now!"

"Unlock number two. Hold for thirty seconds."

"Release number two now!"

"Pause the interval. Stand by for number three."

Everyone worked in fear of being hit by small, sharp pieces of fast-moving metal that might pierce their suits or visors at any random moment, causing rapid decompression that could result in death.

Watching the Earth spin below them was small consolation to the groups who had to get the timing right to send each canister into debris fields far below, which they couldn't actually see with unaided eyes.

Each of the big aluminum containers, filled with rolls of artificial fiber fishnets purchased from Alaskan fishermen, passed through a preselected debris field as it came within range of the space station. Falling through the opening caused each canister to be hit by dozens, hundreds, or even thousands of debris fragments that had once been orbiting satellites. The absorption of these small pieces caused the hole the debris field to get larger.

Time passed slowly for the workers in zero gravity. The expended cans burned up as they failed to properly enter Earth's atmosphere. Civilian observers on the ground recorded the incinerations with growing curiosity.

* * *

Military analysts in many nations took note of the growing hole in the debris field between the space station and the planet. Mainframe computers calculated the time it took for the opening in the debris cloud to orbit the Earth. Planners who had access to data from radars capable of looking into space pondered the significance of this activity. Strategic planning software programs generated hundreds of "what if" scenarios relating to the convenient opening in the debris. These were forwarded to human working groups.

Civilian engineers determined that this activity might be the station's crew clearing the way for their eventual exit from the platform. Military thinkers in Beijing reached a different conclusion.

Mainstream media efforts to contact *Gold Rush* by radio were unsuccessful. Their calls went unanswered, which led many late night talk show personalities on radio and television to concoct their own theories to explain what was happening.

"They're in trouble, so they're trying to get off."

"Suppose they *are* going to fire a death ray."

"See? Do the math. That hole is just big enough to let a flying saucer get through."

* * *

Automatic doors opened with a hiss. Jim Cook, fresh from a nap, shower, and shave, walked into the starport's new media center wearing clean clothes. A pair of armed guards, following close behind, matched his brisk stride.

The trio passed through the silent lobby. Jim halted at the front desk to chat with the administrative assistant, who scanned the badge on his lapel with a wand.

Jim sized up the employee, whom he'd never met before. The young man appeared to be in his mid-20s, with bags under his red-rimmed eyes. He worked deliberately, keeping one eye on what he was doing and the other on his high-profile customer.

"How's it going?" the starport boss asked, as if he were not in a hurry at all.

The apathetic underling looked uncomfortable in his coat and tie. "Billy's already here with what's-her-name," he mumbled through parched lips.

Jim signed the log with a scrawl when it was offered to him. "That's Beatrice Brown. Polar News. Don't you recognize her?"

The desk attendant took the pen and the log. He blushed. "Sorry sir. This isn't my normal assignment. I haven't slept properly in three days."

Jim flicked a stray hair off his forehead and leaned over the counter. "Neither have I. It's all drugs. I'm actually dead on my feet," he whispered.

"Yeah," the youth snorted and put the log away.

Jim stood up in a pose of comic outrage. "You think that, just because I'm the big cheese around here, they only bother me with the big stuff? Is that it?"

"Yeah," the sleep-deprived man nodded.

"You're right," Jim conceded with a flourish. He bellied up to the high, flat counter. "Let me tell you something about what's happening right now. All of it is big. None of it is small. That includes you."

"Yeah," the subordinate yawned and sat heavily.

"What's your problem?" Jim asked sincerely.

"Nobody to take my place," the man complained.

"How long have you been here?" Jim asked with growing interest.

"Four days," the assistant replied glumly.

Jim looked around peevishly. "Where's your I.D.? What's your name?"

The unhappy underling picked his identification card up off the floor and clipped it to his lapel.

Jim forced his weary eyes to focus. "Okay, Mr. Kyle Foss, production assistant. Go get the studio manager and we'll start making things right."

"Gone," Foss replied without making eye contact.

Jim thumped the counter top with his fist. "I suppose you're the only living soul in this building?"

"Yeah," Kyle sighed.

Jim threw his hands up.

"Everybody, come with me!" he shouted.

He turned and charged deep into the building. Foss and the two guards jumped, following at a trot. Jim swiped his I.D. card to pass through a pair of secured doors and rushed down two flights of stairs, into a protected underground structure that housed the starport's new television station and media production workshop.

The quartet arrived to find Beatrice wandering around the camera bay with a coffee cup in one hand and a tablet computer in the other.

"W-where's Billy," Jim wheezed, staggering to a shaky stop.

"Been gone for five minutes," the correspondent explained while sipping coffee.

The starport executive bent over to relieve the pain in his back. He coughed to clear his lungs. "Mr. Foss has been updating me on your situation. I'm sorry."

Beatrice put the tablet computer down and came closer as the guards spread out. "Kyle was helpful when I got here. I think he's been short-handed. You should promote him."

"Think so?" Jim considered as his pulse slowed.

She nodded. "I want you to promote me, too."

"I don't follow," he blinked.

Beatrice held the dark blue mug in both hands. The starport logo peeked out between her fingers. "I've seen this place at its best. Now I'm seeing it at its worst. Your methods are a little unorthodox, but your mission is worth telling people about."

"Go on," Jim beckoned.

Beatrice didn't like explaining her innermost thoughts to anyone. "I've been from one end of this state to the other. I've seen it all and talked to everyone who will speak to me. I have never in my life seen and done what you've put me through in these last few months. It's a chance for something new, and I want it."

Jim licked his lips. "First, I haven't put you through anything. Secondly, you ain't seen nothin' yet. This isn't like running an airline or a railroad. It's like doing both at the same time through jungles controlled by drug cartels run by flying monkeys."

Beatrice knew he was trying to discourage her. She looked him in the eye. "I've been a news director. I've got the experience to run all of this."

"Why would you want to?" Jim asked mildly.

She pointed at the disheveled assistant.

"Why are you still here?" she asked him sharply.

"It's the coolest company I could ever work for," Kyle admitted spontaneously.

Jim glanced at the nearest guard, who was apparently following the conversation with some interest. “What do you think?” he asked casually.

The former soldier took a second look at the man and woman. His boots squeaked on the floor as he shuffled in place. “Little fish stayed when the big fish left. That’s balls. Give him a shot. See what he does.”

“What about her?” Jim asked in a stage whisper.

The officer was thoughtful. “Best PR comes from people who want to tell your story.”

“She’s a journalist. They’re always hung up on the truth,” Jim recalled.

“Nothing’s wrong with the truth when you’re doing right,” the man stated bluntly.

Jim frowned. “I need PR. I don’t need news.”

“You *do* need news!” Beatrice objected.

The guard approved with slight nod. “She’s right. You gotta tell people what goes on around here. It’s a good story, and it’s true. That makes it news with positive PR value.”

“When what we do is legal,” Jim muttered.

The big man laughed. “Look at her. She knows that.”

“I do,” Brown insisted.

Jim eyed her suspiciously. “This *is* a television studio,” he pretended to consider, “You’d be competing with a lot of good infotainment if we made your our official rep. Could you do that?”

Beatrice took a small memory device out of her pocket. “I’ve been auditioning for this job since you hired me,” she bragged. “I just didn’t realize it until I walked in here and saw all of this equipment.”

Jim shuffled closer. “Is that so?”

She brandished the object as if it were a prize. “Everything you’ve been letting me see, or keeping me from, has been a test. Apparently, I passed.”

Jim clapped his hands together to prevent an awkward silence. “Okay, then! Ms. Brown, I’d like to be the first to welcome you aboard our newly created news division. You’ll be our first lead anchor, news director, and senior field correspondent. From now on, our lies will be your lies.”

He walked over to clap a hand on Kyle's shoulder. "You, my young friend. You. Did you like your old boss? No, of course you didn't. He's not here, which makes him not worth liking. So. How would you like to be our new production manager?"

"Top dog?" Kyle responded, truly surprised.

"Lord and master of all you survey," Jim insisted proudly with a sweeping gesture.

"Full pay?" Kyle demanded.

"And a five percent raise," Jim promised.

He pulled the younger man in close to whisper sinisterly. "No stock options for two years. No expense account for one year. You'll go through a full performance review every six months. Make me regret this and I'll break you into so many little pieces, they'll need an electron microscope just to recover your ashes. Are we clear?"

"Yes, sir," Kyle choked.

Jim stepped back. "This has been a lot of fun, but we've got more to do."

"Such as?" Beatrice asked worriedly.

The administrator went to the nearest workstation and tapped on a touch screen until he could show her a satellite image of the approaching Chinese flotilla. He stepped back so that everyone could see the streaming video. "You're going to get a visit from the nice folks over at public relations any minute now. We've made an appointment with a few hundred media outlets to show them something very special."

"First I've heard of it," Beatrice said reproachfully.

Jim took one more step back. "Kyle? Start earning. Get upstairs and make this place do whatever it does so Ms. Brown can do whatever she does."

Foss bolted for the door. Jim looked back to make sure he was gone. "Somebody remind me to call personnel and make sure his promotion goes through. So, here it is. In less than 40 minutes, we are going to sink that aircraft carrier."

Beatrice put her cup down and came closer to study the real-time imagery. "We, meaning the Kodiak Starport, are going to sink—as in destroy—*that*?"

"Yes," Jim declared with more certainty than he felt.

"May I ask how and why?"

Jim swung his arms. "First, we break the bad news to your former employers."

"I should handle that. Better if it comes from me."

He nodded. "Then, we call your lawyer. I convince him that this whole thing is real. We sign a new employment contract, a merchandising agreement, and a few of the usual nondisclosures. Then I'll tell you. Then, you can hate me."

* * *

Sasha had every reason to be pleased with the performance of her crew. They'd moved the station and opened the debris field as planned, with 15 minutes to spare on the estimate she'd given to Jim Cook.

She remained in the operations compartment with her helmet radio off while everyone else changed clothes, got some food, or took bio breaks. The absence of time-sensitive activity caused her to feel self-conscious. She used the station's optical and thermal capabilities to look down on a busy Kodiak Starport. Images on three large screens held her attention for several minutes.

The historical and technological importance of the place wasn't lost on her. Trillions of dollars, billions of man-hours, millions of skilled professionals, all used in one way or another to put thousands of platforms into space that had, until now, only been visited by a mere few hundred people.

She thought about the novelty of her situation. The men and women who'd spent their careers developing the technology she used had never been to space.

Sasha raised her gloved hand and made a fist. The synthetic material crinkled. "Could've been somebody else wearing this glove," she philosophized. She looked around to be sure that she was alone. "I could still be in prison," she thought. "Lucky to be here."

The prospect of failure still concerned her more than the actual loss of life that she was about to inflict. People of her generation weren't easily swayed by nationalist or patriotic sentiments. Corporate loyalties were more attractive than devotions to heritage or homeland.

Sasha, and most of those whom she chose to employ, were part of a growing movement of highly educated risk-takers whose only concern was advancement within their fields of endeavor. Money, patents, stock, and other material holdings, were the measures of their success. Everything else was a distraction.

These aggressive, amoral entrepreneurs maintained that the alleged neutrality of space was a legal construct, created by then-dominant terrestrial governments in an era when space travel wasn't practical, to hedge their bets against future geopolitical opponents.

Sasha knew what she was doing. Successful operation of the rail gun, no matter how poorly constructed it might be, would result in permanent criminal status. She and her fellow engineers understood that they could never openly admit their involvement in the defense of the Kodiak Starport. Alibis had already been established to explain their absence from public life while they were aboard *Gold Rush*. Each of them would have to be satisfied with the large amounts of money they'd make when the nonproprietary secrets of their patented technology, used in the slapdash assembly of this improvised weapon, were leaked to the media…by Sasha.

She tapped the nearest instrument panel. The station's surveillance systems dutifully scanned the ocean below to reacquire the *Strong Prosperity*. Images blurred on several screens until she had the high-altitude view she wanted. Interruptions in the feed caused the picture to distort at random intervals whenever pieces of debris interfered with each camera's view. A countdown clock in the upper left corner of each display showed how much time remained before the opening in the debris field would be directly below the space station.

Sasha yawned. Early sunrise gleamed off the slate gray water. The massive ship dwarfed all others that were arrayed around it as the entire formation left long, white wakes in the Bering Sea, just minutes from their launch point, from which they could unleash a massive air strike on the Kodiak Starport.

"Very lucky to be here," she reminded herself.

Chapter Twenty-One

Sunrise illuminated the Arctic in majestic silence as events continued to unfold. As interested as they were in the battles raging at sea off the eastern coast of Japan, international news organizations still devoted much of their airtime to covering famines and inland disputes.

Representatives for the Japanese government issued proud press releases touting recent success in repelling a series of hostile commando raids targeting the military installations in and around Fukuoka, located near the southern tip of Honshu.

Leaders in Washington paid greater attention to the worsening situation in the Aleutians. Aggressive Chinese troops worked quickly to overwhelm the small detachments of Special Forces and partisan groups on these islands.

Organized resistance in the Arctic was all but nonexistent outside of the Alaskan mainland. The *Gerald R. Ford* battle group was now in headlong retreat. Rumors circulating through the Pentagon suggested that security forces at the Kodiak Starport were somehow involved in defensive efforts. That claim hardly seemed worth considering by the hundreds of analysts who had access to the starport's nonclassified profile. What could a few glorified security guards at a rocket launch complex on a small island in the Gulf of Alaska possibly do to one of the world's most modern militaries?

Political correctness prevented outright ridicule, though pity for the company's employees who might still be on the island generated some sympathy. People who had more urgent concerns quickly dismissed the jokes made in poor taste at the starport's expense.

The last known locations of the *Strong Prosperity* battle group, as discovered and plotted by a series of long-range reconnaissance patrols, indicated a course and speed that would have that formation within aviation strike range of Kodiak Island very soon.

* * *

American aircraft carriers *Kennedy* and *Enterprise* rode high in the water as they plowed through the warm central Pacific with empty aviation fuel tanks, vacant aircraft hangars, and bare ordnance storage bunkers. Pearlescent wakes trailed behind more than two dozen screening vessels from five countries. The midday sun made the water glare in a way that made every sailor inside those hulls wish for the cover of darkness.

Admiral Carlisle ordered entered his combat information center deep inside *Enterprise* without looking at the task force's combined squadron readiness display. *Kennedy* and *Enterprise* could launch and land a total of seven aircraft. That wouldn't be nearly enough to stand off another enemy attack that would be made by at least 50 multirole aircraft from three opposing carriers, much less mount an effective combat air patrol to warn the ships in the flotilla of that approaching air strike.

The senior officer was just sitting down when a communications alarm sounded. Technicians worked furiously to decode and announce, "North American aerospace defense command reports a Chinese ICBM launch. Outbound trajectory indicates it's coming from our part of the world."

"Show me," the admiral directed.

Computer data, sent by encrypted microwave transmitters from the mainland, was received by the task force and fed through local networks until it appeared on the CIC's monitors as an interactive display.

"It's not aimed at us," somebody giggled.

"What are they shooting at?" he pondered.

"It's transpolar," a technician announced.

"Gonna nuke Santa Claus," another voice joked.

The admiral leaned forward, as if the closer look might provide more information. "Can we confirm this on our end?" he asked.

"Positive radar contact," came the reply.

He sniffed when the range became apparent. "Well. Too far away. We're not going to shoot that down. Looks like this one isn't our problem." A ripple of mirth swept through the compartment.

Thurmond took one last look at the rising missile track. "Confirm that flight path to NORAD, then turn it off. Reset DCR and put the alert fighters on standby. Whoever lit that candle may have plans for us and I'd like to be ready for them when they get here."

* * *

A swarm of lawyers wielding pens and tablet computers surrounded Jim Cook as he barged into his improvised operations center. He signed what he had to sign and approved the rest with his thumbprint. The representatives of the legal department's crisis management team vanished just as quickly as they'd appeared.

Cook pulled off his necktie and dropped it on an empty desk as he passed by. Men and women worked efficiently around him without looking up to see what he was doing in the sweltering heat of the bright, poorly ventilated room.

Jim arrived at his desk and discarded his suit jacket. He stopped a woman who was passing by with an open bottle of high-caffeine soda in one hand.

"Would you please get me two of those?" he asked, pointing at her drink.

"Sure," she replied, offering him her beverage.

He took it with an elaborate nod. "Whatever the doc gave me is wearing off," he confided softly.

"Happening to all of us," she replied gravely.

"Two bottles. Find me."

The technician turned and merged into the blizzard of human activity and noisy machines.

Jim guzzled the soda and tossed away the empty bottle without bothering to see where it landed. He went to the newly upgraded communications hub. Several pieces of modern equipment had been added. A number of pieces of old equipment had been removed. He looked up at the nearest big screen to see Beatrice Brown chatting live with representatives from a dozen different news and infotainment groups.

"We should be getting a live feed any second now," she assured them.

Jim burped and cracked his knuckles as he cast a furtive glace over his shoulder. "I hope everyone is ready to make some history. I have no idea what happens next, but it'll be something they talk about for the rest of our lives. However long that might be."

Coughs and snickers, punctuated by moments of silence, seemed to be his reply.

Jim cleared his throat and stood on a box. On impulse, he handed the card General Sachdeva had given him to the closest technician. "Do me a favor and plug this into a preset, will you?"

The communications engineer whistled when he read the handwriting. "This is a classified—"

Jim punched the man hard on one shoulder to make him shut up. "I know what it is! I'm not going to order pizza. Set it up and hope that I don't need it." Turning away from the man, Cook adjusted his footing so he wouldn't fall off the box. The added height allowed him to see overhead screen more easily as he reached for a wireless headset and a separate handheld remote control.

He glanced down at two women working nearby. "Thanks for putting this together. That old gear was just not going to cut it."

A sudden chirp announced an incoming transmission from *Gold Rush*. Jim put on his headset.

"Anyone there?" Sasha inquired, her voice echoing.

"Yeah," he replied without following protocol.

"Thirty seconds to firing window," she proclaimed.

Jim tapped his headset. "Is that our end? I hear an echo. Where are you?"

"Wearing four pairs of thermal underwear and the biggest vacc suit you've got, down in the main refrigerant control bay. It was the only place we could find to hook up the—"

"Yeah, yeah, yeah," Jim loudly interrupted.

Sasha coughed. "Oh, I get it. Company's on the line."

Jim nodded while taking in all the information he could see. "From now on, assume that everything you say is being heard by somebody."

"Fifteen seconds," Sasha announced dramatically.

Jim muted his microphone and pointed to somebody far away. "Cue the media!" he shouted.

"Ten seconds," Sasha whispered melodramatically.

Kyle Foss, working by himself in a cluttered control room, was surprised when a satellite systems board lit up to announce incoming feed from *Gold Rush.*

"Beats working for a living," he chortled, hurrying through his duties.

On set, Beatrice Brown reacted with poise as monitors came to life, showing aerial images of the Chinese naval formation cruising south of Kodiak Island. Text began to move on her teleprompter. She looked at the only working camera in her field of view. "Ladies and gentlemen. You're seeing live images deep inside American territorial waters."

"What?" Sasha asked, apparently speaking to somebody on another channel.

"Eh? What now?" Jim demanded.

"Wait one," Sasha snapped.

Jim's jaw dropped when static filled his ears. "Well, of course. The whole world is listening. Please, do put me on hold. We have nothing better to do."

The frustrated woman came back on the line spewing profanity. "Our lookdown radars are showing that something is on its way up. Seems to be coming from the middle of the Pacific Ocean. It set off our collision alarms. Optical tracking is sketchy, but the computer seems to think it's—"

"Pull the trigger!" Jim shouted.

Confusion erupted over the open frequency as men and women began to shout.

He flinched when a loud burst of static filled his ears. Audio, video, and instrument feeds from the space station stopped transmitting, causing hundreds of readouts in his field of view to go blank.

"Fix it!" Cook bellowed at everyone within view.

Dozens of voices responded as Beatrice Brown reacted. "Ladies and gentlemen, I think we've just seen something terrible. Apparently, the Chinese military has—"

"Not so fast! Hold that thought!" Jim ordered loudly through his intercom. His analytical mind tore apart what it had just seen. He secretly hoped the incomplete station had merely been incapacitated by an electromagnetic pulse unleashed from a nuclear weapon modified to function in space.

"We all saw it," Beatrice retorted.

Jim glanced at his wristwatch. "Just wait one damned minute! We couldn't put a rocket through that hole in the debris field, so what makes you so sure the kids over in China can do it? They're not *that* good."

Network employees around the world who witnessed the live video feed from the Kodiak Starport weren't so patient. Producers and executives wasted no time prodding their presenters to speculate on the destruction of a civilian space station.

Hasty questions for Beatrice came rapidly.

"How many people were on the station?"

"Did you know this was going to happen?"

"Are you sure that was a Chinese attack?"

She shook her head, now grateful that she had just one camera to pose for. "Please, one at a time. You saw what we saw, as it happened. I'm sure that our chief executive has more to say about this. Mr. Cook?"

Jim swallowed and made hand signals to get a wireless camera pointed at him. "Yes. Yes, I do. What you've just seen is a tragedy. I'm hoping it's not as bad as we think it looks. Even so, I would like to point out that the Chinese have exploded a nuclear bomb in space. They did it first. Not anyone else. This was all them."

Beatrice used a touch screen on her desk to allow the audience to hear questions as they were asked.

"Did you know this was going to happen?" the first horrified correspondent asked.

Jim swiped at his watch and began to perspire.

"No. Yes. Yes, I thought it was possible," he lied.

"What made you think they would?" the man pressed.

Jim fidgeted with the remote control in his free hand. "Anything is possible in a modern war. We had to assume the worst. In this case, we turned out to be right."

"How do you respond?" another talk show host solicited.

"I am hoping to have that answer for you any second now," he grumbled.

Beatrice sensed that Jim was playing for time. She interrupted. "Mr. Cook. Excuse me. What about that aircraft carrier we were looking at? Do you think they'll use their planes to attack the starport, now that the space station is gone?"

Jim got angry when the fair question left him feeling exposed and alone. "I'm not actually sure it *is* gone," he insisted.

"You think they're down because of EMP?" a newscaster luridly suggested.

"I like that idea very much," Jim confessed with a nervous twitch.

A technician to Jim's left, out of camera range, held up a piece of paper on which she had written in large, red letters, "no track on G.R."

Jim's head sank to his chest. "I've just been told that we have no radar contact with our space station." He stood up straight and looked at the man. "We had a hard time locating it through all that debris. Is it gone, or just out of sight?"

The tech tore up the page and let the pieces fall.

"Somebody confirm that!" Jim demanded.

Beatrice inserted herself again in an effort to maintain control of the situation. "Sir, what about that aircraft carrier? It may still be on the move. Do you think they're going to attack the starport?"

Jim gritted his teeth. His planned media event was turning into an infotainment apocalypse. He wiped a line of sweat off his rough chin while everyone around him scrambled.

Seconds passed slowly. He glared at the camera. "I think we have to assume that they will attack."

"What will your government do to help you?" an anchorman eagerly asked.

Cook took a deep breath. He thought about the sweat-stained card with General Sachdeva's phone number on it.

A busy woman appeared nearby. She started turning off big display screens that had been showing operations data from *Gold Rush*.

Jim was speechless. The last of his confidence crumbled. Too many things had gone wrong. He'd misjudged the Chinese intentions to take the starport intact. The attempt to arm *Gold Rush* had failed because Sasha and her people couldn't make the rail gun work. He was now faced with an incoming air attack that couldn't be stopped. The air defense grid that they had broken so many laws to install had never been intended for actual use, even though it had performed well beyond its suggested capability.

The same dirty secret also applied to the ragtag air force that Norman and his pilots had put so much work into. None of those old F-15s or their over-the-hill pilots were ever supposed to see combat.

The rail gun aboard *Gold Rush* had been intended to be the real problem solver. Now, it was gone and so was his career, along with the future of the Kodiak Starport.

A gaggle of anxious show hosts and producers shouted to be heard over Beatrice.

"You need a miracle," somebody from a foreign network suggested.

* * *

Admiral Chen Lang watched relayed news feeds from his post in *Strong Prosperity*'s combat information center. He viewed Jim Cook's hesitation through a small desktop monitor.

After a long pause, Cook said, "We're going to deal with this as best we can."

Chen turned off the broadcast from the starport when it became obvious that the administrator and his staff were still in shock from the loss of their space station.

"They've been watching us?" somebody asked.

"Not anymore," another sailor responded, smiling.

The task force commander turned to a swing arm display and reviewed his most recent intelligence updates. His long-range drones and search planes couldn't find any sign of the American aircraft carrier thought to be in the region. That fact was most reassuring.

Destruction of the *Gold Rush* space station wasn't mentioned in any of the dispatches he had access to. This lack of information was no oversight. It was a tacit statement that the matter was none of his concern.

He focused his attention on the most recent reconnaissance photos of the damaged starport. Retail air defenses and an ad hoc air force made up of obsolete fighter-bombers indicated that they planned to fight. Fortified checkpoints on the ground suggested that local resistance would be coordinated.

"Good, but not good enough," Chen decided.

He would've been tempted to put a commando team ashore ahead of the air strike to assess bomb damage and call in targets of opportunity if he still had any submarines with his battle group. The unsatisfied desire caused him a very brief moment of irritation. He had expected to lose one or two submarines by this stage in the conflict. How had he managed to lose all five of them against such pitiful resistance?

His attention was drawn to a nearby workstation with active monitors showing more of the live broadcast from Kodiak at a very loud volume. The starport administrator was babbling and he appeared to be losing his nerve. Hardly the kind of leader to inspire a civilian workforce to resist what this armada was about to visit upon them.

An underling presented the admiral with a tablet computer. He took the device. Ignoring the distractions around him, he focused his attention on the fuel expenditures that were higher than anticipated.

Chen signed the report and gave the tablet back to the waiting man. The subordinate departed, leaving the admiral to think. Aircraft losses had been minimal. Ordnance expenditures were occurring at expected rates. Fuel was being consumed faster than anticipated.

He came to a decision and reached for an intercom phone to speak with his executive officer, who was on the navigation bridge. "I've changed my mind. There is no need to launch this strike at long range. Reschedule the attack. We will attack the starport at point-blank range."

"That will provoke their fighters," the second officer dutifully prompted.

"It will," the admiral concurred.

The man continued stating his observations. "We should also presume that will trigger a response from the American Air Force on the Alaskan mainland."

"It will," Chen agreed a bit more forcefully.

The subordinate glanced at the nearest area radar display. "The engagement will be decisive if they fight."

They talked for several minutes. Orders were changed. Formation resources were reallocated. Combat air patrols were increased. Pilots who had been assigned to strike missions were permitted more sleep and recreation.

The ships of the task force turned in unison when signaled, avoiding traveling on a straight course that would make them easy prey for lurking submarines or ambushing aircraft. The battle group was forced to reduce speed as it drove into an increasing headwind.

* * *

SSN-21 *Seawolf* slipped quietly inside *Strong Prosperity's* antisubmarine perimeter without being detected as the Chinese carrier battle group changed course.

CHAPTER TWENTY-TWO

Jim Cook went to his desk and flopped into a swivel chair. He was bathed in sweat after the worst 20 minutes of live media he'd ever experienced. A pair of open soda bottles fizzed next to a cluster of dusty telephones.

Nobody approached him. The mood was subdued throughout the operations room as everyone recovered their composure and stayed on task.

He emptied one of the bottles in a long swig and tossed it into a nearby trash cash. The sudden rush of sugar and caffeine made his tired body twitch as it battled with his fatigue.

The red phone near his elbow rang. He picked up on the second jingle. "I had a feeling you might call," he moaned.

"You haven't left me a choice," Laura Andrewyuk chided softly from her Anchorage office.

"I won't resign."

"I'm not asking you to."

Jim straightened in his seat. "What—"

U.S. Army General Manika Sachdeva interrupted without warning. "Mr. Cook, I'm conferencing with your board of directors right now."

Jim reacted as if he'd been slapped. "I'm tired of playing to an audience. Can we have this conversation some other time or on a more private line?"

"It's just the three of us," Laura insisted.

"I'm listening."

The general was blunt. "It's time to throw in the towel."

The administrator glanced across the room at a pair of large, silent screens. The first camera shot caught the starport's eastern skyline in relief as the early morning sun continued to rise.

"I don't think so," he replied as he viewed the images. A line of four water tours stretched off into the distance. Two big black sport utility vehicles with starport security markings rolled slowly down an access road parallel to the towers, which were filled with hidden air defense weaponry.

The second video perspective showed mechanics in cold weather gear working on a pair of long gray F-15s. Starport logos stood out on their tails. Ordnance specialists, dressed for working in the cold, moved carefully, mounting missiles on external hard points under each wing.

"You've done all you can," Laura said comfortingly.

The general continued. "Jim, I have this from Washington. The President himself would prefer that you save what's left of your facility. He's given me his word that nobody will lay a finger on you."

The shaken man squirmed. "You assured me—"

"I know," Manika said soothingly. When he didn't respond, she added, "Things have changed."

"Throw in the towel actually means surrender, doesn't it?" Jim asked bitterly.

"I told you he wouldn't," Laura observed.

Manika paused for a drink of water before elaborating. "We've got high-altitude recon that confirms the position of that carrier and three troopships."

"Who was nice enough to give you that kind of assistance?" Jim snorted.

She forged ahead. "I have three stars now. That promotion comes with a lot of things, like two full squadrons of reconnaissance drones. We send 'em on one-way missions to get that kind of intell. No round trip means we can afford to visit *Strong Prosperity* from unexpected directions."

"Does your high-altitude have anything to say about *Gold Rush*?" Jim asked.

Manika frowned. "They used a nuke. Must've been pretty close. All that the observatories can see right now are lots of ionized particles and debris from the missile that delivered the warhead. It's a big stain in the sky."

He leaned an elbow on his desk. "Our people said the chances of getting anything off the ground and up through that moving debris, through the opening our crew was able to make, seemed like one in a million."

The officer raised her voice. "The fact is that they did it. Now, you've got to deal with some facts of your own. You're taking this pretty hard, so I'm going to presume you had something cooking on that space station that some of the folks down here might not like too much."

"Laura told you, didn't she?" Jim accused.

"I did," Laura confessed sheepishly.

Manika expressed herself more forcefully. "Doesn't matter. That can be our little secret. All you need to do now is save the lives of your people."

Jim turned in chair and swapped the phone to his other hand as his frustration grew. "Our air defense grid is still working in the most important areas of the starport. You've got F-35s at Elmendorf. They could be here within the hour. Send 'em to me and we'll double-team these guys!"

"No," Manika refused resolutely.

Laura forced her way in to the exchange. "Jim! You've done enough. Even if you won the air battle, they'd still have soldiers coming. There is nothing on that island worth your life or the lives of anyone who works for us."

Jim's heart began to race. He reached for the remaining soda and took a drink to quench his sudden thirst. "Don't you see what's at stake here? Wreck this place beyond any hope of repair, and it's gone. Loot this place and take all the one-of-a-kind tech that generations worked so hard to make, and *it is gone*."

"He's not rational," Manika said.

"I have to agree," Laura concurred unhappily.

Jim waved the sloshing bottle in his hand. "I may not be rational, but I do have a front row seat to what's going on, which is more than you two can see from Anchorage! How do you know that we win this war? Suppose we don't? Those troopships you mentioned won't stop here. They'll keep on going!"

After a short pause, Laura said, "James Cook. As president of the Board of Directors for Shadow Fusion Enterprises, I hereby *order* you to—"

"I won't let them have it!" Jim snapped and hung up.

* * *

General Sachdeva looked across the conference table at Laura. "I assume you have a contingency plan for this?"

The President of the Board shrugged. "Actually, no. It's never come up. I'll call Billy Richter and have him take Jim into custody."

Members of the board milled around in the hallway outside the locked conference room, waiting to hear from the two powerful women sequestered inside.

Manika took out a handkerchief to dab at a tear in her eye. "I wish I had time to tell him how hard I argued his case. The President is looking for a way out of this mess, and the Joint Chiefs are convinced that Jim's mercenary experiment is interfering with that initiative."

"I do know how he feels," Laura empathized.

"You'll get him back through prisoner exchange," the general said reassuringly.

"What about the others?" Laura worried.

"They won't all survive captivity," Manika acknowledged grimly.

"You don't mean—" Laura stammered, her eyes growing big.

Manika composed herself without replying and put away the handkerchief. She changed the subject. "Win or lose, the President and the members of his party will have to answer for every death in this war. I can hardly blame them for trying to minimize the damage."

Laura felt queasy. She stood up. "Are you still going to think that way when the Chinese have troops in Anchorage?"

"One problem at a time," Sachdeva cautioned.

Laura sighed. "It would have taken a miracle to save the place, anyway."

* * *

Seawolf slowly closed range to the Chinese aircraft carrier by traveling in a straight line. The flotilla zigzagged to make any ambushing torpedo shots harder to calculate. Random active sonar pings were used by roaming frigates to search for underwater mines or lurking enemy submarines.

Outlying destroyers reported intermittent deepwater sonar contacts to the combat information center aboard *Strong Prosperity*. Powerful computers aboard each antisubmarine vessel, supported by sophisticated software, classified most of these contacts as orca and beluga whales, which were common to the region.

Captain Brewster ate breakfast at his post on the command on *Seawolf's* deck. He handed off his empty plate and approached a display, then gestured at the monitor with his fork. "Every second our fish run gives them time to figure out where we are. Get in close. Preflood all the forward tubes. Shoot six. Save two for anything unexpected."

He took a step back as members of the watch nodded. "Reload as we turn. Sonar has a reliable map of their whole formation. Three of those signatures are troopships."

He went to his chair and sat while men and women around him talked. "This isn't anything we can't handle. Back on the reverse course, we take shots at those landing ships. Whatever we get. We're out before they know which way we went."

The X.O. nodded. "Clipping just one troopship will mean they need all hands on deck to get survivors out of the water. Screws up any plans they had for those units."

Brewster fiddled with his fork, using it to tap his wristwatch. "Time to target?" he asked.

"Eighteen minutes," the helm operator called out.

* * *

Sasha Xavier woke to find herself in a cold, dark void. Breathing was strangely painful. The muscles throughout her entire body ached in a way that felt unnatural. Every inch of her skin felt as if she'd been out in the sun all day without any ultraviolet protection. The taste of bile filled her dry mouth.

She probed with her hands. Her space suit seemed to be intact with no tears. A smirk crossed her face when she realized that her eyes were closed. Opening them revealed that her helmet appeared undamaged.

Indicators inside the visor display told her she had 32 minutes of oxygen left in her backpack air supply. Touching an external button on the helmet activated a shoulder-mounted lamp. A second button activated lights located on the sides of her helmet.

She was still in the refrigeration chamber. Bright white light splashed over every wall as if it were a liquid. An unfamiliar milky haze clouded her vision. Sasha reached for her tether and pulled herself to the workstation she'd been using before blacking out.

Hand tools floated freely throughout the airless room as she approached the consoles. Four of the eight screens were blank. Two of the six instrument boards were lit. None of it was easy to see. She put her faceplate up next to each screen and squinted through the haze to see what was being shown.

A small yellow triangle blinked on and off in the lower right corner of each working display. Miniature red lights next to each panel strobed on and off. Sasha cringed when she recognized the radiation and damage control warnings.

A nonstop ringing in her ears competed with a worsening headache to make her nauseous. Three futile shakes of her throbbing skull on a sore neck didn't help. Oscillating wisps of white and gray on the periphery of her vision caused her to stop and think about her worsening physical condition.

Sasha counted off a dozen heartbeats and steady breaths. A modified nuclear device had been set off close to the orbital platform. A wide-area electromagnetic pulse from the detonation had knocked out the station's power grid, forcing major systems into total shutdown or automatic reset.

She decided that she was suffering the effects of lethal radiation poisoning. Every symptom she could feel was consistent with what she knew about the fatal results of extreme exposure to radioactive isotopes.

Sasha looked around the big compartment. Power tools and battery packs bumped against the far wall. She put her faceplate up against the only screen showing navigation data and tried not to think about how she was going to die.

Realization that both legs were starting to go numb jarred her out of indecision. She felt an overwhelming urge to do something, even if it was wrong. She willed herself to make sense of what she saw on the monitor.

Squinting through gradually hazing corneas, she could make out a wide-angle view of the ocean. Debris in low orbit passed in front of the cameras, causing sudden intervals of darkness, each lasting no more than a tenth of a second.

Had the shockwave from the explosion moved the station? Her vision was too poor to read the latitude and longitude projections being picked up from ground-based radio stations. Struggling to read the tiny white numbers made her slow to a stop. Where was *Gold Rush* in relation to the opening in the debris field they'd worked so hard to make?

It took a moment for her to realize that movement on the screen was actually the passage of ships rather than the rotation of the space station. Adrenaline surged through her bloodstream when she realized what she was looking at. The Chinese battle group was passing through her field of view.

Sasha glanced at the nearest panel to see six green lights, indicating that the improvised rail gun was still charged and ready to fire. She laid a gloved hand on the board and began to flip the switches. Each indicator light turned from green to yellow as the individual levers were pressed downward.

She swore softly when the six yellow lights began blinking simultaneously.

"Tell me what's wrong this time," she mumbled.

A short search through a nearby open conduit revealed that the unshielded firing mechanism she had just installed was completely shorted out. "I knew you were going to do that," she complained as she stood.

Sasha went back to the workstation to see if the protected backup somebody else had installed in the operations compartment was still active. Her eyes watered with the effort of focusing. All she could make out was a blinking green smudge. "I'll assume that's a yes."

She unhooked her tether line and pulled herself, hand over hand, out of the refrigeration compartment, up through the central core of the space station, past the lifeless drifting bodies of her crewmates. "Stay there. I got this," she wheezed while reasoning that the piping and ductwork near the refrigeration systems must've shielded her from a great deal of the hard radiation that had so quickly killed the others.

Upper body strength ebbed as Sasha climbed. Fear of her imminent death mingled with doubts about the rail gun. What if the damned thing just didn't work? "Lucky to be here," she reminded herself.

Bones and tendons in her shoulders and spine ached in ways she'd never experienced before while fumbling her way into the shadowy operations compartment. Blinking lights cast an eerie glow over the slumped forms of three men and two women in vacc suits strapped into crash chairs. It occurred to her that she was now seeing what starport salvagers—or government investigators—might see, if they…

Sasha refused to pursue those morbid thoughts any further and went to the big swivel seat that was normally reserved for her.

"I can't take you people anywhere," she ruminated.

Sasha sat and strapped in. Seconds later, she had her air supply hooked up to the station's internal resources. Working from memory, she tapped each console within reach to restore systems that could be easily restarted. Seconds later, she was able to turn on the compartment's normal lighting.

When her surroundings didn't come into focus, she loudly rebuked herself for thinking that brighter lights would help her failing eyes. The agitated woman dimmed the room's lighting with a swipe of her hand. "So very lucky to be here," she reminded herself.

Sasha leaned over her instruments in a vain attempt to see them. One of three navigation radars came back to life, allowing her to guess that the proximity of the nuclear explosion must have displaced a huge swath of the debris field near *Gold Rush*.

"Lucky break," she grinned, her teeth stained with blood from her bleeding gums.

Vision in one eye was now worse than in the other. Sasha had no way of discerning what the radar images meant. Open contours and few solid clumps on the blurry display suggested large intervals, which meant the rail gun's projectile had a good chance of getting through.

She squirmed to see the Chinese naval formation, and the aircraft carrier at its center. A slight nudge of the station's variable pitch thrusters to change the platform's position seemed to improve her aim.

"That's just good timing."

Her heart rate became irregular. She broke out in a cold sweat. Something very warm and upsetting began to spread through her chest. A wave of rising bile burned the back of her throat as it surged up her esophagus. "Not yet," she muttered, grimacing.

Sasha put one hand on the extra module that had been added to her station and opened the black plastic box. Stopping that carrier might not win the war, but it sure would give the American media something to talk about.

A bundle of multicolored wires spilled out, attached to a big red button set into a black socket. Somebody was bound to reveal her involvement in all of this. Nobody among her circle of friends could keep that secret indefinitely.

She gripped the button in her free hand and pressed it once. Several seconds passed while she searched her displays for the green indicators that proved the firing switch was active. How many people would go to her funeral?

"That's the miracle I've been waiting for all day," she rejoiced, her voice slurring.

Sasha's eyes watered. The thought of being known for *this* didn't seem so bad. Not compared to the other things she'd done. Especially some of the things that the authorities hadn't even found out about yet.

She blinked her tears away and turned on the microwave transmitters that would send proof of what she was about to do to the Kodiak Starport.

"Let's be the good kind of famous, just this once."

Chapter Twenty-Three

Jim Cook finished the soda he'd been sipping from for the last several minutes and dropped the empty container into a nearby trash can. Beatrice Brown's voice carried quietly from a far corner as she continued to field questions about recent events.

Norman Ahgupuk, dressed in full flight gear, appeared on monitors around the operations center. "I've got four drones ranging out to sea. More than enough fuel to do the kind of recon we need. We're gonna lose 'em when they meet that carrier's air cover, but it'll be worth it to have the early warning."

"I understand," Jim responded simply. Jet engines roared in the background as he spoke.

"Let's run through this again," Norman said.

"We're listening," Jim replied, nodding.

Everyone around him worked in hushed tones. The loss of *Gold Rush* was more than a financial setback for the company. It was proof that the war was real and headed their way, with life and death consequences.

The pilot knocked on his helmet. "Their pathfinders will come through well above supersonic. They've got full spectrum video equipment that's good enough to take pictures at that speed, so they'll be in and out faster than you can say your own name."

"Yeah," Jim replied glumly.

Norman's voice was momentary drowned out as a taxiing F-15 rolled by just a few dozen yards behind him. "—first real wave of trouble starts with more fast movers coming in on the deck to suppress our triple-A. Ground fire gets 'em or it doesn't. We stay in the racetrack I told you about earlier, waiting for the next wave to approach with ground attack munitions."

Everyone near the communications section reacted with surprise when satellite receivers assigned to *Gold Rush* suddenly activated.

"Hold that thought," Jim urged Norman as the previously dead radio frequencies came to life.

"We'll know in two hours," the aviator assured him.

Jim turned. "You're not going to believe this…"

"Handle whatever it is." Norman saluted and ended his conference call.

Beatrice reacted to the sudden reappearance of data from the space station on her desktop display. "—now looks we're receiving a new transmission from *Gold Rush*, which we all thought was destroyed by a Chinese antisatellite weapon less than one hour ago."

Jim rushed through the crowd, over to a stack of communications equipment as white noise bellowed from ceiling mounted speakers.

"Must be a transmission from the afterlife," somebody whispered nervously.

He stopped in his tracks to stare in utter amazement at grainy video images on big screens overhead.

"Sending at full power," an engineer commented.

Jim pivoted left, then right, in search of anyone with answers. "They've got to crank it up to punch through that expanding cloud of radioactive scrap."

Video quality was poor, but there was no mistaking the now-familiar lines of the Chinese aircraft carrier, *Strong Prosperity*.

"Somebody clean that up!" he shouted.

"Computers are enhancing," a specialist confirmed.

Jim held out an empty hand. "Can we get a signal up there?"

The answer came quickly. "Yes, if we don't care about being triangulated—"

"Do it!" Jim bellowed in frustration and fatigue.

He was given the same wireless headset and remote control he'd used earlier. He slapped it on and fumbled with the remote. "Bea, are you seeing this?"

"We see it," she replied, astonished.

He changed channels, looking for any signs of life.

"There!" somebody called out when sounds of labored breathing were heard.

Jim paused to listen. It wasn't a trick of the transmission. Somebody was breathing!

"Sasha?" he asked tentatively.

"Still wanna see me do these guys?" she rasped.

"More than anything in the world."

Strong Prosperity's image flickered, bounced, and vanished in a white flash.

Jim looked askance at the workers around him. Heads bobbed up and down inside the work group assigned to troubleshoot the rail gun. A heated argument broke out among the environmental systems engineers.

Seconds passed. Air conditioners hummed. Phones began to ring. Dozens of screens went blank, then filled with static.

"Did we hit the damned thing or not?" Jim fretted.

Kyle Foss, working in shirtsleeves, slid from one end of the television station control room to the other on a wheeled chair. He didn't know the full back-story associated with what he was presenting to more than three million viewers worldwide, but he knew good programming when he saw it.

Cook was clearly at the end of his rope. Beatrice looked like she might be about ready to have a nervous breakdown. Acting on a hunch, Foss cut the satellite feed and cued a commercial break.

* * *

Seawolf's captain jumped out of his chair when the entire submarine shook. "What in the Hell was that?"

On-duty sonar operators and electronic warfare specialists were baffled.

"Computer classifies that event as surface detonation, sub-kiloton, nuclear."

"Must be a mistake. The overpressure would have already crushed us."

"Loose radio traffic spike! They're talking to each other about something."

"Somebody hit our carrier," the X.O. decided.

The captain recovered his composure as he studied the flow of incoming data. He whistled as the boat rocked back and forth, again. "Look at those readings. I can see why the software thinks it should be nuclear, but there's no radiation in the water and we didn't detect an EMP. Must be the Air Force, poaching our carrier with conventional payloads."

"Let them have it," the lead sonar specialist suggested.

"We were just two minutes from the firing point," somebody mentioned.

The captain rubbed his chin as the submarine heaved through another deepwater wave. "Helm, hard right. Take us away from whatever they're doing up there. Increase your speed to two-thirds. Reverse course and let's go get those troopships."

"Right turn, aye," Helm replied.

"*Strong Prosperity* is definitely breaking up!" the sonar expert confirmed.

"That was fast," the X.O. observed.

"Recommend decoys as we go," the electronic warfare officer suggested.

The captain nodded his approval. "Prepare two. Set one for an eight-minute delay. Rig the second for 12 minutes. Release when ready."

"Units programmed. Decoys away," E.C.W. confirmed after a few keystrokes.

The captain grinned as a feeling of relief swept through the conn. "I don't care what they're doing up there. Weapons! Flood one through eight. Reset for those landing ships. Swim out one through six as planned, two per target, as we bear. Let those fish do their own passive acquisition. They should go live as we make the outbound turn."

"Active pings from two sources on the far side of the group!" Sonar warned.

The X.O. rubbed his hands together. "Second miracle for the day, Skipper. They're looking in the wrong direction. We could make them pay for that."

The gray haired officer touched a finger to his forehead. "Smarter, not harder. Their best asset is going to the bottom, which forces the rest of them to go home. Any damage or distraction our torpedo spread causes will be sauce for the goose. We're not dead, which means we get to go home, too."

* * *

The lead environmental specialist approached Jim to whisper in his ear.

"Not while I'm on the air," he told her.

"Commercials," she pointed at a far off screen.

He turned to see dancing teddy bears pushing a bottle of laundry detergent.

"You need to know," she insisted.

"Talk," Jim groused, muting his microphone.

The woman cupped one hand over her ear. "Incoming data. All the station's logs are programmed to download automatically when the primary computers reboot after a major event."

"Station integrity?"

"Environmental systems on *Gold Rush* are messed up. Good news is that it looks like they turned off the air and purged all the compartments. Bad news is that radiation sensors were tripped."

"They were attacked," he said, gesturing emphatically.

"Saturated."

Jim closed his bleary eyes. "How much radiation are we talking about?"

"More than lethal. It'll take a while to go through the codes. At first glance, it looks like all the detectors burned out. All of them. That means the entire station—and everyone in it—is Chernobyl hot."

Jim heard Sasha snort and swallow to clear her throat.

"Having trouble," she apologized through static.

Jim keyed his mic on. "That's all right. It's okay. We lost your video. Have your cameras failed?"

He turned his headset off and took a few steps out of camera range to speak with the specialist. "Chernobyl, as in the old Russian nuclear power plant that had a meltdown that irradiated an entire city? Is that what you're saying?"

The environmental systems expert chewed on her lower lip. "Yes. And don't ask me how Sasha can still be alive. She's boiling inside her own skin, as we speak."

"Jim?" Sasha called out.

The administrator touched the specialist on her shoulder. "Put an assessment team together. I don't know what comes next, but I want options."

The expert stepped out his way. "I can tell you right now that the entire station is a write-off. Reclamation to satisfy the environmentalists will cost more than the original construction."

"Thanks." He turned and walked away. Making his way to a chair, Jim sat and turned his headset on.

"Cook?"

"I'm here."

"I can't see," she said with an audible tremor.

The shock was more than he could bear. He doubled over for just a moment. Spectators nearby saw the anguish in his eyes and looked at each other. What should they say? What should they do?

He stood, glaring at anyone who showed him pity. "Does anyone know…? How do we get the cameras on our space station working again?"

The question caused a scramble. Anyone who could find an excuse to be somewhere else did so, quickly.

Sasha exhaled loudly. "Sorry. I almost forgot how much this means to you. Just give it a minute and you'll have all the proof you could ever want."

"How?" Jim demanded mercilessly.

She mumbled something unkind. "I launched a metal telephone pole through a stack of ring magnets. What did you think was going to happen? All that kinetic energy had to go somewhere. We got bumped."

Jim raised his head. The only engineer he could see nodded as if to validate the physics lesson. The remainder of the problem wasn't hard for him to figure out. Jarring the station would mean its cameras, sensors, and antennas would be pointed in the wrong direction.

"What's your fix?" he asked testily.

The delirious woman adjusted her seat harness. "That's better. It's not like I'm going anywhere."

"What have you got up your sleeve?"

She sighed through interference. "We upgraded the flight programs. The same computers that run the autopilot used to keep this bucket of bolts on whatever geostationary orbit you want can now reorient the station after a rail gun shot. It's automatic…happening right now, as we speak."

"Very nice," Jim conceded.

Sasha winced at the rising pain in her abdomen. "You weren't going to think of it, so we had to. Wasn't hard. We borrowed most of the code from—"

"I don't need to know," he interrupted politely.

She giggled. "Tell me when you have signal. I'm too sick to know if we're moving or at full stop."

Jim looked up to see Beatrice talking. Voices, conversing in serious work, murmured around the room, creating enough noise to drown out whatever Brown was saying. Promotional images of *Gold Rush* splashed and faded as a ten-second clip of the rail gun shot was aired for a third time.

"I was hoping for something more impressive."

"Tell me about it," Sasha jeered.

Jim stood up as screens jumped to life. "Okay, here we go! Merge that video with our media traffic. No sound."

Computers aboard *Gold Rush*, reading various forms of ground station location data, used hardwired controls to operate variable pitch thrusters to reposition the platform. The station slowly returned to the orbital location and angle it had been at when the rail gun was fired.

Tiny particles of metal and plastic, propelled by expanding gasses and stirred up by the short-range nuclear detonation that had crippled *Gold Rush*, now adhered to the outside of the space station in increasing amounts. A microscopic film of radioactive matter over the protected camera apertures reduced the quality of visual images now streaming down to the starport's receiving arrays. Two of the three remaining digital cameras activated. Only one rotated when its electrically driven gimbal was directed to so do.

Images of a cloudy sky, captured by ground dishes at the Kodiak Starport, coalesced in a matter of seconds, revealing a high-altitude view from a different perspective than Jim had previously seen.

Two of the five remaining thermal imaging systems in the lower sections of the station came back online, granting observers a view through the fast-moving weather to the turbulent sea far below. High-speed computers rendered the view as a realistic full-color panorama. White wakes from a dozen large vessels could be seen twisting and turning through a vast field of wreckage, debris, and flotsam.

"Looks like they're running away," Jim related for Sasha's benefit.

"Wouldn't blame them," she panted through her pain.

Two long, fat ships were sitting stationary and on fire. Plumes of dense, black smoke billowed high into the sky. A third vessel of similar configuration appeared to be capsizing as series of explosions ripped it apart from the inside, out.

"Where is it?" he pondered aloud.

The picture stabilized further, improving the images being received. New details began to emerge Jim watched. In the distance, wreathed in its own smoke and flames, was the *Strong Prosperity*. The big ship tilted with an extreme starboard list.

"Shouldn't there be a big hole in that thing?" Jim observed resentfully.

"Never done this before. Wouldn't know," Sasha drawled.

Chapter Twenty-Four

Social media networks around the world passed the word about the starport's remarkable broadcast. More than ten million people watched the technically assisted feed from *Gold Rush.*

Two multirole fighter jets were prepared for takeoff from the stricken Chinese aircraft carrier, hastily launched by the quick-thinking crews in an effort to defend their ship. The planes tore mercilessly through retreating sailors and loose equipment as each desperate pilot struggled to achieve enough airspeed to get airborne. This specific event would become one of the most watched and repurposed video clips on the Internet to come out of the conflict.

The flight deck's steepening incline robbed both aircraft of their forward momentum, forcing the pilots to eject. Their planes tumbled into the ocean as their parachutes opened. Only one of them would survive the freezing waters to become a household name in China after the war.

The ship continued to sink. Ordnance tractors slithered across the shifting deck, leaving greasy skid marks as frantic drivers lost control. Men and women in red, yellow, and green uniforms scrambled for safety inside the doomed ship as parked aircraft began to slide. Some were knocked off their feet and crushed by falling ladders and plummeting weapons packages. Others were flung from the rolling ship by flailing hoses that randomly lashed about like berserk animals.

Audiences in China suddenly lost their view of these events as broadcasts were terminated by state censors. Americans and Europeans experienced no such restrictions. They watched as helicopters broke loose from their moorings, adding their weight to the avalanche of men and machinery falling overboard. Three unsecured fighters quickly slid from the carrier's deck, into the churning water, with panicked pilots still strapped into their cockpits.

Jim tucked the remote in one fist and folded his arms. He took a deep breath and let it out with a sense of accomplishment.

"I know that sound," Sasha preened.

Jim watched the carnage unfold with grim contentment as Beatrice struggled through her commentary. "I never wanted this."

"Feels good, though, doesn't it?" the engineer observed.

The truth hurt enough to make him flinch. "It's only good if I can convince them to stay away. Otherwise, all of this was for nothing."

"The world is watching," Sasha reminded him.

"Yeah," Jim replied gloomily, unable to take his eyes off the sinking ship.

"Stop talking to me and go make a statement," she scolded weakly.

He stalled. "Been thinking about that for weeks now. Not sure what to say."

Sasha snickered. "You've got their attention. Now, scare 'em just a little more."

He let his arms drop as *Strong Prosperity* lurched deeper into the water.

"Go," she insisted when he didn't respond.

"You probably won't be here when I'm done," he offered lamely.

After a long pause, she replied, "I know."

The bright light from overhead fixtures, the hot stale air, and the pervasive scent old food odors suddenly closed in on Jim to make him feel smothered.

"Want me to put somebody else on?" he asked flatly.

"I'm gonna pass out," she replied curtly.

Jim looked around, only to see that everyone was fully engaged by what they saw on the television screens or at their workstations. He felt helpless, and he didn't like it.

"Last request?" he invited.

"Yes, actually. Name something large, expensive, and hard to steal after me."

* * *

Billy Richter, in uniform and wearing body armor and combat gear, stopped at the checkpoint desk outside the operations center. His boots left muddy tracks on the floor. A dozen armed guards in similar attire followed him closely. He leaned over the desk to speak with the sentry.

"You know who I am?"

"Yes, sir," the seated man replied, nodding.

Billy adjusted his beret and pointed at the door. "Nobody goes in or out of that door unless I tell you, face-to-face, that it's okay for them to do so. Is that clear?"

"Yes, sir," the man confirmed stoically.

Billy turned to his entourage. "Everybody listen. This is your last chance. I've told you what I know and what I intend to do. You've all got a pretty good idea of what'll happen when I go in there. Make your choice."

Reassuring looks passed between some. A few nodded without speaking. Others joked. Nobody walked away.

"Is there something I need to know?" the sentry asked, a worried expression on his face.

Billy looked down. "Stay here and do your job."

Richter looked up and down the dimly lit hallway. The radio on his vest came to life with a squelch, followed by rapid voice traffic from male and female voices.

"Administration secured."

"Executive airfield in lockdown."

"Legal department under observation."

Norman Ahgupuk's enraged voice blared unexpectedly through a burst of background noise.

Billy keyed his microphone. "I sent them."

The pilot was in no mood for politics. "I don't care if half the Chinese fleet just went to the bottom! You have no business interfering with my flight operations at a time like this! Open that air traffic control tower! Now!"

Billy shook his head in frustration. He agreed with the executives in Anchorage who thought that Jim Cook was unstable. This crisis had obviously worn him out. Even so, the destruction of the Chinese warship—which had just happened—seemed to validate everything he'd done to preserve the starport. Forcing a stand down at this point seemed unnecessary. "I told her this was a bad idea," he huffed.

Each part of the starport's organization had its own role to play in the execution of a larger, choreographed chain of managed activities that made up the organization's successful daily operations. Interfering with the tasks of any division, department, or section could throw the whole enterprise into chaos that would take days to sort out.

Billy gripped his microphone and tried to sound more confident than he felt. "Norman, please. I'm asking you for some patience. Wait five minutes and I promise you'll hear something that matters from the boss himself. All you need to do is give me that much."

Norman leaned on the door of his SUV and surveyed the snow-rimmed airfield. Something was going on that he didn't know about. Several possibilities entered his mind, few of which were very appealing. News of the Chinese carrier's fate had spread as quickly as the raging fires, fed by punctured aviation fuel tanks and clouds of superheated toxic gases, devouring *Strong Prosperity*'s crew below decks.

"Are we gonna stand down?" he asked, his tone chilly.

Billy grimaced when the men behind him chuckled. Norman wasn't the kind of person to be easily deceived. "Five minutes!" Billy said emphatically.

"Five. Then I'm coming for you," Norman promised.

Billy cursed and turned to face his men. "Everybody knows where they have to be. Go there, now!"

He waited for ten of the armed guards to split up and go toward different parts of the building. The last two apprehensive men remained nearby.

"Let's go," Billy ordered with a gesture.

The sentry remained silent as the trio strode into the operations room.

The scene that greeted Billy startled him. Static electricity filled the air. Smells of coffee and overheated electronics offended his nose. People wearing headsets and clutching various handheld gadgets were staring intently at Jim Cook, who towered head and shoulders above everyone. His face could be seen on every large screen in the cavernous chamber.

Billy made his way through the cluttered workstations in an effort to get a better look at the spectacle that was unfolding. The armed men following him were careful to avoid colliding with the people they went around.

The starport boss stood on a large plastic box near the communications hub. His shirt collar was open. Clutching a headset microphone in one hand and a remote control in the other, he spoke in front of a pair of wireless television cameras on tripods that were nearly hidden between stacks of equipment.

Billy's boots squeaked to a halt halfway across the room when Beatrice Brown's confident countenance filled every screen in his field of view. He raised a hand, telling his subordinates to stop. Sponsor logos materialized in the corners of the program feed with slow shimmer, allowing the security man to infer that he was watching a live broadcast.

"Mr. Cook, our audience is eager to hear what you have to say," Brown said.

Jim slipped the remote into the pocket of his slacks and hung the headset around his neck. He took a deep breath and puffed out his cheeks in a long exhale.

His words came slowly. "Thank you. Less than one hour ago, our station was damaged by the near miss of a medium-yield nuclear weapon. It was just dumb luck on our part that many of you got to see that live, as it happened. We have reason to believe the Chinese launched this weapon."

Releasing the accusation relieved some of his tension. "The attack didn't originate from their mainland. We think this was intended to be misdirection on their part." Political necessity made the lies come easily. "Anyone with ICBM technology can make a transpolar shot with some degree of accuracy. Our experts tell me it's just a fluke that their nuke didn't hit our station and vaporize it."

Billy's mouth dropped open when he realized what was happening. Jim was using the media to parlay the Chinese strike on *Gold Rush* to his advantage. The cover-up wouldn't be airtight, but it could be good enough shield the starport and its parent corporation from the worst legal and social repercussions, as long as public sentiment and the opinions of elected leaders could be influenced in their favor.

Jim clasped his hands behind his back as he prepared to deliver the most carefully rehearsed remarks of his career. "Life is not fair. The world is a dangerous place. Climate change, diminishing resources, a lack of useable water, and severe food shortages make these truths undeniable."

He paused for dramatic effect. "With this honest assessment in mind, we have taken it upon ourselves to protect this starport by every reasonable means at our disposal. Losing what we've built here puts an end to manned space flight in this part of the world at a time when that technology is desperately needed."

Graphics and short video segments were added to the broadcast as Jim continued to speak. "We need satellites to survey our dying oceans. We need heavy lift suborbital cargo carriers to move people and payloads to address the Small Rock mining disaster here in Alaska. All that would be gone if we hadn't defended it."

"Here it comes," Billy muttered.

Fatigue and the burden of many miseries inspired outward sincerity within Jim as he bowed his otherwise cynical head. "I never wanted this to happen. None of us did. We're on American soil, and we're damned proud of that fact. So, we worked with the U.S. government to plan for this day."

He looked directly at the nearest camera. "The Chinese attack on our space station wasn't entirely successful. There have been casualties. On my orders, as you can see, the crew on *Gold Rush* has deployed a defensive weapon that has drastically reduced the threat that was headed for this starport."

Men and women safely behind the line of cameras looked at each other with expressions of shock and horror. This was the first that most were hearing about any kind of military systems on their space station.

Beatrice twitched in her chair as she was bombarded with a deluge of text and verbal requests for additional information.

Jim raised a hand to quiet the murmurs of people in the room with him. "Be mad at me. I deserve it. We've got a worldwide audience right now and I need to talk to them for a few more minutes, okay? I'll get back to the rest of you later."

As the engineers and technical specialists quieted, Beatrice recovered her composure. "Jim, what exactly do you mean by a defensive weapon?" she asked.

He cleared his throat. "We're not at liberty to say. That secrecy is part of our cooperative agreement with the U.S. government. Anything I tell you about it could get me sent to prison."

A shiver went up her spine when Beatrice saw the prepared questions that would make her complicit in the starport cover up begin to appear on the teleprompter.

"Are you prepared to use that weapon system again?" she read aloud.

"Only as a last resort," Jim insisted with a show of open hands.

Billy turned around, whispering, "Let's get out of here."

The nearest guard put one hand on his pistol. "I thought you had orders. What about—"

Billy laid a hand on the man's shoulder, turning his head to look each security operative in the eye. "Look up there. See what's on the big screen? That's a win. We're not going to mess that up by taking him away in handcuffs."

"What're you gonna tell Anchorage?" the man to his left rumbled.

"It's my decision to make and I've just made it," Billy replied testily. "We go back to our posts and everybody does their jobs. This matter is closed."

Chapter Twenty-Five

Strong Prosperity's destruction became the lead story on every infotainment network around the world. The action was so sensational that it eclipsed breaking headlines showcasing the start of a Chinese amphibious landing in the Philippines.

Central Committee members in Beijing were outraged by the turn of events and thoroughly embarrassed by the media circus that followed. The matter was hotly debated before senior party leaders ordered the naval chain of command to withdraw what remained of the task force.

Infotainment outlets reaped huge advertising revenues as sponsors bought time on live feeds featuring starport security forces at the ready in and around the shattered complex. Spectators watched as small craft from the decimated armada struggled to locate survivors from the doomed ships, who were still adrift in the frigid water, before they succumbed to hypothermia.

Audience numbers swelled to historic proportions as senior officers, including the admiral commanding the flotilla, were successfully evacuated from *Strong Prosperity* before the vessel broke up and capsized. These command staff members were taken by motor launch to the guided missile cruiser *Vigilant Warrior* (*Jĭngtì Zhànshì*).

Advisors reporting to the admiral quickly reached a consensus. The loss of all three landing ships within the formation was no accident. It also couldn't have been a byproduct of the starport's strategic response, which they deduced was a kinetic strike weapon of with multiple fragmenting warheads of some kind.

"We have an enemy submarine somewhere inside our formation," he decided. The destroyer and frigate captains on the outer perimeter of the chaos had already reached the same conclusion when *Seawolf's* decoy noisemakers went off. The bluff gave the American submarine a free hand, which the Chinese now hoped to find and cut off.

Well-trained officers and crews worked to organize a thorough search. Sonar buoys were set for passive detection and dropped in long parallel lines by fast-moving ASW helicopters launched from the destroyers. Nimble frigates scoured the interior of the formation in an effort to provoke some form of response from the intruder. The sweep for enemy submarines wasn't obvious to the millions who watched the unobstructed view from *Gold Rush.*

* * *

General Manika Sachdeva sat in a high-backed chair inside the underground command post at Joint Base Elmendorf-Richardson watching Jim Cook's spin on the Chinese naval disaster.

"That'll go down in martial history as a new form information warfare," she joked.

Laughter came in reply from the men and women nearby.

The general reached for a telephone. She punched in her clearance code. "Air Ops," a man's voice responded.

"Roll the dice," she ordered.

"Ninety is go?" the voice queried directly.

"Launch when ready."

* * *

Hounded by antisubmarine vessels and hammered by dozens of depth charges, *Seawolf* slipped away from its pursuers without being identified. Its long run through the Gulf of Alaska on a twisting southeasterly course lasted well into late afternoon. The exhausted officers and crew were unaware of the worldwide interest being focused on the action they'd just escaped from, nor did they know about the American air strike that hit the regrouping flotilla.

Spectators were thrilled to realize that the tiny dots they saw were actually a reinforced squadron of F-22s unleashing a barrage of antiship missiles. Chinese fighters left their combat air patrol orbit to meet the threat. They'd been conscientiously maintaining their vigil over the task force because they still had fuel. Radios crackled as pilots on both sides accelerated.

* * *

Very little of the air battle could actually be seen by the millions who flooded social networks with their opinions and observations. Excitement ran so high that much of the global peanut gallery didn't notice the damage inflicted by the few warhead impacts that got past the Chinese antimissile systems.

Six of the 36 missiles released by the aggressor squadron actually hit their targets. Layers of small caliber, rapid-fire, rotary gun systems filled the air with lead and tungsten slugs, destroying the rest before they got close to the warships.

The damage caused by the warheads was minimal. The inner compartments on ships that were hit weren't compromised. Well-trained fire management parties, coordinated through advanced damage control networks, quickly prevailed.

The clash ended anticlimactically. The Chinese defenders were unable to overcome American numerical superiority, despite having better avionics and other engineering factors that experts in the media had claimed would win battles for them.

Surface-to-air missiles from the task force claimed three F-22s. U.S. pilots, refusing to break off when threatened with sophisticated antiaircraft systems, opted for a high rate of closure to force their opponents into a turning gunfight that would rob them of their industrial advantages.

Tactics trumped technology at the cost of half the squadron. The surviving F-22s withdrew from an empty sky after all six of the Chinese fighters had been vanquished. Only one parachute floated toward the undulating sea.

Viewers were still coming to grips with the outcome of the air battle when *Gold Rush's* unattended cameras caught sight of a dozen civilian fishing vessels arrived in the wake of the rapidly departing task force. Each one flew a pair of massive white flags from its rigging. The faster warships outdistanced the slower boats within a matter of minutes.

Inside the starport's television studio, Beatrice Brown told the world what they were seeing. "Radio operators from our very own Fish Net are directing local fishermen to assist in the rescue of Chinese sailors who have been left behind."

* * *

Jim Cook was ecstatic when he spoke with General Sachdeva through a secure landline after witnessing the air battle.

"Sorry for your losses," he empathized.

"Costly," Manika confided.

He lowered his voice. "It's physics. Go fast and hit hard. There's not going to be much left when the trouble finds you."

"Prisoners?" she asked just to change the subject.

He nodded. "Not sure how many, but you'll have them. Word is that the fishermen are finding some sailors. Most are dead. Fish Net reports 200 among the living. I'm told we should expect another 200, give or take."

"What's your next move?" she inquired.

"Look dangerous and talk tough," he chuckled.

"Why?" Manika questioned.

Jim remained calm. "Put on a good show, convince those folks from across the sea that they don't want to come back."

"This I have to see," she encouraged.

"Watch me," he jabbed and hung up.

Frantic phone calls tied up precious landlines to and from the starport for several hours while corporate security forces remained on high alert. Uniformed personnel made themselves conspicuous throughout the installation while pairs of F-15 Eagles roared overhead.

* * *

Alaskan journalists and media personalities were flown in as evening shadows grew long to provide added exclusive coverage in an effort to keep global attention focused on the space launch complex to dissuade Chinese forces from making further attacks on the battered facility.

Norman Ahgupuk was taken by surprise in his hangar, when reporters and television cameras arrived in an unannounced convoy of vans, buses, and catering trucks.

He and his misfit pilots became instant celebrities as night fell. Profiles of the most unsavory aviators drew the most attention from unorthodox fans, who spent millions on starport merchandise.

* * *

Video and data transmissions from *Gold Rush* ceased just after midnight Alaska Standard Time. Astronomers at three different University of Alaska observatories reported witnessing a heat trail in the night sky that corresponded to the last known orbital trajectory of the space station.

Independent observers at various national observatories were able to track the fall platform as it burned up in the Earth's atmosphere. The path of descent was very gradual, but occurring at a very high rate of speed, as if the platform were being accelerated into its crash.

Gold Rush burned brightly in the night sky over mainland China for 28 minutes as it descended on a west-to-east heading. Late night observers, urged on by the media, documented the event with more than 10,000 postings of amateur video to the Internet.

The heaviest pieces of *Gold Rush* rained down on central Beijing just after 2 a.m. local time. Accumulated radioactivity in the debris set off isotope detectors in government office buildings and other high profile locations.

* * *

Military analysts at the Pentagon were stunned by new developments as they reported for work. Briefings given to elected officials before breakfast included a Justice Department summary of recently granted legal immunities that prevented the matter from being more thoroughly investigated.

Members of the House and Senate Intelligence Committees were unanimously irritated by this covert gag order. Information provided by the Central Intelligence

Agency shed new light on recent happenings from a different perspective, which satisfied them.

Reliable sources within the Chinese navy suggested that fleet coordinators had had no reason to suspect the station was armed. China's decision to strike *Gold Rush* had apparently been based on its value as an intelligence-gathering platform. The justification was practical, given the pace and escalating brutality of the war. Senators who reviewed the starport's official specifications for *Gold Rush* had to admit that the station's many cameras, radars, and other sensors probably could have been used to observe enemy fleets in the central and northern Pacific Ocean.

* * *

The efforts to contain information about the extent of starport defensive preparations weren't the only things that Jim Cook lost control of. Overworked engineers, given the chance to mingle with reporters who were willing to spend money on suddenly overpriced liquor at local bars, drank too much and revealed too much. Uncomfortable truths about *Gold Rush* made the local news before many Alaskans arrived at work the next day, prompting starport lawyers to work overtime. Americans in the continental U.S. tuned to the revelations with a mixture of disgust and grudging admiration.

Mainstream media sources continued to cover the withdrawal of Chinese forces from the Arctic. Chinese representatives from official state-run media outlets said only that their government was considering its options. Chinese external media, reacting to the "attack" on the country's capital by the starport's falling space station, characterized it as an act of corporate brutality that was emblematic of America's bad behavior. Anti-American commentators around the world expressed similar views, saying that the crash had been a deliberate act.

"The odds of such a thing happening entirely by accident are astronomical."

"It's a miracle that nobody was killed, I tell you!"

"…just like the Americans to do this."

A brief statement by the United States Attorney General was carried by two dozen highly rated infotainment networks in the western hemisphere during midday peak viewing periods. He expressed proud, unflagging presidential support for the scruffy defenders at the Kodiak Starport. A press release was later supplied to the media, in which the Attorney General apologized for his use of the word "scruffy" when referring to starport personnel.

Conspiracy theorists claimed *Gold Rush* had been deliberately destroyed to prevent anyone from learning the truth about Sasha Xavier's involvement in the starport's plan to build on a rail gun on that space station. Secrecy enthusiasts believed that the infamous Sasha Xavier must have had something to do with it, because Jim Cook mentioned her name during a live broadcast. Some said the U.S. government had paid her to put advanced weaponry on *Gold Rush.*

This claim was lent some credence thanks to statements made to members of the tabloid media by a few less-than-scrupulous starport engineers, who revealed the existence of the rail gun. This antiauthoritarian faction believed Sasha was now on a tropical beach somewhere, being wealthy and lasciviously anonymous. Others with a more creative mindset claimed that Sasha was an alien pretending to be human, using a death ray that only she knew how to make. Her mission had obviously been to defend the starport because her people wanted to encourage human space travel. That raucous faction believed she was now returning to her home world.

* * *

Officials inside China were becoming concerned. News of the Arctic disaster was reaching the domestic population, in spite of a total blackout by state-approved media outlets. Approved media personalities were roused from their beds and brought to work for emergency briefings.

A hastily arranged working group, comprised of psychologists and Communist Party-approved opinion-makers quickly concluded that the allegedly unregulated video feed from *Gold Rush* was actually a masterful public relations ploy.

"No bombs or bullets," one professor with a high security clearance explained. He tipped his glasses. "Those allegedly responsible profess embarrassment and shame. All is presented as if by accident. It's nothing less than brilliant."

The assembled image experts recommended a full-scale multimedia counterattack, using every propaganda tool at their disposal.

"Maintain the outward message that this was American extremism."

"Introduce the international media to our surviving sailors. Let them see the results of such misery."

"Beijing has been irradiated. That fact by itself will sway many opinions."

The admiring academic sobered. "The long view must be considered. This war is not over with, yet. The Americans have won a single battle. Just one. That victory does not wipe away their long string of defeats. Even if this conflict should come to a cease fire, we are still in control of more than we started with."

Central Committee leaders concurred. Western resolve was questionable. American resistance was weak, in spite of recent events. China had more productive military endeavors to pursue in other parts of the Pacific.

Positions in the Aleutian Islands could be held at a nominal cost to maintain a strategically useful northern air defense corridor. Those outposts could be easily abandoned, if the Americans chose to parley for them. Mainland Alaska would be left alone, for now.

CHAPTER TWENTY-SIX

Combat continued in the central Pacific for 16 days as U.S. naval units were forced away from Japan and South Korea. Expansion of their "defensive perimeter" gave the Chinese more than room to maneuver.

Governments in Cambodia, Laos, Myanmar, and Vietnam reached a diplomatic accord with Beijing by the end of July, reducing military tensions in the region. Western diplomats and military personnel were to be interned or expelled, as terms dictated. The agreement, signed by representatives from all five countries in neutral Malaysia, under the watchful eyes of solemn United Nations observers, was hailed by the world's major media organizations as a giant step forward in the resolution of a worsening crisis. American allies were less enthusiastic about what they saw as a consolidation of Chinese regional influence.

* * *

Reconstituted U.S. naval assets converged on the Hawaiian Islands after their drubbing in the Arctic. The undamaged *Gerald R. Ford* was given a new command staff before being placed at the center of a heavily reinforced carrier battle group. The *Ford*'s admiral and her top tier subordinates were reassigned in early August, after the new formation was fully outfitted and on station as a bulwark against northeasterly Chinese naval incursions that might threaten vulnerable West Coast shipping by operating from temporary bases in the occupied Aleutian Islands.

Alaskans of all political persuasions felt betrayed by Washington. Statewide media aired their grievances in every possible format.

"There's no way container ships will come up here from Seattle. We are on our own."

"Are we supposed to rely on Canada for protection?"

"It's like we're behind enemy lines."

* * *

September's storms showered the Tanana Valley in autumn mist. Birch and black spruce trees on and around the University of Alaska campus dripped with accumulated moisture. A large dark blue tilt-rotor aircraft with starport markings roared in, making a fast three-point landing at the hillside airpark. Attendants in bright yellow rain gear rushed out to put wheel chocks in place and open the vehicle's doors. Cargo doors opened on both sides of the long, sleek aircraft. Starport security specialists in urban camouflage and body armor got out with weapons at the ready and formed a loose perimeter as the rotors came to a stop.

Jim Cook stepped out into the chilled air wearing an athletic jacket emblazoned with the starport logo over a suit and tie. His executive entourage deplaned with an assortment of baggage. A uniformed state trooper met the administrator and his group at the edge of the landing pad. He ushered them into the warm, dry terminal building. University Chancellor Helen Hathaway was there to greet them.

"You have a few more gray hairs," she kidded.

"Hard to tell with you," Jim replied coyly.

The silver-haired woman accepted the retort in good humor. "You've had a busy year. I saw your testimony on Capitol Hill."

"Who didn't?"

Helen smiled slightly at the jest, then gestured toward a long corridor. Jim fell in beside her. The entire procession moved forward like a small army.

"I'm surprised you still have your job," she told him as they walked.

"Gee. How many times have I heard that?" he pretended to consider.

Jim slowed his pace and reached behind with an outstretched palm. An aide, following close behind, handed him a round, black object.

"What's that?" Helen asked as they turned a corner.

"A gift," he explained, offering her the sphere.

She took the orb in both hands, examining it as they went down a flight of stairs. "This way. We'll be using the small auditorium this year."

"Lack of interest?"

Helen's expression soured as they turned down another hallway. "Lack of students and faculty. Selective Service has activated the draft. Enrollments are down. Medical deferments are hard to come by, so we have fewer young minds for you inspire."

Jim showed his I.D. card to a uniformed guard, who unlocked the door and allowed them to pass. "We have a new zero-G training program to announce today. Gonna start making our own astronauts."

"How do we get a piece of that?" she asked.

"Math." Jim stood with Helen and waited for his subordinates to clear the checkpoint.

"I hear you've picked up some federal research grants," he mentioned softly.

"Cold weather warfare," she replied, frowning.

"You say it like that's a bad thing," he jested.

Helen refused to look at him as the last person walked by. "I don't want you to get the wrong idea. We all know what you did, and we're all grateful. That includes me, too. I'm just so angry about what's happening. The droughts. The famines. Catastrophe everywhere, like the Small Rock mining disaster that's poisoning Bristol Bay, and now this damned war. No satellites. I hate it!"

Jim reached out a hand to hold the door open. "Give me a few years and we'll fix it."

"I'd like to see that," she replied angrily.

He pointed to the patch on his jacket using his other hand. "'Gateway to the future' isn't just a slogan for me. It's a mission statement. We'll find a way to clean up the debris that clogs low orbit. Then everybody's back in business."

"A better future. Is that it?" Helen asked, hefting the black sphere.

He looked up and down the hall. "I can't believe I have to say this to you, of all people. Think about where you are. Think about what you do. It's your job to educate them; it's my job to get them into space. It'll be a better future as we rebuild."

"Which you'll do at a ridiculous profit," she said derisively.

"Don't bite the hand that's about to feed you!" he warned, arching an eyebrow. "My point is that you and I have to think long-term. Don't just hope for better days. Look for ways to make them happen."

Helen moved the softball-sized weight from one hand to another. "That's noble, especially coming from a capitalist who just did more damage to the environment than we can measure. Tell me just one better way to make those good times happen."

Jim knocked on the door he was propping open. "Pragmatism and persistence. Nations rise and fall. Economies boom and bust. People do stupid things before they do smart things. Know it and plan accordingly."

He pressed on before she could interrupt. "Do what it takes to keep this university going, if that's what you believe in, so the next generation of builders and peacemakers have a chance to learn from somebody who actually gives a damn."

"Victory at any cost," Helen scoffed.

Jim moved closer to her. "Education and space travel. That's what we give other human beings a chance to do. They can keep on doing those things, as long as we maintain their access to what they need. Take that away and…" He let the door close with a heavy thud for emphasis. "No access means no education and no space travel. It's hard because there are a lot of really stupid people out there that want to do things that'll close that door, permanently, if we let it happen."

"You're still justifying victory at any cost," she complained morosely.

"Yes, I am, because it matters who the gatekeepers are."

Helen pointed to a clock. "Talk is cheap. I've got an overheated auditorium full of jaded students waiting for you to sell them on your way of doing things or put them to sleep."

Jim looked at his bored entourage. "A few of these folks are still alert, so I guess they haven't been waiting long enough."

He was rewarded with a few perfunctory laughs and off-color remarks as the chancellor lead the group into a soundproof room behind the raised stage at the back of the auditorium.

"One more thing. Are you ready to announce the Xavier scholarship?" he asked.

Helen turned away from talking to her secretary. "Your endowment was accepted and approved by the board last night. We can make the announcement right now, if that's what you want."

"You don't like it," he realized.

She shook her head. "I don't like the idea of enshrining somebody who embarrassed this institution. It sends the wrong message."

"That's your opinion. I have it on good authority that she got a raw deal."

Helen looked for a way to change the subject. She held up the black sphere.

"What is this thing, anyway?" She asked awkwardly.

"It's a deactivated Chinese cluster bomb," Jim replied with a twinkle in his eye.

EPILOGUE

International events represented here are not in dispute. Audiovisual records from the period corroborate significant wartime activities as they occurred. These were observed by the mainstream media and various government agencies of their day as represented in this dramatic recreation.

Questions remain about the chronology of events at the Kodiak Starport as they relate to defensive preparations made before the start of hostilities. Evidence, in the form of meeting minutes, department briefings, and case studies, has been reported missing from company archives. Official documents granting immunity to senior starport personnel from federal prosecution are a matter of public record. The motives and responsibilities of the individuals named continue to be debated.

After lengthy audits, equipment failures and contractor malfeasance were given as reasons for company losses during this period. Federal officials report comparable gaps in relevant records from this timeframe for similar reasons, leading many to wonder if a cover-up hasn't occurred. A series of privately funded investigations, which initiated Freedom of Information Act (FOIA) requests through the U.S. Department of Justice, have yielded tantalizing clues. They are presented as a part of this narrative to suggest that starport officials did know they were actively engaged in efforts to circumvent federal laws in effect at that time.

There is little doubt among historians, past or present, that the starport, as a gateway to space, plays a vital role in humanity's future. The technologies developed at such installations may be just what we need to save our dying world or relocate to a new planet that has enough air and water to give us a second chance. Is that potential for advancement and expansion so important to our long-term success that it warrants special arrangements with terrestrial governments that stretch the boundaries of morality and ethics?

About the Author

Justin Oldham is a legally blind writer who lives in Anchorage, Alaska. He holds bachelor's degrees in political science and history. Other works of fiction include *Bibix* and *Tales from the Kodiak Starport.* His nonfiction works include *Being Legally Blind: Observations for Parents of Visually Impaired Children*, *Your Ocular Prosthetic*, and *Living with Low Vision*.

Justin has always been fascinated by the pioneers of the aviation and aerospace who took mankind from the ground into the stars. Their examples inspired him to write about a future in which space travel is more consequential to the human experience.

A long-time Alaskan resident, Justin's many interests include collecting books related to the Cold War and 20th century science fiction. Reading, writing, playing strategy games, and home improvement projects keep him busy.

For more information about the author, visit his website at http://www.justinoldham.com. For more about Justin's books, visit our website at http://www.shadowfusionbooks.com.

CPSIA information can be obtained
at www.ICGtesting.com
Printed in the USA
LVHW050551260122
709439LV00003B/149

9 781935 964698